Dancing With Devils

Scott Webster

Published by Scott Webster

Table of Contents

Chapter One

All I could hear were screams, echoing in the moonlight. Huge, orange flames filled the night sky as they raged uncontrollably; the blaze gently met the skyline without so much as making a disturbance to the vast cosmos. As peaceful as it met the night sky, it was causing anarchy on the ground.

Tears and wailing projected loudly and contended with the crackle of the flames. A child could be seen from outside, on the second floor, banging on the window. She couldn't be heard but it was clear she was begging for help, begging for the mercy of God.

"Open the window," I mouthed into nothingness. I couldn't be heard because I could barely breathe myself. I looked down at my blackened hands, as a kind soul raised a breathing mask to my face.

The motion of her small hands hitting the glass was frantic at first but started to slow. The room she was in got brighter, and naturally the blinding light of fire took over.

A sudden crash from the glass as the window blew out. One could only assume the flames enveloped the girl as nothing could be heard aside from the sighs of defeat from the men firing the hoses into the flames. They'd said the fire had the hallmark signs of arson. Someone meant to hurt these kids?

Few people made it out, and when they did, they joined the choir of coughing, crying, and spluttering. I scanned the area and could see the bodies of children scattered across the area, some had jumped from the higher floors of the building in panic, to meet a swifter end. Adults who had made the same jump lay next to them; some weren't moving. One was, I recognised him, and he was screaming in pain, his tibia bone protruding through his trouser leg. It must have been a bad landing, but he was breathing. The servicemen ignored his plight, focussing more on the children in need. Serves him right, I'd call it karma even.

Suddenly, a serviceman carried out the lifeless body of a girl, arms and legs heavy in the night, neck falling backwards; I looked on helplessly and watched it happen as if in slow motion. Everything went silent. I started to zone out and couldn't hear anything anymore. I recognised the youthful face of the girl being brought out. It was the one from the window who had been banging minutes earlier. What a terrible waste... someone started this fire, but why? A nearby nurse's guttural scream as she witnessed the little one's arms flailing helplessly echoed in my mind and jolted me awake.

Silence.

The sound of the world outside couldn't be heard, much like the sudden inception of audio disappearance in the night. The room was dark, with the slightest break of light edging through the top of the curtains. The soft buzz from a digital alarm clock gently simmered from the residual power in the misty light next to my dingy, unclean bed. The timer flicked to 06:00 and with that sudden click, the silence disappeared and a nasally tone echoed to the corners of the room.

"Good morning, I'm Colin Hargreaves, it's six o'clock on October 7, 2019, overcast skies and continued rain expected in the area today–"

With a thud, I made sure I couldn't listen to him for one more second. The sound of my hand crashing on the alarm clock always seemed to perk me up when he opened his mouth. Something about Colin Hargreaves irritable voice spurred me into action. How on Earth he ever found a career in radio, I'll never know. Like nails down a chalkboard, his high-pitched squeal telling me what day it was, reminded me of an old teacher of mine. Contrary to the usual quip of having a face for radio, he strangely didn't have a voice for radio.

Whatever he had on the producers, I wanted to know. Perhaps something seedy? Perhaps he witnessed the manager commit a crime? Perhaps he was naturally a charming guy with the skills of a dark, handsome lothario? I felt myself smirking at the silliness going on in my mind. Maybe I will take a sabbatical Mr Hargreaves. Maybe I'll use my hard-earned time to investigate, detect, and find out. Saying that, I am not one to take a busman's holiday.

Eyes half open and adjusting to the faint light breaking into the room, I exhaled loudly. I couldn't stop thinking all night. I barely slept a wink and when I did, I frequently went back to that night. Seventeen children and three adults died that fateful evening. I hated sleepless nights. Every second felt like a minute, every minute like an hour, until I was living the night like a speck of dust, irrelevant to the passage of time.

It's always when I get anxious that I re-live the memory. I wish I could even explain what happens in that mindless black hole where my mind battles itself. If not foolish questions and scenarios, it's fire and death. Anxiousness seems to find a way into my being, much like the dim light in my bedroom, where even the smallest of cracks is taken advantage of; nothing could keep it out.

I studied the room and thought to myself what a hovel it was. It was never like this before... I could even see stains on the sheets and for the love of me, have no idea what they could be. I don't remember the last time anyone, or anything, was in this room to make those stains and I wouldn't ask my colleagues in forensics to try and decipher the origins for fear of crippling embarrassment.

Wait... I just stopped for a second. Interestingly, my mind was silent; maybe Hargreaves does have his uses, as I was distracted for a beautiful minute; only I felt every second and they were gone before I knew it. Beforehand, I was thinking about everything and nothing at the same time. I was thinking about the depravity of the human race and the next experience I would have of it. It's strange really.

The good we can do and the evil at the same time. Such beautifying, conflicted, and complex creatures, yet so ugly and simple at the same time. We are all walking, talking contradictions, and part of me loves it. I can stare evil in the face and still try to see the good in it. After all, like Yin and Yang, one can't exist without the other. The synergetic equilibrium and balance that one brings to the other is without a twisted doubt, beautiful.

9

I've spent my life trying to understand both sides to that dangerously enticing coin. I swear that in my mind, and as a true empath, I feel it in every fibre of my body. When I was growing up, I would feel everything around me, from everyone else. I was always hypersensitive to thoughts, feelings, and pain. It's one of the reasons I worked myself into my current job.

The twisted elation I get when I walk into a crime scene and see, or feel, what happened. Some of my colleagues call me crazy, they say that I see things others wouldn't; and I've put some very dangerous people behind bars as a result.

No other job would give me the means to get close to the more depraved side of that coin I spoke of, and it eccentrically excites me. I tried some dead-end jobs in college and only felt the stupidity of some of the people around me. Not being involved in such inanity was one of my main motivations to get into this line of work; as well as trying to understand that darker side of our nature, of course.

Most of all, truth gets my heart pumping. I loved to study and assess every crime to find the truth behind it. Three elements could make up any truth: the who, the what, and the why. One of the few mysteries in life to me was that flame-fuelled evening. I didn't know why with that one.

Proudly, I can say that very few people could face the evil I have. I've become accustomed to it throughout life and sadly, was moulded by it from an early age. In some respects, I can say it made me stronger and more resilient; not invincible though. I'm happy to serve and protect the

10

innocence of those who can be spared ever having to see it. The ultimate altruism. Maybe I do have a twisted, yet selfless view on life. Like that irritable friend everyone has, I just know how to take it and darkness, you're my friend.

"So, when is the rain expected to stop, I hear you say—"

God damn it. I hit snooze instead of stop. Hargreaves again. Though it was a suitable encore to thud the silence out of that voice once again, so I felt doubly better about the morning. Interesting point on the radio. It has been raining for a while now. Six days so far. I find rain soothing, it's my favourite type of weather. If it rained that night, maybe more people would have lived through it?

My eyes started to open. Ten minutes past six in the morning. I've never been good with earlier mornings, I'm more drawn to the night. Night is when the magic happens. Shadows creeping, corrupting, and ultimately keeping me in a job. A mildly stereotypical view of the world to assume that only the demons come out at night, but it's generally true.

My eyes started to get heavy again. I heard the awful sound of the vibrating of my phone against the wooden nightstand. Why is everyone against me having even a moment of shut eye?

I barely slept last night anyway. I feel as though I was conscious for most of it.

Still dressed from the night before, I'll admit that I practically fell into bed from sheer fatigue to be robbed of the reward of slumber. Shamefully, I only unbuttoned my shirt from the top, then gave up before collapsing. I had to sort myself out. The bed stunk and the sheets hadn't been changed in weeks. The pillow was wet with my drool and I didn't even care. Well, I did, but just couldn't bring myself to do anything about it. I used to care.

Remember when I said we were complex, yet simple? As much as I wanted to be tidier and sleep in a clean bed, my anxiety made me think I didn't deserve it. My mind made me refrain from actually doing it. Or maybe that was an excuse and I was in denial. Maybe I just didn't want to actually do it.

I will admit, for someone so attuned to the thoughts and feelings of others, I could see what was happening right in front of me but lost control. I became engrossed in the job, lost in case after case, where a murder I was assigned just stayed open, and the trail went cold. I tried to connect dots, to figure out the motive, but nothing fit. Instead, I became obsessed with the anomaly.

Every case made sense; I just hadn't found all the pieces yet. Arianna struggled with it all. She tried to reel me in and keep me grounded but that drug, that obsession, kept me intoxicated and blind to the damage I was doing to the woman that cared about me the most. I pushed away the one person that mattered the most to chase that invisible high that kept me in love with the darkness.

My quest for truth and need to understand felt like nature's joke. The mental jest of someone so in tune with the perpetrators and the victims, and I wasn't in tune with the thoughts and feelings of my own wife.

My anxiety hit an all-time high when Arianna left. I hated being without her. I get lost in my thoughts, and much like last night and the hundreds of nights beforehand, couldn't sleep. When the Sandman makes me drift off, anxiety warps my dreams. I either dream of that fiery night, or I'm just standing in an empty room with no doors or windows. I call that my anxiety dream; where I feel like I'm that girl wrapped in flames. In the dream, the walls stretch and the louder I scream, the faster it happens until sound disappears and has nowhere to go because the room is so large; I become smaller and smaller and disappear into nothingness.

Arianna's last words came to the forefront of my mind. Just a mere two months before, resonating:

"I can't do it anymore. If you can't trust me, Sebastian, you deserve to be alone."

A harsh truth. She uttered those words to me as she walked out the door and told me she needed some space. Sixty miles away seemed like quite a lot of space. I wanted to chase her but the damage was done. She was right. I pushed her away.

The job gets tough sometimes, and whilst I could talk about certain cases here and there and offload and keep her close; this one particular case hit me hard. I seem to attract the worst people in the world because I was assigned the murder of a child born out of rape. By sheer coincidence, we shared the same name.

The mentally unstable father, Arthur Henderson, had been released after seven years for the rape. He was a twisted man and was only caught because the victim, Jessica McColm, in a moment of clarity through the attack, placed her phone in his jacket pocket. When help finally arrived, and the seed of evil deposited in her, the police were able to find Arthur through the wonders of technology. They used the 'find my iPhone' feature and tracked her phone to his car, which indirectly led them to him.

Arthur was what you could call a serial criminal but with his superior intellect, always found a way to commit crime without leaving a shred of evidence. He has a fascination with Norse Gods, Demons, and feels he has a right to spread bile and pain. He was cold, calculating, and so fucking good at keeping himself out of the limelight it made me sick. Arrogantly, he was like me intellectually; he just walked a different path in life.

I fully believe that if not for Jessica's retort with the phone, he'd have gotten away with the rape too. But alas, prison gave Arthur all the time needed to reflect and ultimately plot his revenge. He was a mighty bear caught in Jessica's simple rabbit trap but could only be put away for the crime he was caught for. When he was in prison, even the hardest of men were terrified of him. I was enthralled. I needed to understand him because I was going to be the one to catch him and put him down.

Arthur later tracked Jessica down; unaware she had kept little Sebastian for religious reasons. How I wished his mother's God intervened that night. That poor boy suffered an unimaginable end. Arthur welcomed him into the devil's playground that night.

In fact, I'm sure that Satan himself would have bowed out at the twisted acts that followed. Sebastian was mutilated, tortured, sexually assaulted, and disembowelled. Everything and anything a mother would kill to protect their child from, Arthur made sure to do it. What's worse is, he knew it was his own flesh and blood; but like a predator in the wild, it was a weakness that had to be eliminated.

Arthur strapped Jessica to a chair, forced her eyes open with tape, gagged her, and made her watch as he tortured, sacrificed, and raped the boy. Arthur taunted Jessica and mocked her religion by saying he was purifying her because she gave birth to the son of the devil, who he had deemed shouldn't walk the Earth.

She watched, tears rolling down her face, muffled screams that eventually became silent like the room in my dream. I want to believe that Arthur's original intent was just to repeat his past misdeeds with Jessica and to make her feel pain as he reasserted his dominance, yet his motive suddenly changed upon finding the boy.

I'll never forget that night. I stood at the door, mouthed, "Three, four, five," and entered a trance-like state before walking into what I can only describe as Room 101 in Hell's basement. This was the part of Hell where all the really twisted stuff is dumped and written out of existence.

Immediately upon walking into that room, I was overcome by a wave of emotion and felt the pain in there. For an impromptu murder, it had a coldest, calculated feel to it. Almost artistically, blood painted the walls and left the outline of the boy's mother on the wall like a scene out of a cartoon. Burnt out candles were dotted around the room in a pentagram shape, as if to mock Jessica's religious roots further and fitting his description of the boy being the son of the devil.

What broke me the most as I studied the bloodied room was the image of blood spatter covering a family photo of Jessica and little Sebastian; with pure love and huge smiles on a sunny day, was the dissimilarity and contrast of the evil in the room. What that little boy went through, I couldn't even begin to imagine, committed by the man that donated his DNA. I refuse to use the 'F' word when describing him, though a selection of other appropriate f-words might suffice. It left a scar on my soul looking at that crime scene. A hole in that child's stomach as his entrails were pulled out and hung; no one should ever see. Frankly, it was the most malevolent sight I've ever laid eyes upon.

In my mind, as I explored that crime scene, I could hear the gothic symphony of a child's banshee-like screams, mother's tears, and muffled cries for mercy. That's one of the only reasons why I have learned to appreciate the newfound silence and solitude in my life.

Some of my colleagues couldn't even go in, some of them were being sick, which only served to disrupt the scene. The Chief was on scene and had tears in his eyes. He was on the phone to his wife, asking to put his daughter on the phone to say he loved her; and his daughter is an adult herself. A hardy, older gentleman reduced to a quivering wreck. Even the press held details back to prevent mass panic.

The case had me fired up. I went days without sleep, hoping to find a thread of evidence that I could utilise before the trail grew cold. I was quite literally scrambling for any information, or clues as to his whereabouts. I turned every fucking rock I could searching for him and got lost to the madness. It's how I ended up pushing Arianna away. I dared not utter a single word of what went on in that room because we had been trying for a child for such a long time that I didn't want her to be put off.

Jessica was institutionalised after trying to take her own life and I can't blame her for trying. Whilst her boy was born out of hate and shame, he made her learn to appreciate the fire of love that was extinguished in seconds. Thankfully, she failed in her attempt but part of me would have accepted that it was a quick and easy way to end the anguish. I felt it as I walked in that room, whereas she felt it and witnessed it; taking the proverbial Top Trumps of the matter. It broke her and I strangely felt intrigue, purely for professional understanding so I could tap into the psyche of the person responsible. I HAD to catch that son of a bitch and I was adamant I would torture him myself. That was a year ago and he's still out there. For a twisted bastard, he was certainly slippery.

He taunted me frequently, sending selfies of him outside the station with a smile, right on our doorstep. He even sent one outside my fucking house. Silent calls through the night, some with maniacal laughter. I was going crazy and it all contributed to my sudden lack of ability to sleep. The trail was cold by then too. Good old anxiety and fear became my potion for insomnia; bastard brothers in arms.

Knowing Arthur had the gall to take selfies outside my house and to take photos of Arianna in public or at work; I was the hunter being hunted. She knew something was off, a policeman's wife can sense things. She knew she was being followed, only she knew because she recognised one of my colleagues in plain clothes outside her work, twice. Some of the lads at the station would check in for me and observe from afar when off-duty, all because the Chief couldn't sanction resources for a protective detail twenty-four-seven. I understood the politics behind the decision but didn't accept it. It's the reason some of the lads banded together to have my back. Over time, they had to get back to their own lives and I let my guard down.

When she confronted me, I skirted around the truth and she didn't buy it. For someone naturally able to detect a lie, I couldn't tell a convincing one. She started to worry that I had people following her because I might have thought she was cheating. Far from it, I trusted her implicitly; it was that I couldn't trust her reaction to what I witnessed and the beast I was chasing. Actually, that's bullshit. Bullshit excuses. I couldn't trust myself. I couldn't trust that I could protect her if she knew the truth. She'd get reckless, she'd get frightened, and we'd lose ourselves to madness.

I was too blind at the time to realise we were stronger together and that she'd probably be the sane one between us if she knew.

When she asked if she was safe or at risk; I lied and said yes to keep her close for fear she'd leave. I felt I could protect her if she was close, I knew I could. If she knew Arthur had indirectly threatened me with the photos of her, knowing he could get close; I worried I'd never see her again, or we'd both leave, and I'd forever be looking over my shoulder. My own selfish reasons to protect her and keep her in the dark ultimately made her go. The irony in that I didn't want her to go to her sister's house, and she ended up there anyway.

I received a blatant admission and tip off to my home address in the form of a letter and knew there was something off. Arthur; he was getting cocky. He offered to meet me at a seedy location because he had sins he wanted to confess and if I didn't come alone, my beloved would be desecrated. The thought of him touching her made me sick so I went with it. I had nothing to lose by facing this new evil and I was obviously getting closer to him in my investigation if he needed rid of me. Why else would he leave himself exposed?

Sheer fatigue coupled with my desire to get him overlooked the obvious fact it was clearly a trap. As much as I should have called it in straight away, I told my colleague who was on 'Arianna watch' for the night shift to keep an eye out as I was going to the office for some files; just to try not to arouse suspicion. In a moment of clarity, I called for backup before running into what I can only describe as a clichéd, abandoned warehouse. Powered with almost a year's worth of emotion, anger, and the image of that bloodied boy, justice was on my side.

Despite that fact, Arthur got the jump on me. I took a hard hit on the head, my weapon fell from my grasp and as quick as it did, I fell to the ground. Adrenaline pumping, I groggily stumbled to my feet and swung a few punches in his direction. I got a few hits in and all he could do was laugh. I was concussed from the hit and couldn't stand up straight. Swinging for his face, I suddenly collapsed.

I think the only reason I'm still alive is that backup call. Budget cuts had occasional lone man patrols and despite the fact I wasn't normally reckless and there were fewer patrols, fate shined upon me. The call was heeded and a nearby patrol was about two minutes away at the time. My brief scuffle with the bastard bought my colleague enough time to get on scene. Any longer and I'd probably have left Arianna a widow; though with the distance I had created in the time since that unspeakable crime was committed, she practically was already. I was a shell of her former husband. Lost to madness.

It was in that moment where I collapsed, a sudden pain coming from my head, a persistent Arthur taunted me from above and lifted me by the collar of my shirt closer to him. I was incredibly weak, and obviously losing blood. I looked into the abyss in his eyes and with a serpent's tongue, he told me he couldn't confess as he still had one more sin to commit. He held what resembled a ceremonial dagger with a vine-like design on the hilt; it captured the smallest light and glistened.

Suddenly, a gunshot echoed, and I was dropped to the ground. As if in slow motion, Arthur was gone. Spurred into escaping because of the attending officer. Sadly, the fired bullet didn't catch him between the eyes, but it had come close enough to hit the knife he'd been holding. I mused that it was mildly fortuitous because a bullet would have been too quick for that bastard. The knife is currently in evidence so it might miraculously disappear at some point, and I'll drive it into his heart in my own bid to purify his sins.

I ultimately ended up becoming good friends with the officer that saved my life, Michael.

Michael was my rock in the months after Arianna left and we started to get to know each other. He became a different kind of emotional anchor for me, albeit more of a 'locker room' and lad-like relationship. He reminded me of an old friend from my childhood really. Michael was always trying to better himself and grow. He was a marksman in the army before he joined the force, which explained his deadeye shot to hit that knife. I did ask him why he shot the knife once and he said that as if driven by God, he knew not to shoot to kill. So now God turns up? I didn't believe it.

Michael's aim was to sit for the detective's exam within the next year and put in a few favours to be partnered with me. I wasn't sure how I felt about it in all honesty but humoured him when he talked about it. I'd come to enjoy his company because he was there when I had no one and I suppose if I trusted anyone to have my back, if they were firing godly bullets, it was a solid alliance.

I thought about Arianna every single day. The Arthur Henderson case ate away at me and I didn't open up to her at all, when usually, I would tell her how I was. I tried to save her from the harrowing sights I witnessed, and the mental strain that case put me under. That was the closest dance I've ever had with pure evil and I kept it all bottled up. My advice to anyone that finds their soul mate is to share the good and the bad because if I could turn back time, I would do it all differently.

I actually went to see Jessica once she was institutionalised to tell her, no… to promise her that I wouldn't rest until I brought that beast of a man to justice or put him down. Of course, being expected to uphold the law, I didn't utter those last words but between us, there was a unanimous agreement.

She knew how I felt. I'll admit that just being in the same room with her was hard. I said I was an empath and that moment proved it to me. The unbearable pain I felt as I looked her in her newly-vacant eyes; the same eyes that were forced to witness the devil suck the life out of her beautiful boy. It was beyond intense. With Arianna gone, I may as well put all my efforts into this. I needed something to fight for.

I wish I could say that Jessica's pain was the same pain I felt as Arianna walked out that door and, in some respects, could be compared. She lost the one person that mattered to her and I lost the one person that mattered to me. Though, I suspect I would be dishonouring little Sebastian's memory if I even tried to say that out loud. It was bittersweet in a sense, to have us both sharing different pains but finding one another in the gloominess of the situation. Jessica very sweetly referred to me as her son's bigger brother based on the obvious namesake and my passion for finding Arthur.

The last time I walked out of Jessica's room, there was a slightly defeated smile on her face, knowing that someone was committed beyond the normal parameters of justice to bring pain to her son's killer. If I could bring even a shred of hope to a woman that lost it all, I suppose anything was possible. Maybe I'd one day win Arianna back?

I felt my own vacant smile breaking across my face at the prospect. My phone buzzing suddenly brought me back to the room. It was obviously going to be work, and to be calling me at this hour multiple times probably indicated something quite important. Before all that song and dance, I needed a hit. I needed something to get my mind going again. Coffee was a reasonable substitute in place of hunting evil I suppose.

As the smell of the finest, yet cheapest roast from the store hit my nostrils, I knocked the mug back and gulped with desperation. Such caffeinated bliss hit my taste buds and I felt my already depleted batteries jolting slightly. That would probably keep me going until at least lunchtime.

A voicemail. It was my controller, Carolyn asking me to come in, as there was a new case. I suppose it would have been too good to be true to expect anything related to Arthur Henderson.

I fumbled to the bathroom and pulled on the tap to soak my face. The cold water seemed to wake me up just a little more, probably enough to take me until late afternoon. As the water dripped off my face and I exhaled through the shock, I looked in the mirror. I didn't stop to look at myself much as I'm the furthest thing from vain.

Forty-seven years old, wrinkles beginning to appear across my face. Deep green eyes and soft lips with a contradictory battle-hardened face. I always looked angry, but I swear I wasn't. Those weren't even wrinkles between my eyes, but frown lines that made everyone think I was miserable. I swear that I am the furthest thing from miserable; I just have a look of permanent concentration and thought. Looking into my own eyes, there was a slight sadness in them; they say they are the window to the soul and mine was bruised and always had been really, ever since I grew up.

Today was a day of mixed emotions. As Hargreaves pointed out on the radio, it was October 7th. My birthday. Just another day in that respect, but also the 42nd anniversary since I lost both my parents. Rather antiquated, but I pulled out a pocket-watch and admired it. Inside was a photograph of my mother. Beautiful, long dark hair with a pulchritudinous smile, white teeth showing. I liked to admire the photo as it kept me connected to my past, and my real parents, though my father's face was becoming mentally faceless. I had no photographs of him, and the passage of time was impairing my ability to see him.

The watch was my prized possession as it belonged to my father and was ornate in design. It was silver, with an ivy-branch etching going around the shell with the branches meeting at the button that opened the watch. I had to smile at the sudden likeness between my watch and Arthur's knife. There was also a spiritual comparison with ivy being used to ward off evil spirits and protect. Maybe there was something in it, or maybe it was pure coincidence.

I pressed the button at the mouth of the ivy design, even though I knew the watch didn't work anymore. I couldn't bring myself to repair it, so I left it at the time it has been stuck on. I don't know if it last worked when my father had it, or for all those years, it was stuck at the time since the incident. Twenty-one minutes past twelve. Fixing it would be like wiping out the past and their memory.

It felt almost poignant to leave it in what I felt was its final state.

Chapter Two

"Sebastian, are you getting up? I'm making our favourite. Raspberry and banana pancakes!"

I heard my mum's voice echoing through our cottage. They were my favourite, though I'm sure she just said they were hers so she could keep making me them. It was the day before my birthday. I was four and about to turn five, or 'nearly five' as I told anyone who asked. It was October 6, 1977. I opened my eyes and bounced out of bed.

My room was immaculate and in a good state of repair. My favourite poster for 'Jaws' was on the wall looking at the foot of my bed. I positioned it half way down the wall so it looked like the shark was eating the bed. I loved sharks. They were my favourite animal, because of their acute senses. Fascinated by their ability to detect blood in water, and obviously because to a nearly-five-year-old, they are really cool. The apex of the predatory world of the sea. Only I had never watched the film. I wasn't allowed to because it wasn't for kids and despite numerous protests, came up short. I had one man to thank for that decision and in some respects, appreciate the fact he always stayed true to his word. I took slight victory in the fact I was even allowed the poster.

"Come on, son, you heard your mother!"

My dad was firm but fair and incredibly loving, for what I remember anyway. He was always busy but made time for me. We'd go to the park infrequently and he would do the

26

usual dad-like things, like pushing me harder than my mother when I sat on the swing.

"Son!" His voice bellowed through the corridor and frightened me into action.

"Coming, Daddy!"

Daddy… how sweet and pure. I ran so fast it felt like an effortless glide; through the corridor to the kitchen to find the faint smell of pancakes filling the room. It was a sunny day and my mother looked gorgeous. She was wearing a vintage red and white polka dot dress. She had tights on that wrapped around her legs and made her look very stylish. The sun was shining in the window and reflected off her dark hair. She was impeccable and a true vision of beauty.

That image occasionally creeps into my dreams, like an anchor to a happier past.

"So, how is my handsome little man today?"

I could only respond with a smile, as I was shortly lulled into silence. She served a plate of pancakes and ran her soft fingers through my hair. The magic touch of a mother's love stroking me as I ate still makes my heart thud to this day, and almost acts like an off switch for me. Any time my hair is played with, it's like a time-machine and takes me back to that moment of sheer ecstasy and contentment.

"Eat up, champ, because your mother and I are taking you out shortly for some family time. I might even look for your birthday present when we are out," my father shouted across the table.

Even his quiet 'in the house' voice was like a stage whisper. He went back to his morning newspaper and sat there like a stereotypical dad. He was well dressed but not overly fashionable. He wore a perfectly ironed shirt, with a sharp waistcoat expertly draped over him. His silver pocket-watch sat on a chain into the waistcoat breast pocket. Beyond that, his tan trousers and socks just completed the look of the nineteen seventies dad; all in all, very plain. His thick-rimmed, business-like glasses sat atop his nose as he looked down on the newspaper like an angry headmaster. I could see where I got my natural frown.

My mother went over and kissed him. They were a good couple; there was clearly a lot of love and respect between them, as I had never witnessed so much as an argument or disagreement between them.

They had been married for six years, but had been together since they were young adults, having met at a local university. My mother had studied numerous sciences, history, and law, and was a part of a debate team whereas my father had centred his studies solely on law and became a high-flying barrister, pegged to become one of the youngest judges in the county before the incident halted his progression.

Their mutual interest in psychology and law drew them together like fire and wind, in one passionate flame. My father had been known as a bogeyman around the local lawlessness, as he could expertly construct a case and dismiss even the smartest defence attorneys. He practically played verbal chess with the defence, and embarrassed

28

even the country's best lawyers with his one hundred percent prosecution rate; only he was the grand master and they were the initiates.

I obviously didn't know much of this at the time, and only found out most of the facts when reading back on them. I saved a number of newspaper clippings and kept them together in an old hatbox as a shrine to my past.

It turns out that my father was insanely popular amongst local lawmen, and equally hated by the villains. Though he was clearly respected by his peers, I suspect there was jealousy from other lawyers.

I remember one such newspaper clipping where the defence attorney's closing statements after the verdict were a defeatist, "We knew to enter a plea deal from the offset as arguing a case against my learned friend James Blackwood is like thinking about arguing with my wife, or any woman for that matter; although you haven't even started – you've already lost!"

Of course, newspapers from the seventies allowed such comments to be printed given the culture back then, and the comment intrigued me. I always wondered what it would be like to engage in debate with my father. I'm quite a wordsmith but I suspect I'd be bumbling around like my younger self. I didn't get to know that side of him, so I almost glorified him based on that comment. He must have been invincible. I viewed it like pitting man against God himself: omnipotent and infallible in his stance, showing no weakness to his opposition, and struck down with power and righteousness.

It's funny though, I'd hoped that if there was an afterlife, he would be proud of my career choice as even my family danced with the scales of justice; good and evil.

My mother on the other hand was incredibly smart and a genius in her own right. She had a fascination with cryptography and ciphers; even going so far as making us our own secret messages with letters, numbers, and cryptograms for fun. Every weekend she would write me an encrypted message and I would have to figure it out. They were basic given my age; but always made me smile. We kept a simple code and sent messages frequently; easy ones we could read almost instantly, like, "Mummy loves you," and one of my favourites, "You are the brightest star in the sky." I smile thinking back to it, as I was always her little star.

Albeit little messages designed to make me feel loved at a tender age, I've carried them with me through my life. Sometimes, if it was for a treat or surprise, she would throw in some curve balls and riddles, really confusing me but ultimately, she'd coach me on where I went wrong if I couldn't complete them. I've always been thankful for that, because from a young age, she shaped my young mind to be sharper and see things differently.

Sadly, I didn't know too much about her past because I never had a chance to ask her, but she always said that her father, my absolutely terrifying grandfather I might add, used to do the same with her.

He was allegedly a very secretive man; high ranking in the military and never talked about his work. General Harvey Axton was his name. I can only speculate but for him to know a lot about ciphers, codes, and being involved in the Second World War, even the dumbest rocks could put two and two together with that one. His entire presence exuded power and authority. I don't ever remember seeing him smile other than in a photograph of my mother's graduation. Her graduation was obviously such a happy event that when the camera clicked, it captured the fatherly pride and real man behind the armour.

Sadly, the only memory I have retained, aside from that photograph, was of him shouting at my father over the kitchen worktop. They had a disagreement and strangely, his voice made my father's sound like an actual whisper. It happened about three months before my fifth birthday. My mother hurried me out of the kitchen, took me into my bedroom, covered my ears, and kissed me on the forehead when it transpired. She slowly removed her hands from my ears and said everything was okay, but she really needed me to help with a new code. She left me in my room with a challenge and a message to decipher. I tried to focus whilst I heard verbal thunder crashing through the thin walls.

"It's not all about you, Harvey!" I heard in the distance.

"You don't understand. What did you ever see in this man, Lillian?"

That cipher my mother gave me, I didn't finish de-coding because I left to investigate when curiosity got the better of me. I stood at my bedroom door and counted to ten in my head before plucking up the courage to step out. Vocal discord echoing through the house, I couldn't do it on the first count, so counted to ten again about three times. On

31

my current attempt, I took a deep breath, counting out loud this time for the extra confidence, "Three, four, five," and it wasn't until I heard an ungodly screech coming from my mother that I stopped counting and just opened the door, without a second thought.

I think back to that exact moment whenever I need to psyche myself up, or if I need to prepare myself for something mentally exhausting. It takes me in to my 'zone.' My mother was screaming at my grandfather to let go of my dad. He said something about taking away the most important woman in his life and that moving away was him willingly breaking up the family. He barked about not being well and with a newfound confidence, I shouted at the giant of a man with his fist clenched, and that turned the room silent. My grandfather let go of my father and left without another word.

Ultimately, we didn't move away so whatever the reason or argument; my grandfather won. I suspect that's the only time my father lost, and I'm not sure what, or who, stopped the plans for us to move. My grandfather actually died a few months later from an illness unknown to me and it broke my mother. I could feel her pain from a young age and remember cuddling into her for weeks to try and make her feel better. She'd stroke my head every time, so I suspect it was as soothing for her as it was for me. I would say that as a child, I certainly felt loved and cared for; at least in earlier years.

After I had eaten my breakfast, we all hopped into my father's car on our day out. The nostalgic sound of the old radio being tuned in as we set off and the break of a voice coming through was quite enjoyable, unlike my radio nowadays. I vaguely recall a news statement about a case my father was involved in, but my mother hurriedly switched it off and tutted about it not being appropriate. Laughably, when I think about it, I've taken on my mother's ability to slam the radio off.

We were like a picture-perfect family, having a day out. We went for a walk by the lake, I had an ice-cream in the park, and I reached dizzying new heights as my father ejected me into the sky on the swing, to my mother's over-protective protesting.

It was the last day I remember being happy as a child.

The next day, my birthday, was sadly the day that everything changed. I barely slept a wink out of excitement, hoping I would be spoilt rotten. After all, five was a big age. It was a half-way stop on the road to ten. Maybe I would get the Star Wars doll that our next-door neighbour had? Maybe I would finally get to see 'Jaws' now that I was about to practically enter adulthood?

When I woke up, my parents were already around the table, almost as if regimentally repeating the same process as the day before, and every other day for that matter. I was given breakfast, they gave me a card that had another cryptograph in it courtesy of my mother, which read the promise of a bigger surprise later in the day.

The phone rang and whatever was discussed on the other line left my mother in a state of reaction. I wish I knew what was said, whether it was that a birthday cake was ready at the bakers, whether it was genuinely bad news, I'll never know – but I was left in the capable hands of Miss Battersby, our next-door neighbour. She was a younger woman who lived on her own. She seemed quite wealthy and had inherited the house she was in but had an air of immaturity to her.

My mother gave some instructions to her, then walked over and kissed me on the forehead, before running her fingers through my hair. Although brief, as I recall that moment, that seemed to last forever. My mother referred to me as her little star and wished me a happy birthday. My father on the other hand put his coat on, told me that he would give me the surprise later. Only he never did.

That was the last time I saw them.

The morning started to evade us and then the sky started to turn grey. Rain began to fall and before long, Miss Battersby was panicking, trying to gather her washing from the line. As anticipated, she sorted her own first and then helped with what was on our line, though it was already soaked.

I sat on the porch and watched the rain falling, leaving Miss Battersby looking like a drowned rat. I focussed on the raindrops bouncing on the ground as they formed the smallest puddles. Fascinated with the movement and flow of the water, as well as the soothing sound of the rain hitting the porch roof, I must have spent hours there. Though in my youthful innocence, I know part of it was for the surprise that awaited me, the rain just helped pass the time.

Miss Battersby was on the phone in the kitchen, muttering dejectedly to the person on the other end about how rude my parents were for lumbering her with me for hours longer than they said they'd be. There was a slight pause where the recipient was obviously offering their tuppence worth of gossip before the sound of laughter erupted from the room. She mumbled that my parents were off to pick up a few bits and pieces and in a forced whisper, mentioned that I was going to be the recipient of a new bicycle. I still think to this day that she deliberately 'whispered' to ruin the surprise and get back at my parents for inconveniencing her longer than originally intended, though I guess I'll never know what my actual birthday present was.

As the rain continued to fall, a terrible sadness started to form over me as I watched a policeman pull up outside the property. He looked at the house, then at me before exhaling loudly. He was psyching himself up for something I could tell, despite my young naivety. He had an awkward look on his gaunt face, with droopy eyes and a long nose. He wore a thick waterproof jacket that was already dripping, as though he had been outside for some time already. His female partner stayed in the car, perhaps to avoid the rain.

"Hello, young man," he said in a monotonous voice. "Is anyone in?"

"Miss Battersby is!" I exclaimed proudly, like I was the guardian of the castle.

He walked up the porch stairs, and as his hand reached out to the door, he knocked to signal her attention; she

35

sorted her hair and made him welcome. Miss Battersby gestured for him to take a seat and he popped his jacket off and hung it on the back of my father's chair. He sat down and started talking; gathering information as to what the relationship was between us.

I walked over to where the officer sat and out of the corner of my eye, I was suddenly drawn to the pocket of his waterproof jacket. In the pocket, was a silver watch. I expertly, and innocently pulled it out and recognised it was the same as my father's.

The officer was distracted and engaged in conversation with my next-door neighbour so he hadn't thought that his own pocket could be picked. Caught off guard, I inspected the watch and pressed the button at the collection of ivy-branches. As the case popped open, I could see my mother's face on the photograph inside. Why did the officer have this?

In hindsight, with my current level of experience, I would have immediately suspected him as being a corrupt copper based on his stereotypical elongated face. He looked like a petty burglar, not an upstanding lawman. To this day, I don't know what motivated him. He would have been paid a reasonable sum by the state, but it clearly was not enough to get by; evidently, he made a point of robbing others who couldn't fight back or were gone and wouldn't care.

Either way, as if by fate, the watch found its way back into my possession and I sneakily put it in my own pocket. It filled it out considerably given my young, petite frame and shallow pockets. Youthful innocence at the time suspected the officer found the watch and was returning it, so I decided to keep it safe for my father coming home.

That's when I heard the real reason for the visit. The officer explained there had been a crash, and at present, there were two fatalities and foul play was suspected. He provided a description for my parents and advised he'd inspected my father's wallet to find out the address for next of kin, as both individual's next of kin was the other person.

That's obviously where he found the watch that miraculously found its way into his pocket. I didn't know what a fatality was at that age, so I didn't know how to react or what was really being discussed. Miss Battersby explained I was on my own and didn't know if I had anybody else but with a sudden change of heart, advised that she was charged with my care for now.

The officer gave me a sharp look as if studying me. I froze, thinking he knew about the watch. In my head, I was preparing every reason for why I decided to keep the watch safe; my father would want me to be the one to look after it until he got home. Little did I know at the time, he never would.

I slept at Miss Battersby's house that night, which was strange. I'd never been in her house before, but it was dark. The room I was told I was sleeping in was stacked with china sets in ornate cabinets and sat atop were some old Russian dolls. It felt like they were looking at me and it made me uneasy. It was a very antiquated collection of items and certainly not what I would expect from someone as young as Miss Battersby.

It's clear she didn't or couldn't afford the lifestyle the house provided, as it was stone cold with the radiators off, and everything seemed to be gathering dust. There was no love or care that went into the upkeep of the house or the trinkets within, as they had clearly been left for a long time; which led me to the assumption she did, in fact, inherit the property. I attempted to amuse myself by exploring the trinkets, rather than the number of colouring pens and paper thrown in front of me in a poor attempt to entertain me. What a Happy Birthday...

I looked out the window and the rain hadn't stopped. As if competing with the sound of rain on the window, I heard the competitive chimes of an old grandfather clock from the hallway outside. I studied the room and focussed my eyes on one of the dolls. Tick, tick, tick, was the only sound resonating through the house. I was spellbound by the doll and felt like it was following me around the room. Suddenly a large chime crashed to break the silence. I let out a slight yelp as I foolishly anticipated it being the work of the doll. Miss Battersby came through to the room to check on me to find the source of the yelping. I asked where my parents were with youthful innocence and she broke.

She told me, in as gentle a way as possible, that my parents had gone. I asked where they had gone to and she said they had gone to heaven.

"When will they come back?" I asked.

I was met with tears. The poor woman agreed to watch me for a few hours and now had to tell me my parents were dead. What sick, twisted being mapped this experience out for Miss Battersby?

Fate is cruel sometimes. That said, my newfound sense of emotion made me run up to her and asked her not to cry. I told her that everything would be okay and said thank you for looking after me.

In a bid to start our friendship, I pulled out my father's timepiece and pressed the button and showed her the picture of my mother inside it. Miss Battersby smiled and said my mother looked beautiful; then hugged me tight, saying that for as long as she could, she would look after me.

I stayed with her for three days and I've never seen her since.

Chapter Three

I found myself still staring in the mirror, snapped back into reality. I pressed on the mirror to reveal the contents of a medicine cabinet behind. Within, bottles of pills, vitamins, and anti-anxiety tablets stood in a neat row. I ran my fingers up the anti-anxiety container, popping the lid off like a true professional.

Benzodiazepine: a mildly effective drug I'd been taking since I was a younger man, with few side effects. Then again, whenever I crashed mentally; I don't know if I would be able to tell if it was my mind playing tricks on me, or it was a side effect.

I stopped taking medication when I was with Arianna. She truly kept me grounded, and she was my safe place. I felt invincible with her around, capable of doing anything and strong enough to battle my mental demons.

Trust me when I say that it doesn't matter who you are, or what you do; mental health issues can affect anyone. I did think it made me weak, especially in my line of work. I felt conflicted quite often but always managed to push on. Thankfully, none of my colleagues really knew how I felt, or the challenges I faced. I kept them hidden like a serial philanderer would an illicit affair.

It's tough to explain because everyone experiences it differently. Sometimes the same crippling thoughts could cycle around my mind night after night; experiences from my past would knock on the door and remind me they were there. I'd mentally re-enact entire situations from my life as if I was right there, but with the freedom to explore and treat them like brand new, active scenarios. In doing so, I could almost question why I ended up where I did; I would question whether I made the correct decisions, or if I could have handled them better. Then I would be overwhelmed with worry and dread.

Sometimes, I couldn't escape them, and I'd enter what I would call my own personal 'black hole.' Mental demons anchored to me like a physical ball and chain. Lately, the medication helped. I could suppress them but even when down, they aren't out. I was strangely capable despite them, professionally speaking. When I was exploring a crime scene, or hunting a killer, I came alive. To come alive when surrounded by death... I was a high-functioning bag of contradictions really.

I knocked some of the pills back, swallowing them with a sip of water directly from the tap. I took an extra one as a personal birthday present. Soaking my face again, it was like a reset button. I deeply exhaled and shut the tap off and closed the medicine cabinet. It came loose slightly as I closed it with force and seemed to hang from one hinge, balancing diagonally.

I smiled at the man in the mirror and thought I really had to do some work to get the place out of a state of disrepair. Now wasn't the time, I suppose I had to get to work. I snapped back with a sudden jolt of life, heading to the door, power-walking through the room. I effortlessly picked up my jacket hanging on the back of the couch, flung it around my back and slid into one of the sleeves. It felt like my own montage as it all happened without so much of a hiccup, except for the fact I grabbed it upside down and had fumbled my arm into the wrong sleeve.

As I walked outside, I sorted my jacket and observed the weather. The rain was gentle, but still showed no signs of stopping. I smiled at my classic muscle car, a 1975 Chevrolet Camaro. I didn't know if it was the same car my father drove, but it looked similar and gave me a sense of nostalgia, as though I was honouring his memory. It had its flaws though, it was completely impractical and frequently breaking down, but incredibly sexy. I unlocked the car and jumped in.

The crashing of the drops hitting the window and the metal above me sounded quite melancholic, given the anniversary of the incident as a child. Rain seemed to follow me on my birthday, or at least it felt that way. I turned the key and the engine struggled. I turned the key again, nothing. I punched the steering wheel in anger and had to laugh at the comedy of errors the day was turning in to already. First the cabinet, then my jacket, and now this... they say it all comes in threes, so I seemed to have achieved my quota for the day.

It was still dark outside and out of nowhere; a shadowed pedestrian heard my plight as the engine choked. I got out of the car to check under the hood and he waved his hand at my car signalling he had mechanical knowledge and asked if I needed help.

"Bad day for a bit of car trouble," he cheerfully stated. He was of a stocky build and bald, with a slight birthmark on the back of his head. We joked a little about the misfortune and how I broke down at the best possible place, home.

He seemed to identify exactly what was wrong with the car almost immediately and reconnected a few bits and pieces. I couldn't even begin to think how things had become disconnected unless it was a prank by one of the neighbourhood kids. He asked a lot of questions about me in such a short space of time and seemed intrigued when I told him I was a detective. He multitasked and sorted the car out whilst asking question after question. The normal interrogator became the interrogated. It was harmless really, and I felt happy to engage with him rather than stand in silence.

"That's you sorted," he said as he extended his hand out to shake mine.

"Sebastian." I offered my own hand in return. "Thank you."

My tone rose inquisitively as though to suggest I was asking for his name. He had an incredibly powerful grip and practically interrupted me with his jovial tone, sensing my request. "Al."

"Thank you, Al. You've honestly done me a massive favour," I exclaimed.

"Hey, no worries, Seb. I heard the car choking and figured I knew what it could be. Plus, it was an option to get up close and personal with a classic. Fantastic car and fantastic taste my friend. Until we meet again, I guess!"

I nodded in approval and hopped back in the car. Seb. I hadn't really been called that since I was a child. I smiled at the wistfulness of the reference, turned the key and with that slight hand motion, life seemed to pump through the car. The sound of hard, old school muscle regurgitating that vintage roar in the morning air was music to my ears. I looked at the radio dial and it was similar to the one I remembered in my father's car as a child but not identical. Everything I seemed to look at took me back to that day. It was always the case on my birthday.

I put the car in gear and eased off, turning onto the road. Al, a few feet down the road turned around to watch me set off and gave me a friendly wave so I waved back. What a nice guy, the world needed more people like that considering the Arthur Henderson types out there.

As I pulled up to the station, I was always left impressed with the architecture. Our station almost felt like the younger brother of the Washington Capitol Building with a large oval at the centre of the roof. Large pillars kept an overhanging ridge over the side of the building where some small stairs led up to the main entrance. A modernised disability ramp almost ruined the vintage feel of the building but was a mandatory requirement for public access. It felt more like our station was better placed as a museum given the wow factor.

I slowed the car down and as I rolled into the car park, nearby passers-by with their umbrellas looked at me like I was a low-rider, some sort of gangland thug. I revved like a boy racer just for effect, a pointless exercise to motivate me.

It occurred to me how strange it was for the town to have so much life this early in the morning, as it was only around seven. Then again, this city always had some sort of seedy life coughing up at unsociable hours. Like I said earlier, it kept me employed.

I hopped out of the car and the rain hit my face. It was refreshing almost, feeling the drops bounce off my forehead as I looked up to the dusky sky. The faint light of the sun breaking through gloomy dark clouds brightened the view and reflected from the metallic sheen of the car. A slight breeze in the air made the surface of my skin chill.

The slam of the car door broke my concentration, as I almost unwillingly closed it, as if in autopilot. With a slightly hurried jog, I bounded towards the grand stairs leading to the main door of the station, unsure why there was a call.

"Two, three, four," I mouthed as I headed in the main doors. It wasn't even a nervous tick or anything this time; I just needed to bring myself into the room. Whatever the day had in store for me, it was enough for my phone to be buzzing before the day even broke.

The main foyer of the station was rather grand with a large statue in the middle of the back wall, and balconies of the second floor following around the wall above. The statue was nothing short of magnificent; a knight on horseback holding some scales in his left hand, with a blade in the right hand. I meant it when I said the station had museum-like tendencies; though I struggled to connect the dots between police and medieval knights, other than the faint connection with the scales.

45

The statue had a grand plaque brandishing a Latin phrase at the hilt, "Et aequalitatem iustitiae," which meant, 'The Equality of Justice.' With the clicking of my brogues simulating the noise of horseshoes, my footsteps echoed in the hallway as I headed to the elevator.

As I walked, I looked down at the precinct badge painted and varnished into the floor expertly; Island Heights Police Department. There was a certain grand feel about walking in the front door of the station; it made me proud to serve and protect. Equality and justice, two words I did tend to live my life and fulfil my duties by. Unless of course, I was fortunate enough to get my hands on Arthur Henderson, the one man who didn't deserve equality. How do you balance out his sins on the scales of justice?

I pressed the button to open the elevator doors and was met by the horrible buzzer sound it made as it powered on and recalled the cabin. As the doors opened to greet me, I gesticulated with my hands and re-enacted Moses parting the sea, with old steel doors. As badass as I thought I must have looked in my mind, I probably came across as quite eccentric to my colleagues. At least I amused myself at this early hour.

I suppose I was quite odd. From the classic car I drove, to my mannerisms and dress sense, I was the stereotypical 1930s detective, in the 2010s. Waistcoat, shirt, brogues, and smart trousers. I was only missing a bowler hat, or fedora, for the truly unique noire feel.

As the elevator reached my floor, I headed to the situation room I had monopolised since the Arthur

Henderson case. It had become more of a storage room really. People didn't like to go in there, as I had photos and mug shots sprawled across whiteboards. This was a reminder to me, a daily motivational tool to find the bastard and gut him; whereas to my colleagues, it was like glorifying the devil in his own twisted shrine. We used to host team briefings in the situation room but had almost turned the upstairs staff room into it now. At least you could have a coffee whilst you got the latest case, or staff update. I think that's why I was never told to vacate and relocate the proverbial shrine.

I scanned the room as I walked in the door. Everything from the crime scene images, a map of the country, dotted and pegged with expected whereabouts of Mr Henderson. Inclusive of a city map with similar pegs and string linking everything. You could tell I was obsessed. No one really wanted to come in for fear of disturbing my process. Images of cryptic messages left behind at Arthur's latest hideaways, or crime scenes. The worst was the bloodied room. Images of that one covered an entire whiteboard with some coded messages that were found there.

That was a unique crime scene. When we first got the call, my phone buzzed about seven times before I answered. The Chief asked for me specifically, to try and decipher what the hell was going on. Arthur had made it clear it was him. He had found a seedy hotel room that had quite a unique architectural set-up. There was a small hallway into the room, with a step down into the main bedroom area, leading into what can only be described as a small subterranean pool.

He'd booked the room out for almost six weeks in one of many fake names, and in that time had somehow managed to fill the room up with about six inches of blood, with the occasional addition of entrails in amongst it. Forensics identified a mixture of the victim's blood, coupled with various animals DNA, specifically pigs and lambs. Suggesting it was all for show and painfully deliberate. It was strange really, having to dress in a full plastic protective suit to observe a crime scene.

I dressed with intrigue, as I prepped myself to go into that room. Excitement brimming at the unusual nature of preparation, I walked down the small hallway to the stair, as the blood bobbed just millimetres away from being able to spill over the hall.

Anyone that entered quite literally had to slowly wade through blood just to get anywhere in the room, as walking and splashing could inadvertently disturb anything above ankle length. Bizarrely, one wall was left completely blank in the room: like a blank canvas. Blood spatter was riding up the other walls. A bloodied bone-saw was plugged into the wall, which was the obvious implement used to create the mess. When it was taken away as evidence, a perfectly white gap with plug sockets stood out like a sore thumb. It was probably yellow, murky, and dirty, but comparatively to the rest of the room, shone like a dentist's front teeth.

One of the bloodied walls had a message written to me in blood: *Detective Blackwood, 'X' marks the spot.*

On the bed, the once white duvet, sheet, and pillowcase were scarlet in colour with the slightest breaks of white dotted over the bed, somehow untouched by blood. The shape of a human body could be seen through the covers, tucked into the bed so tightly it was like looking at a sarcophagus; at the head of the body was a lamb's head, being worn like a crown. Once the flurry of photos had been taken of the crime scene, we peeled back the covers to reveal the body of a stout old woman; she must have been about seventy years old but had a fairly youthful body, it was her neck and face that was the give away. There was no ID on her, her fingerprints had been cut off, and her dentures prevented us from identifying the body through dental records.

She was Arthur's first Jane Doe. Upon removing the lamb-head crown that covered some of her face, it's almost as if she died from the terror. It hadn't left her expression. She'd been dead for quite some time. In fact, the smell of the body was what brought the case to our attention, that or the entrails that were in the bloody pool at our feet. Wilted carnation flowers of various colours; whites, pinks, purples, and yellows were sprawled on the bed in a beautiful array, damaged by time. The flashes of forensic cameras capturing their saddened, death-like bouquet felt like such a waste.

As we inspected her body, there was an 'X' carved into her stomach and stitched poorly back together, with a small black implement inside. I let the forensics team take plenty of photographs and to the protesting of my colleagues around me, opened the wound to reveal a small lockbox.

It was one of those wooden puzzle boxes that required me to figure out and input the pattern. It was a simple fix, etched into the side of the box were some images of a bird, an egg, a worm, and a tree. I suppose it was subject to interpretation, however, I twisted the cubes around until I presented my desired 'circle of life' was presented. A slight click unlocked the box and the pattern revealed the contents: a UV torch.

"What on earth is that?" my colleague asked as I turned the torch to the proverbial blank canvas, the untouched wall in front of me.

Only it wasn't blank at all. My colleague shook his head and muttered I was obviously in the right job as I connected the dots before he'd even analysed that it was a torch. It was a simple answer to a simple question. 'X' did mark the spot. A hidden message for me, a game I was starting to enjoy playing. My colleague immediately started snapping pictures. The torch couldn't cover the full wall, so I shouted to the Chief outside and asked for some black lights.

What seemed like an age, and after intent studying of the message with the inadequate torch, some larger black lights were brought into the room. What few colleagues were present, they looked on in awe, and I started to decipher what was on the wall. Lots of symbols and letters turned the blank wall into something that resembled the Rosetta Stone.

A riddle, addressed to me, was written and centred across the wall.

Sebastian, Before you doth see, the Head of a Lamb,

Desecrated and carved is the Middle of a Pig,

With her Serpent Tongue remains the Hind and Tail of a Dragon,

Remember and brand this bitch the animal that she is?

For she does the same.

Arthur, what a creative game you play. I deliberated the riddle for days and my answers were scrawled on the whiteboard. I didn't know if the lamb symbolised youthful purity, the pig could be a red herring symbolising me as a lawman? Perhaps gluttony, greed, and mess? The dragon could be the sign of wisdom, myth, and grandiose imagery? But what animal was she? The answer for the animal was simpler but I could sense there was a hidden message amongst the choice of animals.

I broke the riddle down for days and settled on a solution. The Head of a Lamb — "L," the middle of the Pig — "I," the Hind and Tail of the Dragon — "ON." She was a Lion? Or the bitch, Lioness?

I didn't know what Arthur was trying to tell me or symbolise. Her serpent tongue? She lied? For 'she does the same' — does the same as a lion? Lion? Or maybe, she's not really an animal and she was lying? As if laying on the bed, or lying in general?

It was a small part of a bigger picture, but I couldn't see it right now, though 'lion' felt right.

51

Either way, it was a grand picture he left behind and almost left me fascinated. As much as I hated Arthur for what he had done, I almost awaited the next instalment in our game. For a second, as I got lost in the puzzles, the riddles, and the meaning behind his gesture, I was reminded of home. Of my childhood and my mother.

I physically spat at the ground for even bringing her into my mind and comparing any shred of likeness and resemblance between the two. Professionally speaking, that was a stupid move: to let an assailant get under my skin so much, but my stomach did turn at the prior comparison.

That mild, fleeting thought of that crime scene dissipated as I re-focussed to my surroundings; I caught myself staring at the history of the case on the whiteboard, surrounded by my own spittle. I had to find him. I had to beat him. Why did he even target that woman? She was in her late sixties, had no priors; a seemed like a bystander of life. No family, otherwise, they'd have reported the disappearance. Sadly, by being alone, she was easy to be forgotten. I'd keep her in my mind until this case was closed, as a mark of respect. How empty though, living a full life and having no heirs, nobody to continue the family name, a speck of sand on a grand beach by all accounts—

"Blackwood!" the Chief exclaimed as he walked in the door behind me. He startled me as I was lost in thought. I acknowledged him with a simple, "Sir," like he was the General of a small army.

I suppose in a way he was. I respected the Chief. He was always prepared to go with my wild theories, settle on my crazy concepts, and gave me breathing room to work. He never micro-managed me because I made him look good. He loved a press conference, I didn't. Whenever I pulled in a few sharks, he'd get the public credit and I made the precinct's stats look good.

I enjoyed hunting the sharks, like my old childhood poster. I was the predator amongst predators and I fucking loved it. Arthur was more than that. He was no mere shark; he was a whale and the Chief knew it too. Ever since that fateful night of Jessica's and he called his daughter through teary eyes to say he loved her; he wanted me to catch Arthur, bag him a whale so-to-speak.

In fact, I'll never forget the words he said to me. "Blackwood, whatever you need, whatever you've got to do, you find this evil cunt!" Oddly, that's the only time I've ever heard the Chief swear, and he went straight to A-grade swearing. Something punched him in the gut that night and the devil on his shoulder got full control of his vocal cords.

His voice softened, in a defeatist tone. "I'm afraid I'm going to have to have you cut back on the amount of time you are spending on this case."

"What?" I responded in shock.

"Sebastian." He never called me by my first name. This was serious, like a father trying to educate his son; he lowered his voice even more. "You know how much I want this guy off the streets. But I've had the steer from above that they think the case is going cold. Other cases are piling up, the others can't get through them like you can. Upstairs, and the mayor's office – they think that Henderson is unlikely to do anything again so soon."

"How the fuck can they predict that from their ivory towers?" I protested.

"Listen Blackwood." He was talking to me like I was an employee again. "I appreciate this is as much a kick in the teeth for you as it is for me. Call it bureaucratic bullshit. Office politics. But the closure rate for cases since you've been working on Henderson isn't as good as it has been before. See it as a compliment, you're one of the best. I need you out there closing cases or you, or any of us, won't have a job at the end of it. They want to merge us with nearby precincts and solving crime keeps us in front and gives me some ammo to defend the necessity for our station. Granted, solving this one and bringing Henderson in would close a lot of unsolved cases and bring the closure rate up but so would working on others. You invest less of your time." He coughed. "No, less of MY time solving this, and solving some of the petty shit to bring the numbers up. I know I'm making it sound like you have a choice, but I'm sorry – you don't."

You're damn right it was office politics. Complete and utter bullshit. Little Sebastian, Jane Doe, the others. They were just going to become statistics. Numbers. Their lives were nothing but numbers on a pie chart where the bigwigs would push bullshit and finances around to justify their own high salaries. I'd heard the rumours of the precinct merges and the Chief inadvertently confirmed it to me. Probably figured I was eccentric enough to be trusted with the knowledge and that people wouldn't try to engage me in small talk. Naturally, I wasn't one to cause needless drama in the office so his foresight was probably well placed. It still reeked of political bullshit though.

"How long do I have? I feel like I'm getting closer every day, Chief!"

I was left disappointed with the answer, as he pushed a stack of files against my chest, leaving me to fumble with the paperwork.

"In other words, son, take your pick."

Before I had a chance to respond, he walked out the room. That's why he wanted to talk to me this morning. I should have picked up, as I'd have had the satisfaction of throwing and breaking my phone, the bringer of bad news. With no real options, I threw the files across the floor and paperwork went everywhere. A childish gesture that ultimately achieved nothing, but I was seething.

I was beyond angry that Arthur was getting a reprieve because some political dickheads decided that our time was better spent pissed away on other cases. Surely, they could sense the gap was closing, and I was starting to connect the dots. The fact that Arthur would taunt me so blatantly and attempt to frighten me with his selfie submissions and photographs of my wife was proof enough. Surely, I was turning over the right rocks and I'd get a hit.

A stark sense of reality hit home as the loose paperwork started to fall to the floor. The photograph of a smiling woman was on the front of the page. I started to get a surge of empathy, and my attitude quickly changed. A small sense of calm overcame my body, as I weighed up the fact that the other cases were people too. Victims and families left in grief and in pain and they deserved my time as much as anyone else did. Just like that, one quick glance and I was resigned to accepting that Arthur had a reprieve. I'll be back, you bastard.

I suppose that's exactly what made my wife leave. I was falling into the quicksand of the case again and if I didn't tread carefully, I'd be consumed. I suppose I could turn my attentions elsewhere for a short while.

I sorted through the pile; frustrated about my lack of control with the news I received. I pieced together sheets of paper to restore the packs to their former glory, albeit slightly creased. I took a seat at the table, with my back to the door, whiteboard in my immediate line of sight. I looked down at the table to peruse my wares. I felt like a funeral director, flicking through a catalogue of death, deciding which case to pick. It was odd really, how my job could trivialise something as final as death.

Suzanna Holmes; she was a very alluring woman, a stay-at-home, married mother of three, thirty-four years old. Low flier in terms of academic ability; passing grades at college before landing herself in trouble. Record for public indecency after a night out, and not with the husband. Suzanna hasn't worked in eight years, previously a secretary at a powerhouse of a law firm, seduced by the magnetism of her rich boss. Married a childhood sweetheart, who later went into in the army, Sergeant Brian Holmes. Decorated soldier served in four tours.

I could almost figure it out. Stays at home, alone, kids at school; inviting a few people home whilst her husband is away, protecting overseas. Blunt force trauma to the head with a claw hammer, clearly suggested a crime of passion. A fleeting drift over the case, solved. Send some units down to his usual hideouts; crack his network of soldier friends until the right rock is turned over. I scrawled a few key pointers onto the front of the case file and started a new pile.

Richard Weston, forty-eight-year-old father of two, mechanic. Richard was a career man, who started as an apprentice in the field, thirty years prior after an underwhelming academic output. Incredible knack for vehicular technology and featured in a number of local newspaper articles for his charitable endeavours, one of which, he modified a vehicle so a disabled man could drive.

Seemed like a genuinely nice fellow, my interest piqued slightly. Valued in the community for his efforts in dealing with a local charity about underprivileged teens and teaching them skills and abilities to find work. Richard ran the business on a part-time basis, leaving the shop in the hands of his own apprentices. Mildly stereotypical to assume the underprivileged kids could be at the nucleus of the crime but still the most likely.

Richard was found crushed between the wall and a vehicle in a clearly malicious attempt to run him down. Not everything on the surface was so pristine, however, as initial reports of the property found what was suspected to be an

57

illegal chop shop. Either Mr Weston was aware of the goings-on and found himself on the other side of a seedy deal, though unlikely; or perhaps the likely outcome, he found evidence of the illegal goings-on, confronted the teens he was helping, and one took offence to his proceedings. Best place to start really, even the rookie detectives could do this one. Check the books to see whom Mr Weston paid, cross-reference with any known gang ties; crime solved. Another scribble on the file and into the new pile of 'too easy for me' cases.

Mildly narcissistic of me, I know. Maybe I should give this to Michael? I could consider it a bit of professional courtesy for him saving me from Arthur in that warehouse? Give it to a patrolman to solve and bring him in, as that could give him the rightful recognition to realise his dream of being a detective. I pondered the decision and then texted him to come and claim it: *I've got just the job for you to get you some recognition with the Chief. Situation room. Green file, middle table. You owe me a beer.*

Well, that was my good deed for the day with a possible beer at the end of it all. Michael deserved it. He'd be like a dog with a bone as well, even working in his spare time to show his dedication to his superiors. As I went to grab the third file, the Chief burst into the room again. My back was to the door and him.

"Blackwood!" I twisted my head slightly, as he stood above me at the door. It was that authoritative reciting of my name where I knew I was about to be told what case I was doing. A new case had just been called in anonymously and I wasn't given a choice.

It had the same modus operandi of previous Henderson cases. A sigh of relief almost left my mouth. The next move in our game of chess had been made and it came at the perfect possible time. I'd be lying if I said that the next person's unfortunate demise made me smile. I didn't smile for the obvious tragedy but smiled because it was fated to happen. I was ready for action and didn't need to be told where to go. Even if I did have a shred of doubt this was Arthur, it was an order and I always followed them; it had been ingrained in me from a young age to respect an order from authority.

The Chief should have done that before when he threw me the pile of cases; as he would have combated any risk of sudden indecisiveness I may have had and got me straight onto work. There was a professional level of respect between us though. I don't think he liked to order me around too much as I did have a habit of making him look good.

I walked from the room to head to the car. As if he was shadowing me the whole time, Michael could be seen walking across the foyer over the balcony, briskly walking to the elevator. He hadn't seen me, and I didn't want to bump into him, so I opted for the stairs. Probably best to avoid him anyway, that way nobody could report back I had tipped him off or given him the steer to find the solutions to the cases I left upstairs. If he willingly found the file, put two and two together and sorted it out on his own, it might give the bosses the perception he was much better than he was. It was enough to demonstrate the drive, the passion, and embodiment of the spirit of the statue in his desire to deliver justice and equality. That's not to say Michael couldn't have figured this one out; he'd likely never get the chance to, or opportunity to view the file under normal circumstances.

I clambered down the stairs and gave it a minute before I cleared the set of doors back into the foyer. That was to give Michael time to get into the situation room and not see me. Some might say I was just unsociable, irrespective of my good intentions to avoid. I hopped in the car, enjoying the rain hitting off the windscreen. A quick text came through to my phone from Michael thanking me for the tip off. I smiled casually.

I drove out towards the scene of the crime, stopping first for a coffee. That was the problem with not sleeping; I did occasionally need help injecting some life into me. It was still only the morning, so I didn't really know how I was going to survive the day. I stopped off at a burger van parked at the side of the road that served coffee. I was fairly familiar with the man that ran it and he always started his days early.

I did feel bad, as he often didn't charge me because a few years prior, I had stopped an armed robbery of his station, completely by fluke. I was just in the right place at the right time. Karma's way of thanking me was to have the owner fuel me with coffee and such on occasion. We exchanged mutual pleasantries, he moaned a little about the weather, whereas I claimed I was an advocate of it and liked the rain.

He said it was bad for business, so I felt quite bad for being mildly supportive of it.

As I sipped my coffee under the canopy of his van, I felt my phone buzzing. It was Arianna. As much as I wanted to answer, I was frozen in place. I didn't really have much to say right now. If I said I was about to head to another crime scene where it was deduced that it could be Arthur Henderson, she'd hang up. I fell on the proverbial sword and watched the phone ring out.

She didn't need another harsh reminder of why we had gone our separate ways. I was dying to hear her voice. I was desperate to see her. I needed to fight my corner and defend my actions as a professional, though I'll never truly understand the mind of a woman, nevermind a woman who has been hurt emotionally. There are just some things in life that can't be explored and closed like a case.

I bid my coffee friend a farewell and paid this time. I gave him a larger note to make up for the last few freebies and hopped in the car before he had a chance to give me any change.

I could see his point with the rain being bad for business; though there is something magical about the elements. It always reminds me of just how insignificant we all are and how helpless I felt as a child on that fateful day as I watched it at work, transfixed on the puddle while I sat waiting for my parents to come home. I awed at how truly magnificent nature is and how we just ruin it; impede on its ability to flow freely, or as humans, blatantly destroy it with our cars, industry, and...

In automatic mode and not focussing properly, I suddenly had to slam on the brakes. A homeless man was casually strolling across the road, mind numbed to the traffic flying both ways. Unbelievable. What an idiot!

Then hypocritically, despite my earlier contemplations, I slammed my foot on the accelerator and heard the engine guzzle down the petrol needed to move on again. A slight and unnecessary wheel spin broke the homeless man out of his trance, and he gave me thumbs up, as if in thanks.

Nature, how intriguing... the fact I was hunting a very freak of it and I suppose, could probably be compared to one as well, but with much better intentions. I realised I meant exactly what I said to myself when I said we were insignificant. The thought made me feel quite anxious. Of course, now wasn't the time to be thinking like that. I had to focus!

I wondered if Arthur's mind was as conflicted as mine sometimes. I knew I fought with justice on my side, but my mind really played tricks on itself. I could swear I was a good man but to contend with feelings of nothingness felt contradictory because without good to trump evil, we'd be mindless debauches of nothing anyway.

Did Arthur feel like that when he was committing his crimes? Did he feel like he was operating with a twisted sense of justice? Based on some of the things Jessica told me about the night he killed his own son; he operated with a sick conviction that he was doing the right thing to kill the son of the devil. To live in his head for just a minute; to understand how he felt and why he considered himself the devil would be like an astrologer's desire to go into space. Maybe we needed each other in a corrupt cosmic hoax. Maybe we balanced each other out.

I almost envied Arthur because he did have such strong convictions with his actions, as misguided and twisted as they were. I felt horrible thinking like that; and to practically envy a cold-hearted killer just made my anxiety build up some more. I felt myself struggling to breathe as though I had hands around my neck squeezing. I'd only felt like this once before when I was younger and I felt the need to slam the brakes on again, to the displeasure of the car behind me.

I pulled over for a second and started to focus on the sound of my own breathing. How could I be so weak? Indoctrinated by anxiety, the feelings washing over me. I felt like I was losing control and the proverbial hands were starting to tighten their grip around my throat. The phone started to ring again, and it was Arianna.

I answered without even thinking about it. Hearing her voice brought me back to earth. She was my rock, even though she might not have felt it, or knew it.

"Hi Sebastian... do you have time to talk?"

I didn't, but I said I did. We talked about everything and nothing at the same time. We talked as though we would talk over the table at breakfast. We laughed like we used to laugh. Then she heard a crack in my voice. It hurt realising just how much I needed her and didn't have her.

"Are you okay?" she asked with a soft, loving tone. She still cared but left for the right reasons and I'll never hold that against her.

"I'm okay."

My real father always said not to lie, as you never have to remember anything. I said I was okay, although deep down, I really wasn't. I needed her more than anything. I felt alone. I felt like I was back in the day when I lost it all. I felt worthless, alone, and insignificant. Arianna could tell. She asked me if I was free the following night. She wanted to meet me to talk about what happened. She said she had been seeing a therapist, who believed she had to face her loss, and she suddenly felt strong enough to face me.

That term hurt, when she said she felt strong enough to face me. It made me out as though I was Arthur himself. It's like she needed to face an evil in her life, and it was with the very thought, I realised Arthur and I truly were balancing each other out. I agreed to meet, citing it would benefit me as much as it would benefit her.

"Darling," I said carefully, as I didn't want her to get the wrong idea and reject me by saying she was no longer my darling. Rejection was the last thing I needed right now.

The pause felt like it went on forever. I could hear her sobbing softly. I obviously hadn't called her that in a while and it brought back memories, both good and bad.

As she fought back a flood, and sharply inhaled, she weakly responded, "Yes?"

I said it. I said that no matter what, I would always love her and even if she didn't feel the same way, I would always be there. She was the best thing that ever happened to me. She cried on the phone and said she had to go but looked forward to seeing me.

I took a deep breath and realised I felt better, just at the comfort of knowing she loved me. Anxiety had crashed over me like a wave before, but now, it subsided, like a tide retreating to show a golden beach. I felt invincible, knowing I would see her the next day.

I pressed on my indicator and moved off again, casually driving to the scene.

With increased rejuvenation, and mental equilibrium, my heart sped up almost excitedly, raindrops crashing on the windscreen.

Unlike that wave of emotion however, I was perfectly dry and now felt perfectly safe.

Chapter Four

Miss Battersby obviously didn't like my company, or she was just too young for the sort of responsibility she thought she was ready to grasp on day one when she made her promise. After I stayed at her house for those few days, I found myself in the custody of the child protection agency.

I'd been in one of their halfway houses for a short while with a cantankerous old woman, though I don't remember an awful lot. I'd been told the truth about my parents; that they were dead. I was emotionally raw. I had a few nights where I cried; I had a few nights where I didn't. The nights I didn't, that woman beat the tears out of me. I didn't even know her name, as she insisted on just being called Madame.

The irony of being in the care of the child protection agency and being beaten was lost to me at that tender age, though I often reflect on it. I had become a number in the system, a mere statistic. Unloved, emotionally scarred, and lonely. I grew accustomed to the dark in the time I was with Madame. Time merged as I lived, embracing the dimness. The only thing I kept close to me was the watch. As she beat me, I clutched it so tight she couldn't force my hand open. Recognising what it meant to me, with one particular beating, the pain became so much I lost my grip and she succeeded in plying it from my weakened grasp and proceeded to laugh at me.

I suppose that's when I started to like the dark. When you spend enough time in it, your eyes adjust. You learn to see things, and sometimes see things in it that aren't there. My imagination ran wild as shadows pirouetted to the sounds and clambering of the house around me. The smallest faint light broken under the door on occasion, depending what time of day it was; though largely, darkness filled my new home. It was a dusty, old cupboard full of cobwebs, with a few creatures to keep me company. A used, dirty dog-bed was my only comfort to prevent sitting or sleeping on the concrete floor below me.

I was told my parents were murdered. Their car had been run off the road by a large van that had ploughed into the driver door, rendering my father incapacitated. It wasn't until I was much older that I read masked men had jumped out the back of the panelled doors and proceeded to shoot them at close range with an automatic weapon.

My mother must have tried to escape because she was found hanging out of the car, having seemingly taken the lesser blow from the T-bone, being on the passenger side of the vehicle. The masked men were never found, having fled in the van. The sounds of the gunfire eliminated any hope for witnesses who seemingly would have taken cover and considered their own safety first. Not to mention, my father's list of enemies was too great for even the best of detectives. It could have been anyone.

Sadly, for the truly innocent one in this scenario, I was the one in jail. Young and naïve, I didn't quite realise whether I deserved my fate or not. The recent loss of my father's watch, my final connection to them, caused me to cry silent tears. They ran down my face and I was frozen on the spot. Eventually my eyes dried out and the smallest of puddles had formed on the floor in front of me.

I had become quite dehydrated and was so thirsty I licked my own tears from the floor. I think back to how low a point that was, but as a child, I didn't see it. I remember the hunger pains, where I hadn't eaten. I protested and pushed the food back under the gap at the foot of the door. When quizzed why I wouldn't eat, I said I wanted the watch back, begged in fact.

As much as Madame didn't particularly like me, and that much was certain; through my resilience and desire to see my prized possession returned, it obviously struck a chord in her blackened soul. Strangely, in her only spark of humanity, she returned the watch to me, unscathed. I like to think that that was my only element of control I had in that place. Though the truth of the matter was she couldn't explain a malnourished, or dead child should something have happened to me and someone came to check on me. I prayed that someone would, but no one ever came.

I was happy no more than a few weeks before, sleeping in my own bed and I only had a dusty, smelly dog-bed as a replacement. At least I had that watch. Madame left the door ajar that night to let in more light; but I didn't leave, as there seemed to be little point in doing so and the threat of another beating kept me in position.

Then one day, it all changed as a well-dressed gentleman finally liberated me from my new cell. He went by the name of Cyril. I listened intently from my room, or prison, and heard Cyril speak to Madame. He addressed her by her name, but I didn't catch it through the walls at first. The sound of footsteps started to bounce around the exterior hallway, so I stepped away from the door and sat on the dog-bed. An extra sound, tapped in unison with their walking, which I shortly comprehended, was the end of a metal-tipped walking stick.

"He's remarkably strong for a little one. I'm sure he'll be just fine," Madame said as the door swung open. "He's barely said a word since he's been here, cried a few times but got on with it."

"What is his name?" the suspicious man said.

"Names, Cyril? I don't have time to get attached to these kids."

"Have a heart, dear Gretchen. They are beautiful. Innocent. Pure."

The two shared a chuckle between themselves. Gretchen was a wicked-sounding name, suitable for a wicked woman. *How stereotypical of you, Gretchen.* He stepped towards me and crouched down looking into my eyes with intent. His hands clutched the large, silver chrome knob atop his walking stick. It was beautifully decorated; silver streaks that led down the ivory stick and met at a chrome-tipped bottom.

Looking from beyond his hands and chrome orb, was a rather round face, perfect cheekbones, and a rough five-o'clock shadow. He appeared like quite a handsome man in hindsight, but also with flaws, namely his putrid breath. The smell of coffee and cigarettes corrupted his words to the point it felt as though I was being spoken to by a carcass. "What is your name, boy?"

"Sebastian. Sebastian Blackwood, sir."

"Polite, too." He smiled wickedly and gazed through ice blue eyes. "You'll be coming with me now, son. We leave immediately. And what is this?"

His eyes shifted towards my father's timepiece. Madame told him to leave it. As if honour among criminals, or thieves, he didn't so much as look at it again. He left it with me and without any grumblings whatsoever, allowed me to keep it in my pocket on the road home.

We left swiftly, with Cyril carrying a small bag containing a few of my personal belongings and a change of clothes. I felt rather uneasy going with this strange man. Whatever fate had in store for me next, I was leaving the alleged care of Madame Gretchen and anything seemed better.

It was a strange journey to wherever we were going. I sat in the passenger seat, with Cyril driving. He put his hand on my knee whilst looking dead ahead at the road in front of him. He didn't break his concentration but rubbed his hand suggestively against me before muttering in a paternal tone.

He told me that where we were going, there was a set of rules. I would have to refer to him as "Father" for a start, though he cited he liked when I called him sir. He said there were other children and it started to sound appealing. The second rule was that the kids were to respect each other and not fight, unless asked to. *Asked to?* I was puzzled. The third rule was curfew had to be adhered to. Anyone who broke any of the rules would be put into the cage.

"Do you understand?"

"Yes, sir!"

I felt his hand run up and down my leg. I'd spent days in that dog-bed without so much as human touch, other than my watch being taken. If not for being a total stranger, I might have enjoyed the soft feel of Cyril's stroking. I was a child after all; it was like a soft tickle and I wasn't aware of the obvious inappropriateness of the stranger's touch.

He started talking softly. "Son, I don't think you've listened to me." That softness in his hand and his voice turned in to fire as I felt a little sting on my leg. His grip got tighter and started to hurt.

"RULE ONE!" His nails dug into me. His concentration still didn't break as he focussed on the road. I weakly reacted with moans of discomfort and the sharp inhalation of air. *Rule one, rule one.* I didn't dare speak until I recalled what the rule was. Suddenly, it hit me, and I responded, "Yes, Father!"

Cyril, sorry, Father, released his grip with a smirk on his face. I felt a sudden pang of loneliness. What I would give to be back in Miss Battersby's antiquated old room with the old dolls. I could feel the conflict in my soul; not sure what I had done to deserve the sudden hurt. Not sure how to engage with my new caretaker.

The road was long. It started to rain again, only this time; thunder followed. I sat in the passenger seat in complete silence. Relief washed over me as father removed his hand to adjust himself around the groin area and later flipped his main headlights on. My young naïve self sat dumbfounded, unsure what was going on or what gratification he got from inflicting pain.

My mind went to my mother, as she had been in the same position as me no more than a few days, or weeks before; I had lost track of time. Part of me sank emotionally as I thought about that. I was hurting on so many levels that I almost wanted a van to run into our car and take out my fake 'father.' I was only five, yet I was having deranged and damaging thoughts about my own well-being, and my driver's well-being.

71

Hours passed in the car and then we turned off the main road. The cover of trees only served to darken the road; nor the moonlight, nor the rain, could break through. It was like nature's very own tunnel, eerily beautiful. Artificial light eventually started to break through the proverbial tunnel from the lights of my new home. A crooked wooden and metal sign read: *Fort Rose Orphanage*. Fitting really, I hadn't quite thought about it, but I truly was an orphan. A title and a statistic.

The car was still silent as my new father pulled up outside the main doors to avoid as much of the light rain outside. As the handbrake of the car was pulled up and the engine shut down, he turned to me and just stared. The raindrops steadily hitting the window and the metal roof of the car broke the silence. His face was gaunt, and he had a rather evil stare on him.

I could feel my heart thumping through my chest, and I started to zone out, focussing on the beats. Thud, thud, thud. The sound of the rain started to lower until it was gone; I focussed more. His stare matched mine and then a slight smirk appeared on his face. That was my first ever dance with evil. I felt it in every fibre of my body. This man was not to be underestimated.

In that moment, my body sensed I was in dangerous clutches. Fight or flight and despite my youthful innocence, I was choosing to fight. I consumed his stare, refusing to break eye contact. His smirk fuelled the fire inside me. His lips started to move but I wasn't hearing him. He mouthed a few words and I tuned back in.

"...belong to me now. You're home now, child. I am your father and you'll learn to love me."

Our stares were still matching. That was it; I opened my mouth with a foolish sense of pride.

"This isn't my home and I won't love you."

Those words, I regretted them instantly. The next thing I knew, I was looking at the floor, dazed. He had a hard slap to him. There was a ringing in my ears. Everything from the Mexican standoff stare to that final slap played in my head. Home? What an idiot. This wasn't home. This was a desolate pit where people came to die. I could feel it. The sense of danger I was in and sadness that fuelled the air was evident, even to my younger self.

I almost laughed when he said I would love him, but my youthful bravery and strength decided to keep that one to myself. Madame could hit and I cried, but I had cried enough tears. My vow was that I wouldn't cry for someone like this ever again. Like a phoenix rising from ashes, despite my tender age, I was a new person.

I snapped my head back up at 'Father' and looked him in his eyes again. The depravity in his look, his urge to adjust himself again after striking me; he enjoyed it. I wouldn't and couldn't let it get to me, despite thinking all the right things in my head. Hating my current predicament and despising the company I was in; with a twisted stare of my own, and matching smirk, I just uttered the word, "Home."

He guffawed at the fire in me, snorted, and brazenly said, "You'll be dangerous one day, boy." Before laughing some more. His awful breath carried across the car and almost broke my gaze. I think back to that moment and know that if I could face Cyril as a man, he wouldn't be guffawing.

Quite a backhanded compliment and accepted with silence; we then proceeded to break the stalemate and got out of the car, my bag in hand.

The air outside the car was unlike anything I'd taken in before. The mild freshness of the country air was poisoned with sorrow and wretchedness. It felt like I was walking into Amityville. Bright lights illuminated a stained-glass archway above the coveted, crooked doors. He pushed me up the stairs from behind with his ornate walking stick. My bag over my shoulder and watch in one hand, he said, "Don't ever forget I am the one letting you keep that. It's important to hold on to things from our past. Things we hold dear. I said you'd learn to love me because I am your protector now. Keep that trinket as a reminder of where you were and what you can become here. Keep it as a show of how generous I can be if you do what I ask of you."

The only thing I ever thanked 'Father' for teaching me is that one part of his statement: where it's important to hold on to the things dear to you.

He reached for the large metal handles and I started to count in my head. *One, two…*

He opened the door and as much as I expected it to creak ghoulishly like in cartoons, not a sound. *Three, four, five…*

The light that illuminated the stained glass shone on my face. I looked in the entryway at a tall desk, presumably a reception. It was late enough that no one was around so the place was a little lifeless. He didn't say a word, just pointed with his stick and nudged me. Echoes filled the hall with that stick: 'Tut, Tut, Tut;' a sound I would later learn to abhor.

Ornate dressers and cabinets filled a wide hallway that infrequently topped up with light from a few dusty wall lamps. Pockets of light were leading the way to my new home. It wasn't that long a walk in reality, but the unfamiliar surroundings, feeling of sadness, and tutting of the stick added to the length.

We got to a large blue door, childlike in design compared to the old feel of the rest of the orphanage. It was the most authentic and innocent part I had seen yet. He opened the door and sudden mutters and whispers went silent.

The room was deathly quiet and in absolute darkness, with the windows covered by shutters to block the light out further. I felt like I was on parade. The faint glints of eyeballs were barely visible, following me as I walked in to the abyss.

The sound of shuffling could be heard as people moved around in the darkness. I felt intimidated and a little frightened to the point I looked back at "Father," who had become a silhouette in the doorway, enlarged by the lack of light and outline of shadow; giving the false perception of grandeur.

I'd never felt so small, and equally worthless in my entire life. What surprised me more was the unknown entities in the darkness almost mentally manipulated me into thinking I needed him to protect me from whatever sat around me.

He chuckled at the door and announced that I was a new brother for them all. He flicked a switch and light filled the room immediately. Sudden movements around the room as children shifted their gaze to me, some turned into their duvets and feigned slumber, some looked at the door in fear.

I felt every single emotion in that room. Fear, dread, hope, and worry at the front of the queue. A few of the older children looked at me in disgust, which I never understood at the time. As I scanned the room, there were old rickety beds, filling both sides of a large room, with a small play area in the corner. A small blackboard with chalk was at the end of the play area, and some building blocks; clearly for the younger children.

That's when I caught the eye of a rather picturesque young girl. She had bright red hair, amazing blue eyes, and a dim nightie on. She smiled at me and the purity in her eyes relaxed me. I smiled back.

That's when I heard the "tut" and brisk walk of Father behind me. He pushed me out of the way and started shouting. "How dare you disobey? The rule after curfew is no talking. Everyone up!"

All the kids stood up, as if on parade. I froze in place, in the centre of the kids lined up either side of me. Father demanded they line up and show their hands, palms up; I watched everyone throw their hands out and felt obligated to do the same.

As Father patrolled up and down, he walked in front of me and came down to my height. "Son, I admire your respect, but I know this wasn't you, come with me."

I followed and he led me to a bed, put my bag down and told me to get comfortable. I sat on it and watched as he went back to his patrol. Looking over my shoulder, I gazed upon a note on the blackboard: *I hate father.*

That's when he found the culprit with chalk on his hands. I vaguely recall his name being George. He was berated in front of the other children, tried to defend he didn't do it, and was immediately threatened with 'the cage.' He was dragged out of that room and never seen again. Ultimately terrifying.

As I sat on the bed, the room was left in darkness again and tensions eased off. Father was gone, the tutting of his stick against the floor now distantly merging into nothingness.

Some of the children spoke. Such phrases like, "Who is the new person?" echoed in the room. I much preferred the more innocent comments like, "I hope he likes us," as opposed to the more aggressive hisses of, "I hope he doesn't get us in to trouble!"

Then I understood. The small break of light through the shutters fed directly into the play area, where moonlight was able to show the small blackboard. The children were using it to communicate more sensitive matters safely without waking or notifying anyone, namely Father.

I couldn't believe George was taken away. If that was even his name. I met him for only a few brief seconds, didn't so much as exchange conversation with him and he was gone. Our meet was ever fleeting, and the memory so faded I even doubted whether or not it actually happened. If it did happen, I suppose based on the exchange in the car with Father, it was a direct way to disrespect his good will. After all, he did put a roof over us and we were permitted to see daylight, unlike my recent resting place.

Wait. I just defended him? Had he made it under my skin already? Our exchanges had been painful, full of hatred, and I defended his supposed good will? Fatigue must have been setting in. I somehow, after hours of worry and silence, drifted off in the hope that this was all a dream.

That moment of silence in the night, listening to the drips outside the window from the weather as my only comfort made time stand still; as still as the broken watch I clutched hold of for dear life.

After a night of broken rest, and as light began to fill the room, some of the children came to see me.

Rather eerily, they stood looking over me without saying much so when my eyes adjusted to the sight of numerous kids looking over me, I staggered, and tried to push away in the bed.

"It's okay," the young girl said. It was the same redhead I saw the night before. Her sky-blue eyes relaxed me again. Her voice tapered off to a whisper when she realised she was talking too loudly. "My name is Alexia! What's yours?"

She stuck her hand out to welcome me with a handshake, which was a little odd for a girl probably not much older than me. I figured she was about nine or ten years old. The other curious children looked on in delight as I put my hand out to meet hers.

"Sebastian, Sebastian Blackwood."

"That's a long name," she said, as if disappointed. "We'll have to call you Seb on the blackboard, for when we need to talk."

"Why do you talk on the blackboard?" I asked, matching her whisper.

"It's the only way we can talk about the things they shouldn't hear. They don't like when we talk about bad things, even if it's on the board."

"Why don't they like it?"

"They don't like it because they are stupid!" A boisterous young boy blurted out. His eyes matched the girl in how bright blue they were. He had an ice-like stare with fiery locks to match his fiery personality. He looked similar to Alexia, to which I later found out they were twins.

"Robert," Alexia blurted out.

Anyway, we will catch up later. Alexia went to the blackboard and rubbed out the message already on there, before putting up her own. She wrote 'Seb' with a small smiley face and love heart and a badly drawn arrow pointing to the face.

Footsteps and tutting could be heard; the children retreated to their respective beds and pretended to sleep. I was still sitting up taking in the sights of the room. There were about fourteen other children in the room with me, and seven empty beds. The door crashed open, and Father marched to the window with the shutters before opening them. As soon as natural light filled the room he spun around and noticed the message on the blackboard. The poorly drawn arrow made him rant about the devil as it looked like an inverted cross.

Disapprovingly, he enunciated every word. "That. Is. Not. What. The. Board. Is. For."

He walked back into the middle of the room. "Line up!"

The children jumped up and I knew he would find out it was Alexia. Robert knew it too. He looked on petrified for his sister. As he was about to speak, I did it for him. I wasn't scared of Father. "It was me, Father. I wanted everyone to know who I was and that I was ready to love my new home."

Father came down to my height with that walking stick.

"Well, well, boy. Aren't you just adorable?" He could obviously sense the lie. He screamed, "Hands!"

Still dressed from the evening before, I quickly thought on my feet, aware of what he was looking for and wiped my hands against my already dirty clothing. Father knew what I was doing and gave me the death stare and laughed as I put my hands out.

"A warm welcome then, think yourself lucky you aren't getting the cage for that."

Then he came down on my hands with an almighty crack of his cane. Fire embodied my hands. Pain felt. I exhaled sharply but I had said to myself in the car the night before that I would not cry, and I meant it. My eyes watered, teeth chattered from the pain. *Whack.* He hit me six times.

"You know the rules, children. Don't speak with a forked tongue, like a serpent. Don't ever lie to me."

Father looked at me both disappointed with my lie, but proudly for not breaking under the pressure. He muttered that what he said in the car was true, turned around and left.

The room was silent again, other than the chattering of my teeth. My hands were shaking so I paced up and down to take my mind off the pain. I looked at the board again and the arrow looked nothing like a cross. He just wanted another excuse to inflict pain for his own twisted pleasure.

"Seb." I wasn't really listening. "Seb!"

It was Robert. He came over to me with a face softer than when we were first introduced. "You didn't need to do it. I would have said it was me and gone to the cage instead."

I muttered a little, he came over and put his arm around me, then hugged me. He said he was lucky to have a little brother as strong as me, and that his sister had a new protector. He whispered his sister was all he had, in a childlike yet deeply loving fashion.

I suspected everyone had a similar story of grief and abandonment to have wound up here. Impressed by my bravery and unwillingness to quiz me the night before, the other children made up for it there and then and kept asking me question after question, curious who their new brother-in-arms was, and where I came from.

I shared what I knew about my parents and exhibited the watch I had, with my hands still shaking from pain. I struggled to press the button to open it so they could see the image of my mother inside, and it just resulted in more questions being asked.

"How did you get that in here?" Alexia quizzed with shock. "None of us have stuff like that."

I told them the truth. I told them about the policeman that had the watch and how I took it back. It made some of the children laugh, thinking I had stolen it.

"You're like Robin Hood!" one of the children proudly spoke up.

"Or a pirate that found treasure," said another.

"You're so cool," said Alexia.

Smiling at the flattering comparisons of adventurous do-gooders and riotous sea-faring highwaymen, I felt quite proud. I didn't have many friends growing up, as I was normally solving puzzles with my mother and out on family days. Here, I was like yin and yang in this new group of friends, brothers, and sisters. I was the cool one. It felt quite good; I'll admit.

I continued my story about staying with Miss Battersby, then being with Madame. I said I was left in a cold cupboard with a dusty dog-bed. Three of the other children said they stayed in the same place; and like a brotherhood of lost and unfortunate souls, we bonded from the shared experience.

I told them I refused to let the watch go when she tried to take it and when she finally did, she eventually returned it.

"You are like a magician," the first boy stated.

"How did you?" the second spat out.

"You are so brave, like a knight," said the third.

I mentioned I angered Father in the car, then had a showdown and stared him right in the eyes before telling him I wouldn't love him, which is why I said the blackboard was me.

Almost all the children were in shock at the revelation, and the fact Father hadn't punished me by taking it and instead gave me advice on keeping things that were important.

In the space of a night, I went from being terrified by the glazed eyes in the room, to sharing experiences of hurt, pain, and strength, with the children around me.

We talked quietly for a while, only quietening down when it sounded like people got close by.

After feeling every emotion in the air while living with Madame, to the drive, and the walk through to my new bed, the atmosphere changed. For a short, sweet moment, I felt joy and elation. I was happy to have found similar lost souls and was determined to make the most of my time here.

I closed the watch to protect the image of my mother, much like I had protected Alexia from her inevitable punishment. My hands were still tingling from the beating I received but were feeling a little better.

The tutting of Father's stick could be heard coming down the hallway. I stood and looked at the door, ready to once again show my bravery to the children by standing proud and tall. Then the tutting got quieter, as our room was clearly never the destination and he had bypassed us.

Other footsteps could be heard, and a beautiful young woman welcomed us instead. She was like an angel, with flowing black hair, a petite frame, and stunning smile. The children seemed happy to see her and she was welcomed by hugs from some of the kids. As soon as she was done greeting everyone, she could see I was the only one who stood back.

"Who might you be?" the mysterious woman questioned.

"That's Sebastian," Alexia said as she released her hug from the woman.

She walked up to me and extended her hand to me as though to shake it. She had a soft perfume scent that was so magnificent and so pleasurable, I've never found anything that compared.

Whether this woman was a flower in the desert and my senses were amplified in her presence, I'll never know. All I know is everyone's guard was down and all the children felt safe with her. If they felt safe, I knew I could as well.

She reached out, and with beautiful pearl-white teeth, she smiled at me. Her warm smile put me at ease, and I felt the love she had for the children here. I felt her passion, her pride, and her sheer adoration for the lost souls in her presence.

"Hi, Sebastian. I am Mallory. It is a pleasure to meet you."

She sounded so proper. Her accent was very strange to me and not what I was used to. I could only mutter out a weak, shy hello. I felt so allured by her presence.

"Sebastian, you were the lovely lad I heard was coming last night. Cyril–"

The children reacted at his name and she didn't notice.

"Left to get you but I had to go home before you arrived. You look exhausted, my little lamb. I think we will get you cleaned up and in some new clothes."

She was probably the closest thing I had to a mother and I had only just met her. She shared a number of similarities to my real mother but was much younger. She couldn't have been much older than twenty-five. She talked and her voice was soothing. It was soft and her accent accentuated the beauty of her words. She announced to the children it was time to eat and led us out of the dormitory.

Walking down the hallway behind Mallory was much different than with Cyril, err, Father. The room felt brighter, unlike the feeling of being devoid of joy the evening before.

I was learning the layout of the building following her. Seeing new rooms, new hallways, and then she opened double doors leading to a large canteen area. Some staff members were working behind a counter, clearly preparing food for us.

It didn't seem so bad after all. My welcome may have been tough based on how Father acted but this was the closest thing to home I was going to be able to get without the actual thing.

I was curious how often kids came and went within the facility. I didn't ask as I felt as though I would be touching on sensitive ground after the situation the night before and truthfully didn't want to disrupt the positivity going around the room.

Mallory spoke with the staff serving food and laughed, and the place felt rather joyous. To hear the sound of laughter felt good. I felt the elation in the room. The kids all felt at ease and were smiling as they ate from their bowls and plates depending on the choice they made at the counter.

Whatever happened the night before had to be an anomaly. This felt great, we got food, options on what food, and the people around us genuinely seemed to care.

As we ate, we laughed and engaged in mindless small talk, after all, we were kids; we were then told to go out in the garden and play.

We had so much fun. I was kicking a ball with Robert and Alexia, when suddenly, another boy Timothy tried to muscle in and ruin the enjoyment whilst screaming inanely. He kicked the ball with such force that it went to the other end of the garden and into a colourful bed of flowers.

The kids froze and I chased after it, unsuspectingly. I hadn't realised I had crossed an invisible line. The rules of the garden had not been explained to me. I skipped along after the ball, realising it was the first bit of fun I had been privy to since my real father pushed me on that swing.

As the garden stretched on further, I ran past an outhouse with a small porch on it. It was immaculately decorated with flowers, varnished wooden panels, and rather pleasant on the eyes, unlike the dreary hallways the previous night.

I looked back to admire and from the corner of my eye, could see the other children had stopped. I challenged them. "The last one to the flowers is a rotten egg."

No one reacted and I pushed on and started to clamber through the flowerbed to retrieve the ball. A small cross was in the soil beyond an array of beautiful flowers, including daisies, chrysanthemums, carnations, and a large, beautiful amaryllis. Each brought a splash of colour and happiness to the dreary garden, decorating the cross; seemingly a small memorial site.

Then he came.

I had never seen him before, but he had a chilling look about him. His face was full, with hamster-like cheeks, meeting to a pointed chin. His hair was bright white and wire-like, pointing out in all directions but kept in control on the top of his head thanks to a trilby. His face had layers and layers of wrinkles, stacking on his angered forehead like building blocks.

He grabbed me by the arm with such force that I protested with a whimper. He picked me up and raised me to his face.

"You dare come to my end of the garden and ruin my flowers! I should ruin you, boy."

As he spoke, spit left his mouth through his missing front tooth and covered my face. I felt it splashing on my face as I recoiled in fear at the reprimand I was receiving. I thought Father had an evil look in his eyes, but this man was just as bad, only I felt a different kind of danger with him. He spoke as though he had conviction in his words; like he would hurt me. My fears hadn't seemed unfounded, as the kids were quite quick to stay in what I learned to be our part of the garden.

As he shouted some more and showered me in sputum, it only served to alert Mallory, who was quick to run up to help.

"Get off of him," she shouted as she slapped him on the side of his arm. Still at his eye level after being picked up, I kicked him in the stomach and he didn't just drop me, he threw me to the ground so hard I twisted my ankle.

He swore at me and Mallory looked at me worryingly, assessing whether I'd been hurt. The strange man turned his attention to her, grabbed her by the wrist as she swung at him again and bellowed across the garden, "Don't you dare touch me, you worthless slut. Maybe I should teach you a lesson later? I'll get *him* to bring you to my cabin."

Mallory immediately settled down and the strange man whispered in her ear. Her eyes widened in fear and I sensed how uncomfortable she was. She lowered herself to her knees to check I was okay and raised my leg. My ankle hurt badly, and I said as much. It started to throb, and she asked me where all my other bruises had come from. I said I didn't know but had a feeling it came from the beatings Madame gave me, or the incident in the car with Father the night before.

The strange man, in the eeriest and most suggestible method possible, commented that being on her knees was the only thing Mallory was good for. I didn't get the reference. He left and clambered back into his outhouse.

She looked on confused as to the origins of my bruises, clearly worried for me, as though she'd seen it all before. That's when I knew she was going to look out for me, and I could trust her implicitly.

Without even thinking, I put pressure on my tender ankle to straighten myself out and jumped in to hug her. She seemed to appreciate it and I felt her mood change, as I held on as tight as I could. "Now, now, my little lamb, let's get you inside and have a look at that ankle."

The short belief I had, that this place might not be so bad seemed to quickly come crashing down. The mask was falling and the evil face that sat behind it was beginning to show. I'd enjoyed nothing more than a few hours of enjoyment and the only spark of decency and humanity seemed to be Mallory, and the kids I shared a room with.

She led me to a small office, and then lifted me up on to a gurney. A slight creak suggested just how old it was and the cushioned panels seemed tacky and worn. I looked over at an impressive, large medicinal cabinet. It was very ornate, with large glass panels revealing the contents inside. Held together by a small lock that Mallory could release with the small key she wore around her neck. She went inside and grabbed a bandage. I was asked to stay put and she left the room briefly.

It was peaceful for a while. I jumped to the floor and felt fire tingling up my leg. It didn't seem so bad before, but the adrenaline was obviously pumping. I went over to explore the room, accompanied with a slight limp. I looked into the cabinet to see a wealth of different medicines and didn't think much of it. I couldn't read what most of the drugs were, as the names were too complex for my young mind. In fact, I could have sworn the labels on the bottles were just another complex cipher left behind by my mother.

My mother...

I pulled out the watch and pressed the button to see her face. It hadn't been more than about a few weeks since the incident and I clearly felt quite raw. It made my heart sink thinking I was never going to see or speak to them again. I wondered how they would react knowing how I felt.

As I looked down at the watch, a slight glint out of the corner of my eye revealed a small air vent, at ground level. It was a slightly loose vent cover, and I pulled it back to reveal a small diary. I looked down at my watch and something in me felt that it was a weakness, an anchor that could be used to exploit me; and it felt prudent to hide it in that safe place, hoping it couldn't be found.

I flicked through a few pages of the diary and tried to read some of it. A lot of the writing was tough to read and my abilities at that age were far beyond my years, but still not quite as honed as I would have hoped.

An excerpt from the diary read:

He did it again. He used me and I feel dirty. I want to hurt him as much as he hurts me. Thankfully I cannot have children again, since the last time. Just as well, because the thought of fathering his ilk makes me sick to my stomach. But I feel like I have to be here. I have to keep the kids–

At that point, Mallory came back in the room and rushed over to me, frustrated. She was panicking, as I had clearly stumbled upon her own treasure trove of memories.

"You shouldn't be reading that, Sebastian." She quickly pulled everything together and hurriedly closed the pages in front of me. "I told you to stay put," she said in a raised voice.

The sadness in my eyes clearly hit home and she quickly apologised for shouting and said that it wasn't my fault.

"I... I'm sorry, Mallory," I said, upset I had let her down and read her private thoughts.

She hugged me and said she obviously hadn't kept the diary hidden well enough. She laughed and called me her little detective, a comment with hindsight, was suitably apt.

I pulled out my watch and showed Mallory the contents. "That's my mummy."

Mallory was flabbergasted. "How did you get that in here?"

I explained that Father let me keep it, much to her shock. She covered my hand with hers, keeping the contents nicely shielded.

"But I wanted to keep it safe. I don't want someone to take it from me out there."

"Oh, my little lamb, you beautiful little boy. Of course, you can hide it here. I'll keep it safe for you. We can have our own little hiding place. Pinky promise?"

I stuck out my pinky and her full cat-like smile filled me with such hope. I hugged her again and she kissed me on the forehead, stroking my head like my mother did. It was my little slice of heaven, that moment. The safest I had felt in a long time.

"Now, where were we?"

She had left the room to grab some frozen peas. She wrapped the peas in the sheet of bandage and wrapped it around my ankle. The sting after jumping off the gurney, then the contrast of ice was mildly pleasing. The icy sharpness on my skin was enough to take away from the pain in my foot, leaving me quite placated.

"Why are you here, Mallory?" I asked innocently.

"I grew up here, Sebastian. Well, not here as in this building. This town. I never knew who my father was, but my mother knew the proprietor–"

"The who?" I interrupted, quizzically.

"The person who owns this place. He gave me the job and when she died, I was taken care of, at first. But, over time, things changed. That's when I started to write in my diary. I couldn't leave though, because I learned to love all of you." She pressed on my nose and smiled as she said that.

"I take care of all of you children because I know what it feels like to have no one around. So, how did you end up here? If it's okay to ask?"

I felt quite emotional but told her about my parents and the last few weeks. I felt like I'd told the story a thousand times and it did get easier with every re-telling.

Mallory could only hug me; with the promise she would look after me now.

She truly was an angel; a beautiful ray of light, in a place where darkness was contented to reign.

We both smiled as we placed our belongings in the air vent. Mallory pushed a small table over the vent to try and hide it some more.

"If you ever feel you need to see it, just tell me and we'll come together, okay?"

I nodded in agreement.

Chapter Five

I was only a few miles away from the crime scene and I had driven through what could be considered the rough part of town — Blackridge.

I'd come to learn the streets and alleyways like the back of my hand around that neighbourhood. Drugs, assault, larceny, murder; you name it, it has probably happened there, including the bloodbath with the lamb-headed woman a few months before.

What surprised me more was this crime scene I was heading to was in an upstanding part of the city, Doveport; the more affluent of folks lived there fairly peacefully with little to no issue. You had to have some serious cash to own a property in the haven of Doveport.

As I drove, the sky seemed to clear somewhat as I entered the rich town. Even the rain daren't shed on the pristine inhabitants. Bystanders stared at my vehicle, somewhat surprised as it didn't really suit the fancy SUV-style that most residents opted for.

I drove past large, decorated, gated homes, some of which were so grandiose it reminded me of Fort Rose Orphanage, which sent chills down my spine. As I approached some blue lights, the gate was left ajar and I pulled up an ornamented driveway with a beautiful garden. Multitudes of flowers sprawled over the pathway made for a rather eye-catching welcome. Reds, purples, blues; a flurry of colours lit up the driveway amidst the grey skies. The rain had begun to subside briefly.

I pulled up outside the house and even some of the attending officers looked at my car with envy. My brogues tapped off the concrete as I hoisted myself out of the car, locking the door behind me. I don't know why I even felt the need to lock the door, given the heavy security on scene.

"Sebastian Blackwood, homicide," I recited for the umpteenth time and flashed my badge to the officer that had cordoned off the scene.

I asked him if the neighbours had been questioned, if there were any witnesses, and if anyone had disturbed my crime scene. All of which culminated into a resounding, "No." At which point I chastised one of the officers smoking outside the property as he could be unwillingly and unknowingly corrupting the scene. He scurried off in the distance, full of apology and embarrassment. Amateur.

I'm pretty sure I also heard a muffled, "Fuck you." I chose not to engage. The accompanying officer I was with led the way and I eagerly followed.

I entered the hallway of the property and was admittedly quite envious of the owner. To have something quite so grand was a dream come true. Arianna always fancied herself as a designer of sorts and would have loved to work on a home brimming with potential and space, although lacking the budget to do anything with it.

I smiled thinking about how amazing she was. She managed to turn our seedy little flat into a home. Touching up on little bits here and there. I protested often, thinking we didn't need a new table or a new shelf; but whenever I put them up, it filled out the room more and I reluctantly agreed.

This home was incredible though, with a very Gregorian feel to it. Beams, large windows illuminating every cavity of the rooms they proudly served. Marble tiles in the hallway leading guests to various rooms boasted to the wealth of the owner. I was curious to find out more about him.

The officer motioned to his right and said I was in for a surprise and that the victim must have pissed someone off to suffer his fate.

Surprised, I was. The room I had been led in to was a marvellous study, with long, tall bookcases stacked around the sides, full of first edition copies of rare works. I looked around in awe of what the books could be worth alone; suspecting well into the millions. Some rarer books were actually presented in tall, glass stands; safely protected with impenetrable looking locks on them. One antiquated book in particular had a mechanical page lifter and mechanism designed to prevent fingers ruining the pages. It was a pristine copy of, *The Gutenberg Bible.* Unbelievable! Only forty copies exist in the world.

Who was this person and who could have sought his death? That book alone was probably worth half of the buildings on the block. Such a shame it was ultimately without an owner. I felt tempted to keep my eyes open and ears to the ground as to whether or not it would reach auction.

Those fleeting, selfish thoughts soon came to a close as I walked further into the room to a secluded desk area, surrounded by a grand wall of books. This had Arthur written all over it again, clearly. The sight before me was as twisted and demented as the lamb-head scene.

Our victim was strung up and hanging about six feet in the air by barbed wire, flesh hanging from razor-sharp metal with his body torn and cut beyond normal means. The victim's face was looking down towards the ground and difficult to identify based on the blood. As I inquisitively approached, I looked more closely to find he didn't have a face at all. It had been skinned off his skull, revealing thin layers of muscle.

Without his face, or eyelids present, bright blue eyes looked on. Whatever his final moments, as the life left his body; his last look of fear was etched into that look. I felt a sudden surge of pain as I imagined the scenario. It was tough to identify much from his face.

It had to be Arthur as the room was rife with clues as to it being him. Books on codes and ciphers littered the floor. He'd obviously learnt to appreciate his hunter and knew what I loved. For a twisted son of a bitch, I admired his sudden confidence to try and inject some wit into the chase.

I observed the room further, and a bloodied trail led to a smaller bookcase with some seemingly unimportant journals. Dated as far back as 1961.

I opened the first journal and was presented with immaculate handwriting.

They crowded around me and beat me. My tormentors enjoyed inflicting pain and I suppose I learnt to enjoy it, too. It made it easier. It happened enough, so I figured I had no choice but to become one with it. As they kicked me, one of the bullies spat on me and kicked me in the face, breaking my nose. As much as it was painful, I felt the blood running... only, I felt it somewhere else. I realised I had an erection. I recoiled from the kick to the nose after hearing the snap of the bone and my tormentors seemed frozen in place after hearing the crunch. A certain line was crossed as the kick delivered made everyone stop. I curled into a ball so that the sudden embarrassment between my legs wouldn't be seen but my shorts tented all the same. I'll never live down the fact that they spotted me, erect. Nothing compares to the crippling pain of shame. They removed my trousers and briefs and left me, coughing and spluttering blood, with my member standing to attention. At least the beatings stopped after that, as people mistakenly thought I was gay. They didn't want to be associated with the gay man and beat me in case it turned me on. I was mocked. Every. Single. Day.

The journal continued and I felt empathy for the writer. The book I read from was quite old and worn so I gently put it down for fear I would damage it. Whilst the presumed writer was the man hanging in front of me, my care was almost a mark of respect for their belongings.

The journal didn't seem to have anything to do with the case so there was little point in reading on at this moment in time. I highly doubted that bullies from the late sixties would have committed the crime before me. Given the age of the journal and the victim's body shape, I could only harbour a guess at this point but figured our victim was late seventies to mid-eighties. His style, the way his home was decorated, and even his sense of dress; pretty much all pointed to a more established gentleman. Without a face, and it nowhere to be seen, I was unable to pinpoint exactly how old.

I had to recap. The victim was an elderly gentleman, and I had little to go on in terms of motive at the moment. It was, without a doubt, a rather passionate crime for an elderly gentleman. No signs of forced entry, no witnesses, nothing. However, he was bruised, battered, and bloody, from the addition of the barbed wire; clearly placed here on display like a cheap, trophy kill. He was deliberately hoisted up in a torturous manner to be above the ground; did it signal his wealth and desire to be looking down on those less fortunate?

No real smell, so the body was fairly fresh. His hands were mangled and broken in many places, as though they had been crushed with a large hammer, blood under the nails with the skin unbroken. The assailant clearly wanted to torture and hurt the victim. Although mangled, his left hand was forced into a fist like shape, as best it could anyway, with the exception of one of his fingers snapped into position and pointing towards the general direction of a sideboard. Directly where the finger was pointing, a wallet could be seen.

It dawned on me that the anonymous call wasn't exactly what it seemed. A pristine yet chaotic crime scene, with very little out of place, except the victim's face. Seemingly, and most logically, the culprit was the caller, as there was no realistic way to lure anyone else here. Someone was mocking from afar. We were led here because the killer wanted to show off; had everything about Arthur's showcasing and boasting mentality written all over it and I knew it was him.

Arthur was prone to hurting and being dominant over those weaker than him, or in a lesser position to defend themselves; so no one better than a frail old man to have his wicked way. I vaguely recalled that Arthur, when in prison for the rape, made sure he was well read and constantly reading; though to attack a book collector seemed a far-fetched connection. Maybe I was off? Maybe I was trying to make it Arthur because I wanted him to be the one responsible and needed to catch him?

It was a rather glorious and extravagant method of killing, which fit Arthur's style given how he maimed and disembowelled his own son. Hanging by barbed wire and torturing was a cakewalk in comparison. There I went again! Almost applauding atrocity. Snap out of it, Sebastian.

I assessed the room. Oh, the wallet where the victim was pointing. Little cash, numerous expensive credit cards, and the kind only the ultra-wealthy have access to apply for, and a key card to a bus station locker. Now I knew he was playing with me. Locker 25A, Row X. Fitting.

Any doubt in my mind about it not being Arthur was immediately washed away. Like the woman with the UV light in her stomach, this clue led me to a locker in row X – 'X marks the spot' after all.

It was a deliberate plot, as no wealthy gentleman with such obvious wealth would be storing his possessions in a bus station. This was another addition to our game of cat and mouse. I was being lured and I was happy to take the bait. I should have logged the key card as evidence but slipped it in my pocket instead, electing to play in the twisted game.

I reassessed the wallet and found there was no ID. The man really was a John Doe right now, just like our Jane Doe from before. Other officers and detectives had explored other areas and hadn't so much as turned up a fingerprint. The place had been cleaned down thoroughly, with special care taken to make our job that much harder.

"Does anyone have a name for me?" I shouted out impatiently.

The beckoning through the house encouraged an officer to come forward. He had found an old letter addressed to a Mr Xander Hardiman. Another slight smirk hit my face. Another 'X,' which was far too much of a coincidence to not be relevant. Xander, who are you and why have you been brutalised?

I had to better understand who he was. I went back to the journals in the study area and assessed some of the more recent ones. As if slightly out of place, a fresher journal sat on the end of the bookshelf, not damaged by the sands of time. It was dated for this year, and by far more pristine than the one I had read earlier, a white chrysanthemum flower had been used as a bookmark. Flowers on the scene just like the lamb-head Jane Doe.

It was mildly frustrating in a sense because as much as the crime scene was cleaned up, it felt like every scene was a scene from a movie, where we transitioned from scene to scene, clue to clue.

The paper was crisp, white, and still smelt quite new, slightly perfumed by the flower. I held the page open as I was obviously being drawn to it, and briefly assessed the rest of the journal; speed reading to take it in. A few entries caught my eye where Mr Hardiman was rather sorrowful. He wrote a lot about how he always went back to what he referred to as 'the night' but didn't allude to whether that was a specific date or not. Shame really, as I suspect I could have reviewed the relevant journal coinciding with the date, like a children's make-your-own-adventure.

I stopped flicking and went to the desired entry that the flower brought me to. The first was dated a week before today. I scanned through trying to decipher any sort of motive or understanding as to the horrific sight before me.

The writing was still as elegant and stunning as the journal from the sixties I scanned earlier.

Something in me can sense that my time is coming. God knows I deserve it. As my saviour, I would also accept his judgment as my punisher.

Would I say I am happy with my life? Probably not.

Would I say that I am a good person? Definitely not, though... I tried to be.

Darkness enshrouded me from a young age, and no matter how much I fought it, it always won.

Hatred always built inside me, but it made me strong. I feel like that same darkness is coming to reap me, return me to dust and ash like that night.

That glorious night!

Nothing excited me more, to the point I felt alive!

Everything has a price. At the height of that orgasmic height came an overwhelming shame. I was reminded of when I was the victim, when I was the one in pain.

That world swallowed me up and that shame told me I had to veer away from my current path.

With a sigh of relief, I knew I had taken the first step to absolution. My God, my father in Heaven saved me. He saved what was not worth saving.

I buried the truth, my past, and my shame. I started anew, quite literally as a new man.

My journals kept me true to my path for salvation, as, like now; I would always transfer my twisted thoughts into black and white. Pen and paper reminded me of what I was and refocussed me to being better. I could not tell a soul about who I really am, so my journals frankly are my only friends. If anyone ever reads them, do not pity me. Dig up the truth about who I am, hate me, and rid the world of cancerous souls like me.

I often wonder if time seeks to claim me? Perhaps the devil seeks to present me with his own form of karmic intervention?

Either is fine and either would have a right to end me.

I cannot help but laugh though. I have been writing in journals since I was a boy and bleat on about how I was saved by God.

As I write about my story coming to an end, I laugh because who am I kidding? If I can be truthful to myself for once: was it self-preservation or was it absolution that I pursued these forty years?

I have felt the shadow of the past looming over me lately that I do not even leave the house now, so, I suppose it is the former.

I have not actually been out in months. My cupboards are finally starting to empty. My garden starting to get out of hand, the flowers beginning to wane and wilt, the grass growing. There is a certain beauty in knowing life can continue as normal without me. It would be a jungle out there if not for a kind neighbour tending to my garden. He is the only thing keeping life in this place because I have been dead inside for so long.

Certain sadness is in me as I write knowing that these words may become my last.

I am ready.

I had to question this gardener. Maybe he witnessed something? Someone?

I felt empathy for the writer though. Whoever he was, pain followed him, and I almost sensed it. Amplified with my surroundings, I felt it tug on my heartstrings. The writer wallowed in such self-pity and shame that it was almost enough to bring a tear to one's eye. How could anyone feel so helpless? I suddenly felt quite good about what anxieties I had, as they clearly didn't match Mr Hardiman.

I went back to the journal. The writing on the next page was different. It was rushed, and not as well formed as previous, and almost as if written by a shaky hand. Was he made to write the final entry under watchful gaze?

Wherever shadow forms, beasts lurk. I have been caught and hunted by a righteous one. I am almost happy. The torment can end. I don't know if anyone will ever read this, I don't know if anyone will ever know. I was a terrible father and I am sorry, so, so sorry. Jesus, son of the Lord, died for our sins and I have shamefully banked one too many and do not deserve his forgiveness. In the eyes of my own, allow me to repent. Let the father die for the sons, the youth of the world, and let my garden grow. Wherever I may go next, whether my later repentance and penance gains me entry at the gates of heaven, or the fires of hell light up the feelings like that night; I know I have earned my true reward. Peace.

Peace at last.

Thank you.

The final words were smudged as though soaked by a tear; the paper mildly warped. The writer's journals intrigued me. It felt like a final apology of sorts. That's when I saw it. The victim's body was hoisted up like a cross, albeit, a sharp, shard-like metal one. I was almost frustrated I hadn't seen it before. Everything around me had been meticulously planned to the final faceless scene of our harrowed writer looking down in a scene hardly comparable to the story of Christ but envisioned as one.

He cited being a poor father, was this Arthur's father? It would be eerily poignant if he had killed his own son, then his father. Was Jane Doe his mother? Was Arthur purging his entire family and expecting me to do the same to him?

I shuddered with excitement at the thought.

Shame washed over me with the acceptance that I wanted to kill Arthur. This wasn't me. I wasn't a killer but was almost being baited into being one. I felt the world expanding around me like my dreams, a sudden loss of air and fumbled helplessly for my watch. I quickly pressed the button to reveal the photo of my mother and felt a wave of calm soothe my soul. This hunt was dangerous. I felt myself being twisted, warped, and ashamed like Mr Hardiman.

The name didn't match though. Arthur Hardiman? Did he change his name to Henderson?

Did the father change his name out of shame for his own spawn or out of shame for his past?

Too many questions right now and I needed a quiet place to ponder. I allowed forensics to do their bidding and headed back outside to the car. I felt trapped, battling new emotions, and desires to inflict pain on Arthur. The sound of my brogues against the marble hallway reminded me of the echo in the police station when I walked past the statue. Justice and equality. Those two words kept me mildly sane.

It was still quite early, but I needed some quiet time. I slid into the car and had a desire to drive straight home. I didn't care if the Chief disciplined me for going AWOL. I needed some peace. My mind full of possibilities and questions, no real answers. I placed my hands on the steering wheel and lay my head against my wrists, exhaling loudly.

Slight raindrops started to crash on the windscreen. I closed my eyes and took in the sound of the dewdrops. The purity of the rain, the peacefulness, the silence in my mind…

A crash of thunder jolted me awake. Talk about sleeping on the job. The rain was torrential and must have shielded me from any wandering colleagues going in and out of the crime scene. I could barely see out the car. I looked at my watch and to my surprise; four hours had passed in what felt like mere seconds.

Six missed calls, two from the Chief, and a text from Michael who had clearly folded at trying to call me. His text was a simple offer for a beer later as he wanted to chat about the case I'd left him. I needed one about now actually. I responded to his text to say I would meet him at the usual spot later.

Despite everything I had seen, I was more concerned about meeting with Arianna the next day. She needed to talk to me and there was pain in our voices as we spoke. A mutual love. Conflict filled my brain; my desire to want to see Arianna now, combined with the desire to find Arthur and put a stop to these killings merged my heart into chaos. Maybe something as simple as a beer would help.

Our local, just a five-minute walk from my house was the destination. I walked there in the rain, wise enough not to drive as I knew Michael was prone to plying me with one too many. As I walked down the pavement, splashes from the puddles started running up the leg of my trousers. I looked up at the sign of the bar: *The Queen's Head. It was* swaying in the wind, with droplets forming all around it. It wasn't much to look at and was fairly seedy, but it was close to home and a convenient drinking hole.

The barmaid, Kirsty, was always a welcoming sight. She wore red lipstick, tight tops, and her ever-so-pretty face religiously welcomed the patrons. A number of months after Arianna had left; we had a little fling after closing time. A rather rough individual was getting a bit too close despite repeated protests and I drunkenly defended her honour, flashed my badge, swung my fists, and forced the ruffian to leave.

I wasn't usually prone to fighting and wasn't even a violent person, but I was in a dark place, plagued by Arthur's taunts, Arianna's departure, and a desire to get pissed beyond mortal contention. With a slightly bruised fist to my assailant's ego, I turned back to my drink and raised a glass to Kirsty.

I presumed her desire to have me was driven by the fact that I'd always treated her with respect. I never once leered over her, though did fire a sly compliment her way a few times. We had arguably become good companions, with her occasionally stopping off after her shift and sharing a drink with me. There was nothing much to it other than that one evening.

After getting rid of the scumbag, I was the only one left in the bar. My proverbial white charger primed and ready outside, I gallantly raised myself from the barstool I had frequented most of the night. Kirsty followed me to the door and thanked me. Only, her thanks translated into a click that killed the silence. She locked the door. Before I could react, her wanting eyes and a passionate kiss powered my drunken libido. It was nothing short of an animalistic coupling, fuelled by whisky; no words were spoken.

I ran my hands over her tight body, sat her on the pool table and spread her legs. As anticipated, she wasn't wearing anything under her skirt, so I quickly used my fingers and tongue over her pretty little sex. Minutes later, sheer sexual frustration followed, and we became one. It was the most aggressive sex I'd ever had; egged on with the guttural moans she released as I drove into her. It was quick and frantic and over as fast as it had started.

I did stop drinking there for a short while, almost out of embarrassment for the mess left on the pool table. Truthfully, my heart ached as I wasn't over Arianna and didn't particularly want Kirsty to get the wrong end of the stick, or pool cue as it may be. I bumped into her a number of weeks after our tryst and she said she was disappointed I hadn't been back and wondered whether it was her fault.

With a pang of guilt at her beating herself up, I lied, denying there was an issue and that I was working a case that had swamped my time, committing that I'd pop in again soon. She hugged me, thanking me for that evening once again, and that if it made me feel any better, we could forget it even happened. An element of relief swept over me, as some things were better left forgotten.

It was an incredibly erotic night with Kirsty, but the guilt of it was intensified as a mere few days after the frantic tryst with my tempting barmaid, Arianna came to the house to pick up some items she left behind. I hadn't seen her in about seven months or so and in a most unusual show of charm, I said I still loved her. A long story short, we ended up making love, passionately and without protection. We weren't together when my dalliance with Kirsty happened, but my feelings for my wife were still so powerful that it made me feel like I was cheating. Perhaps not cheating in the traditional sense but cheating on my own heart. Cheating on what I truly wanted.

Alas, I made a promise to go back to the bar and I swanned in, shaking off excess rain, scanning the room in the process. It wasn't particularly busy that night; a few patrons playing on the pool table raised a sly smirk from my face, thinking back to before.

"Hey, handsome, you're back," Kirsty exclaimed before pouring my usual. She hit me with a double and said it was on the house for her favourite customer. I raised the glass to her, and she gave me a sexy wink with her red lipstick in tow.

"Well, now my feelings are hurt, Kirsty. What makes him so special?" said Michael, who was propped up on the bar stool next to my usual spot.

"If it makes you feel better, I'll take it off the next twenty you give me when you top up?" she retorted, causing Michael to sheepishly laugh.

"I wasn't expecting to hit the strong stuff early, I only came in for a beer," I jested to the seductive barmaid. She responded by skilfully taking the cap off a bottle and sliding it in place next to my glass.

"Thank you, Kirsty." I placed money on the bar to cover it. She left it there, ignoring it as though I was welcomed to another freebie.

"So, what makes you need a drink so much today, Michael?"

Like an excited child, he took a swig of his drink and started to talk about the file I had left about Richard Weston, the mechanic who had been killed. He talked about how he followed the tip off, jumped down the proverbial rabbit hole, and started to question anyone and everyone connected to the victim.

Michael said he followed the coaching I had provided about baiting techniques in interview, he had managed to close out the case in half a day. He said one of the apprentices he had taken in was the one to commit the crime. He had turned up the heat and played on the murderer's emotions by building up how great a man Mr Weston was, taking in all these kids off the street, and how it would take a special kind of bastard to want to hurt him.

Michael said he let on that it was like a wounded dog being nursed back to health by a vet and then proceeding to bite and maim them. He said that as he watched the disappointment and anger building up in the killer's face, he kept pushing and pushing until he managed to break him and get a defeated confession.

"I couldn't do it without you, mate. I don't know how you can piece things together so quickly and effortlessly. You've got a rare talent my friend!" He raised his glass.

"I've been promised the option to fast-track to detective for the way I closed that case, Sebastian. So, tonight is almost a celebratory drink, as much as a thank you."

"Does that make us even?" I jested, referring to the fact he saved my life from Arthur in the warehouse.

"It'll take more than THAT to make us even! How is your case coming along?"

"It isn't… it's the most challenging, infuriating, and exhausting case I have ever worked on."

I knocked back the double whisky I had been given, admitting defeat. A few bursts of laughter from around the room echoed in my head as I tilted my head back. Patrons merely having a good time and sharing jokes, in a brief element of madness, I knocked the glass back onto the bar loudly, with a short scream. "Shut up!"

The room fell silent. People looked in my direction, before moving back to a whisper, and sound filled the room again.

"Sebastian," Michael said empathetically, sensing my own defeatism.

"Sorry, this is just getting to me. I'm not seeing sense. This case has slowly become my life. I've lost my wife and I seem to be losing my mind. Chin chin!"

I chugged the beer and before long, Kirsty had topped up my whisky glass. She put her hand on mine and smiled. Her hand was so soft. How I longed for it to be my wife.

"What is eating at you so much with the case though, mate?"

"Him. Arthur. That scumbag mutilates his own son, rapes his own flesh and blood in front of the mother—"

Kirsty yanked her hand away from mine, struggling to listen to what happened to little Sebastian. She went back to tending the bar and serving the men at the other end by the pool table.

"Then kills an older woman and older man, who I presume symbolise a mother and father. It doesn't make sense. The old man had written some cryptic entries in his journal as if forced to do it in front of Arthur. The woman? I can't see the motive or whether they are connected. It feels like they are, mate, but it's nothing more than fucking speculation at this point."

I downed the new glass, slammed it on the bar, and motioned for Kirsty to top it up by slapping another twenty on the bar.

"Every crime scene is like a picture or a movie that I have to reverse engineer to find the hidden meanings. Flowers, 'X's, riddles. This bastard is fucking with my mind and what kills me is that I know I can figure this out. I know I can find this motherfucker. But Michael, what's worse is I want to see him burn. I want to see him bleed."

Michael looked on in astonishment, with a few earwigging customers sitting nearby in darkened booths adjusting their line of sight to my general direction. Some faces looked familiar, people I clearly shared the bar with on previous days without so much as taking in their names or faces.

"You've got to be careful, mate. It's just another case and you know what happens when you get too invested."

I barked at Michael for generalising and comparing it so much.

"Just another case!? What do you know? Marching up and down the beat, only getting a whiff of the big time because I help you!"

I felt guilty at the admission, even if it was the truth. Michael was clearly hurt at the outburst.

"Michael, I'm sorry. That was totally out of line. As you can see, it's getting to me. The images etched in to my brain aren't going anywhere. He's a sick fucker and I would honestly love to see that c-word burn."

I dared not to utter the c-bomb; even though my wife and I weren't together, I knew she hated it.

"Listen, Sebastian. I know this means a lot to you. Don't worry about it. No offence taken. I'll help you. If I make detective, we'll hunt this guy together."

I smiled at the fact that I clearly had a good friend, even if I was an extreme introvert and didn't particularly make much effort. Michael was a good guy. My barking at him probably made him feel inadequate with my scathing testimony about his abilities, or lack thereof.

"You've got something in you, mate. You do. You'll easily make detective. What I said earlier was out of frustration, I truly do apologise."

Kirsty came over with a top up.

"From the gentleman in the booth! You're popular tonight, sugar!"

I turned over my shoulder. It was the man that helped fix my car that morning. I raised my glass in his direction with a smile and asked Kirsty to reciprocate, and that his next one was on me, reciting the story of how he'd sorted my car.

"Listen, Michael..."

He listened intently. I told him how I was running on empty; physically and mentally exhausted. I told him from a sheer position of weakness and slight drunkenness, that I was having anxiety attacks and didn't know what to do. I referred to only feeling that helpless when I was a child and some of the time in the orphanage.

He sat and listened intently, realising he was learning a lot of new information about me. Kirsty looked on almost in sadness and pity; like she wanted to hop over the bar and embrace me. I felt vulnerable enough where I would have allowed it.

Michael patiently listened to me talk and then told me that after his time in the armed forces, he went through phases just like it. He said that having witnessed some of his friends take a bullet or get blown up; he felt he had experienced his fair share of pain. He told me specifically of a younger gentleman who had signed up like a typical patriot, wanting to fight for his country. He said the younger man, whom he and the squad referred to as 'Buck,' as in young buck, was a constant reminder of the youthful enthusiasm they all shared.

They were on a tour in Afghanistan when they were tasked with defending a small village from assailants who were raiding and pillaging to try and draw out allied forces. Michael said that Buck would keep the entire camp laughing and joking by reciting silly anecdotes and how he intended to propose to his high school sweetheart on his return. By this point, Kirsty was listening as intently as I was, perched over the bar with her head in her hands, flickering the occasional glance at me. Michael talked about how Buck kept them all grounded, despite everything going on, and the entire squad felt primed and ready to take on the world.

One night on watch, Buck confided in Michael, telling him why he joined the forces. Buck, realising that his lesser redeeming qualities might be enough to put off a good woman, felt that signing up would teach him some of the basics in life. I quizzed what sort of basics Buck meant and Michael told me he was always prone for being quite tardy, and ill-prepared, even turning up for a drill with his shoes on the wrong feet once.

Michael couldn't hold back his laughter as he thought of Buck marching up and down the camp with his shoes on the wrong way and how it caused a slight limp in his walk. The drill sergeant refused to let him change them over as a punishment. It was nice to see Michael laugh, and forget about some of the external frustrations we were having.

Buck continued to confide in Michael that night, saying he had just written a letter and was going to send it in the morning to his sweetheart but alluded to not being too strong with words and needing some help. Michael could still remember most of what Buck told him. He recited most of the young man's letter to us at the bar. It was beautifully simple. A commitment of love, longing, desire, and hope. It made me think of Arianna.

Before he had a chance to finish reciting the letter to Kirsty and me, Michael welled up. An incomplete letter, a message of hope diminished in a second. Buck was reading the letter to Michael when a bullet hit him in the neck. Michael struggled to continue but said that Buck's last words were to have him promise to deliver the letter before dying in his arms.

He said his own panic attacks started to happen after he left the forces and delivered that letter. He said he would often get choked up and start to feel like the world was caving in, that he couldn't breathe. I felt transfixed to Michael as his symptoms were similar, but not exactly the same as mine.

Michael cited that no matter how much good was in the world, or how many good people; there was always a dream shattered by another person's unjust action. How apt, and how true he was with that statement, as I thought back to my childhood and the loss of my parents.

We shared a bond that night. I felt closer to Michael, and to Kirsty by proxy. I opened up about my earlier anxiety attack and that it was Arianna's phone call that brought me

118

crashing back to earth with a sense of calm. Kirsty tried to listen in on occasion whilst serving other people; and almost sounded disappointed when I told them that my wife and I had agreed to meet. Whatever faint hope she had of us rekindling our meaningless tryst was shattered by my words.

We sunk a few more whiskies and kept the conversation flowing. I'd never known me to be so free in conversation, but the anchor on my feelings was being lifted. The weight removed. It felt good to finally talk. Time was flying, drinks were flowing, and the night grew quieter as patrons left. The man from the booth behind me stood up, tapping me on the shoulder as he left and thanked me for reciprocating with the drink. I thanked him again for fixing the car and went back to sharing stories with Michael.

Michael was entirely positive about meeting Arianna, going so far as to bring it back up.

"You should do it, without a doubt!"

"I won't lie, Michael, I'm terrified because as much as I love her, my love for the job is there too. My lust for justice. My desire to strangle Arthur pushed her away. I was putting unis on watch to make sure she was safe when the prick was sending me selfies from outside our house and her work."

Michael laughed. "The balls on that guy! Maybe I should have shot him in the head, eh?"

"Maybe you should have. Those two old people might be alive..."

Michael looked into his now empty glass, with a slightly guilty look.

"Oh, I didn't mean it like that, mate. I meant that I wouldn't be running up the walls dealing with a mad man."

"No, I know. I don't know why I felt the urge to shoot that knife. I thought about saving you first."

"That's not to say I don't appreciate it."

"I wonder if Buck would still be here if not for me encouraging him to read the letter to me. Maybe he'd have kept his wits about him. I'd have kept mine and he'd–"

"It's not worth thinking about. You couldn't have known. If there's such a thing as fate, it's all pre-determined. It's all aligned. It happened for a reason. We are here now, in this moment."

I rambled in my drunken, loud voice and cited some nonsense about the stars aligning and that we would end up being partners and hunt Arthur down together. We had a bit of a manly embrace and truly became united in our anxious, depressive selves; renewed and re-energised.

Kirsty gave us some final whiskies for the road, which we sank before merrily stumbling out the door. We went our separate ways and the walk home was blurry, dark, and mildly forgotten. I'd stopped to vomit in a bush and vaguely recalled having to run my house key up my arm and finger to line it up with the keyhole, unable to find it on the first few attempts.

For once though, I actually managed to sleep. Alcohol had helped will me into a peaceful slumber, though I'd like to think that some of it was because I had offloaded my inner thoughts and feelings. It's true what they say. It's good to talk.

I awoke the next morning to my favourite, hated radio DJ and not even he could get me down; as today, I was going to see my wife. Although separated, we hadn't officially divorced.

A wave of excitement, fear, and anxiousness hit me like a freight train. Or was the freight train the hangover? I hadn't decided. Like a child at Christmas, my excitement made me bound out of bed and get ready. I had my 'three s's: a shit, a shave, and a shower; before getting some of my nicer clothes out and ironing them. Arianna wasn't even coming to the flat, but I made a point of tidying up. That way, if she asked if the place was in a good state of repair, I was at least telling the truth.

What would I say to her?

What would she say to me?

I set off fairly early to make it to her before lunchtime. The drive was long, due to traffic build-up, but the sound of the same tape lodged in my Camaro stereo was enough to make it worthwhile. Thankfully, it was my day off and I intended to keep it a day off. I told myself I wasn't going to think about the case today, all of my time and energy was going into her, as it should have always done.

Arianna had resorted to staying with her sister since she left; taking control of a spare room and using her free time to look after her nieces and nephews, two boys and two girls. They were nice enough kids, well-mannered which felt like a rarity in this day and age.

I smirked at the thought of them trying to act up in front of her anyway. It was a very suburban neighbourhood, much like Doveport and...

I slapped myself in the face for going back to the crime scene. I was just around the corner and seconds away from seeing the love of my life. I mentally counted in my head like I did the day I left my room to check on my parents, and then put my foot on the accelerator and moved off.

I parked up against the house and she'd obviously been waiting for me, and whether that was a good sign or not, I'm not sure. I turned the key of the ignition, bringing the guttural sound of the engine to a swift silence. I pulled myself out of the driver's seat and closed the door, looking up at the door. She was standing there with a faint smile on her face.

"It's good to see you, Sebastian."

"You too, darling," I weakly responded, almost choked up.

"How was the drive?"

"Fine, I guess."

We were engaging in mindless small talk and walked up to each other, keeping a distance. God how I wanted to hold her and repeat the scenario from the evening we made love about four months before. Her beautiful eyes, saddened by the past looked at me longingly, lovingly. As if an invisible wall was between us, we were frozen in place, speechless.

My desire to kiss her was so strong but the fear of rejection was too great. I needed her, I loved her, and I felt powerless without her.

Being with her was the best thing a man could ever want. She kept me sane, she kept me grounded, and made me feel invincible the whole time I was with her. I looked at her, with a tear forming in my eye. I felt extremely emotional, but it was driven by what I felt just being with her. I could sense the hurt in her. Her body language told me everything too. She was sheepishly playing with the sleeves of a mustard-coloured cardigan that complemented her complexion.

That's when we awkwardly motioned to each other for a hug. I held her so tight, taking in her sweet perfume and the smell of her hair. I pulled back slightly to kiss her on the forehead and gently told her that I missed her.

"I've missed you too, Sebastian. Thank you for coming."

I went back in to embrace her, and she did the same. I felt a strange sense of calm, like none of the last year or so had happened, excluding our dalliance. It felt that the world around me was finally normal again.

"Come in. Let's not do this by the side of the road."

I followed her into the house, and she closed the door behind me.

"So, where are your sister and the kids?"

"They are away for the next week. They've gone to see Margaret and Alan."

I looked on confused, not really sure who she was referring to.

"Seth's parents."

We made some more mindless small talk about the kids, how she was finding things with her sister and then, over some tea, started to talk about what this was really all about.

"You are probably wondering why I needed to see you, Sebastian."

My heart immediately sank, assuming the worst. She was going to ask for the divorce. She was ready to be done with me. Or was she? The way we hugged before and said we missed each other, wasn't how people acted if they had reached the end of the road, surely?

She told me about how she had gone into therapy and started to address how she really felt. She said that when she left, she appreciated it was sudden and hated the fact that her last words to me in person were as scathing as telling me I was destined to be alone. She apologised, profusely, though I didn't need to hear it. I knew she spoke from a place of anger, hurt, and disappointment, and that I was fully in control of how I could have helped her with that.

"I'm sorry, too, gorgeous. I could have been a better husband. No, I can be a better husband."

Her smile made my heart skip a beat. The little dimple she gets when she smiles is one of my favourite things about her. She truly is beautiful, and I'll never know what I did to get so lucky to find her.

"Do you remember how we met, Sebastian?"

"I'll never forget. The double date?"

"No, not that. Though you're right, that's when we first met properly. But I actually saw you once before then. You turned up at a barbecue, Marcie Cunningham's?"

"That, I don't remember."

"We were never introduced. I was leaving as you were coming in, I watched you drive up in your Camaro and assumed you would be some arrogant classic car collector. Some egotistical tool that felt he was God's gift. You walked in the door and as you did, I turned my back to start saying my goodbyes to Marcie. That's when Gareth collapsed."

"That I do remember, everyone thought he'd had a few too many when it wasn't the case."

"I'll never forget how you dropped everything and went over to help him as everyone looked on. I was so ashamed in myself, and everyone else for not reacting. They only did when you told them it was serious. You didn't see me because you were doing everything you needed to in order to make sure he was okay. You waited with him in the recovery position until the paramedics came and then left with him, made sure he was still okay, telling everyone to have a good time and you'd see them later. I was meant to be going elsewhere that night; I meant to catch a train. I waited and watched you. I never caught that train, Sebastian."

"Where were you meant to be going?"

"Here. I was supposed to be coming here. My sister had set me up with a job and offered me a room to start a new life. I'd split up with Christopher about five months before and didn't see much of a future. I missed the train and something in my mind told me I had to see you again. I was totally wrong about you. My perception of you being this arrogant big shot was so wrong. You were kind, caring, and compassionate. Not to mention handsome."

I smiled at the compliments. "You've never told me that before, darling."

"I didn't need to. That double date we were on, I was so nervous that day. I knew who you were and had the biggest crush on you after seeing how selfless you were. I was star struck when we spoke across that dinner table, and you made me feel so comfortable. That's one of the things I miss, Sebastian. In therapy, I've been talking a lot about it. My life could have been so different if I left that barbecue five minutes earlier that day. If I hadn't seen you. If I hadn't been so transfixed on this handsome man helping that innocent, collapsed man. I could have been on a train and ended up here and gone a completely different way in life. I've thought so long and hard about it, and whether this last year would have been worth it. I'm hurt, Sebastian, so hurt. But also, quite proud. I know that whatever kept you lost in your head was the same reason you helped Gareth that day. You've been doing things in your own selfless way and you've indirectly pushed me out by doing so. That's what hurts."

"Darling."

126

"I need to say something, and it's not going to be easy to hear Sebastian."

My heart sank. I felt every painful beat. Thud, thud, thud. Speak Arianna. The silence is killing me.

"I still love you. But I can't be with you, at least I don't think so."

She was fighting back tears and the world was swallowing me whole. I was veiled in black, haunted by images of helplessness.

"I can't put myself in a position where I am second to your job. You do so much good and I am so proud of you, but I can't ever be in a position where your thoughts are hidden from me."

"Can I try to explain?"

She nodded, as though waiting for me.

"I know I am difficult emotionally. I see myself as a black hole of sorts. I can be fine one day, then the next; I'm wallowing in my own self-pity. I may appear strong and headstrong on the outside, but inside is a daily battle. I am selfless. I do everything I can for anyone who deserves it because I hate the idea of someone feeling like I do. I hate the thought of someone being so far gone they are beyond help. That's where you were perfect for me. You and that perfect heart, that perfect smile."

She smiled through tears.

"I have never stopped loving you. On the run up to you leaving, I was scared. Terrified. I'd bore witness to the most harrowing sights. I faced evil. I watched a young boy with his insides disembowelled by his own father."

Her face changed, as though trying to picture it.

"I saw a poor boy, maimed by his own flesh and blood, and thought about me as a kid. How I wished that fate upon myself sometimes. When I was a kid, there was this nurse, or caretaker if you will, at the orphanage I grew up in. Her name was Mallory. She was the only good thing I had in my childhood there. She kept me safe; she protected me and was like a mother to me. When I thought I had no one, she turned up. Like an angel, she always looked out for me. She kept my watch safe when I was frightened it would be taken away from me. The only link to my past, my real parents; she guarded with her life. Then, fast forward a few decades, you come along. Whatever vision I had of Mallory being an angel was shattered. You, gorgeous, were my true angel. I felt connected to you, entwined. I guess that in some twisted logic, by seeing that boy brutalised, who I should mention, had the same name as me, I felt as though I was facing my own past. Something in me snapped when I started to hunt Arthur. It took me to a dark place. I was hell bent on finding him and I suppose, myself in the process. The only person I couldn't tell was you."

"Why not?"

"I was worried that you'd leave. If I told you how that beast had gotten under my skin, and how I sort of matched it up to how I felt as a kid, you'd have called me crazy. I couldn't and wouldn't let your opinion of me change over something so trivial, which was at the time, so big to me.

What I looked at when I was at that crime scene, I felt it. Coming home to you was my safe place, and by keeping you in the dark, you weren't tainted by its poison."

"That doesn't sound so stupid."

"What I couldn't tell you was that Arthur, the man that killed this innocent boy, knew I was getting close. He was taunting me. He would send letters. He would take pictures of you at work. He would take pictures of him outside our house."

She looked on stunned and practically shouted, "Why wouldn't you tell me that?"

"I kept you in the dark to protect you. I didn't want you to get spooked and come here, then be vulnerable. I didn't know how serious the threats were, or if they were even threats at all. That's why some of the lads from the station would watch over you when I couldn't."

"They weren't exactly subtle, Sebastian. That's one of the reasons I started to step away. I felt as though you were watching me because you didn't trust me or something."

"God, no. I trust you implicitly. I know how stupid I was not telling you. I know I could have trusted you. I felt as though I had it in hand, that I had everything under control. I didn't want to be hunting Arthur and then, all of a sudden, not be able to protect you. Our home wouldn't have been the safe haven I needed it to be. You wouldn't have been you, beautiful and unblemished. I'm sorry for pushing you away, Arianna. I am so fucking sorry that words cannot express just how sorry I am."

"If you'd have told me, we would have been stronger together."

She was crying again. "I told my therapist I thought you had changed. That I thought you assumed I was cheating, or worse. This whole time, you were shouldering this burden and you couldn't tell me. I wish I..."

I waited for a response that never came. I could only hug her. She fought back deeper tears and I felt powerless. I was an idiot keeping her in the dark. If I had been honest from the beginning, things might have been different. I might not have pushed her away. The twisted irony is that by trying to keep her safe and protect her, I orchestrated the complete opposite of what I wanted. I felt incredibly injudicious. I held her and let her beat out some words of pain; she weakly punched me on the chest out of despair.

I had to tell her, I had to try and make it right. Any hope of keeping her in my life or losing her forever; now was the time to man up.

"Darling. I appreciate it's as if I breached your trust by not telling you. I promise you that you were never in danger. I would have protected you, and if you can't be with me and want me out of your life, I'll understand. Just know I will always be here for you. I love you, Arianna. I'll never stop."

She interrupted my emotional monologue and kissed me deeply. Through pain and tears, we shared the most powerful kiss, a combination of souls and hearts. This was the woman that I loved in her most pure, most vulnerable form, and she was completely safe in my arms.

"I love you too, Sebastian. Thank you for telling me that. It helps."

"Where do we go from here?"

She led me by the hand, upstairs to her bedroom. I took the flattering mustard yellow cardigan off her to reveal that she was fairly underdressed underneath. She was wearing rather enticing lingerie, black and white, wrapped around her beautiful upper body. The dimly lit bedroom, pretty void of sunlight kept an air of eroticism in the air, augmenting her caramel-like skin, and I kissed her as she unbuttoned my shirt.

"I always loved seeing you in a shirt, Sebastian."

She kissed me and our tongues explored as if we were two experimenting teenagers. In an entirely unsexy way, we clambered to take our trousers off and I was rewarded with the scene of matching lingerie. She always was classy like that. She'd sooner go without than to wear a mismatch.

I lay her down gently on the bed, ran my lips and hands all over her body, and felt the energy in the room. I started to slip off her lingerie then fumbled around excitedly to become fully naked. I kissed her in her most intimate of places to be rewarded with soft moans and hands running through my hair in a very sensual form of encouragement. As I worked my way back up her body, we looked at each other, deep in the eyes, as we started to make love.

It was the most amazing, most passionate lovemaking.

We fumbled for hours and talked deeply and emotionally in a sweaty embrace.

"I love you." I placed a soft kiss to her forehead.

"I love you too. I have to tell you something... I promise it is good news, what say we do it over dinner tomorrow?"

I nodded enthusiastically. Any chance to see her was a welcomed invitation.

We emerged from the bedroom, retreated to get some coffee, and after more loving embracing, and honest conversation; she politely asked me to leave. She told me that what we just shared was special and gave her a lot to think about, and she wanted to think about the possibility of coming back home. No doubt that's what she wanted to share over dinner, the logistics of moving back in.

Realising what she was suggesting was everything I wanted the last year, without even thinking, I made sure to give her the space. I told her to give me a call later that night, or the next day, and we parted with a deep, loving kiss. I hugged her goodbye, making sure to take in the scent of her perfume once again.

I put my jacket on and reached in the pocket to grab my car keys, to find the locker key card for the bus station I had taken from the crime scene the day before. I quickly stuffed it back in before Arianna could see it and see me snap back into 'work mode.'

We blew kisses at one another, before parting ways. I left, incredibly content, incredibly happy, and excited at what the future could bring. I figured the quickest way to kill time until I received that phone call was to go to the bus station and see what awaited me.

The drive was blissful, full of positivity, and heart-warming thoughts, thinking back to our lovemaking. I laughed, thinking how happy I was considering I thought the conversation and day would have, and could have ended much different. Telling her the truth lifted the mental and emotional anchor that bound me to negativity. I felt free. Rejuvenated. The drive was automatic almost, with little thought going into the actual driving, more into my mental happy place. Before I could even look at the time, I was at the bus station. No rain either, just a dusky grey sky.

I pulled out the locker key card from my jacket and assessed the scene. The station was fairly quiet and not very used. A couple of busses moved in and out, but you could tell that most people were opting for rail travel. It was quite desolate, which was a shame as this used to be one of the biggest transport hubs in town. Locker 25A, row X. Arthur better watch out, as I felt so alive and I knew I was getting close.

I hopped out of the car and walked past the few people in the station. I asked a rather cheery individual where the locker stations were, and he merrily pointed in the general direction and wished me good evening. He had to be the happiest person in the place, until I turned up and took the crown after my afternoon. There was a definite spring in my step as I found the correct row and scanned the lockers. I inserted the key card and an almighty buzz released the magnetic lock.

The contents of the locker were quite anti-climactic considering. The contents included a bloody letter opener, and an envelope? I was half expecting a severed head, or the remains of Mr Hardiman's face. Upon closer inspection, it was evident that the blade was what was used, as remains of flesh were noticeable on the knife-edge. I opened the envelope and found a letter inside, addressed to Detective Blackwood.

Another riddle and a flower were pressed inside, a gladiolus. He was trying to tell me something else with the flowers too. The riddle was far more convoluted than the last:

Formed in an instant, lasting a lifetime; I draw you back to where it began.

A bare-faced lie; he carried something new, weightless unlike the guilt of the past.

Deities Apollo and Artemis protect us, he defiles us.

Chronos mistaken affiliation, despite devouring his own, puts reflection on who the victim may be.

Even I wasn't that good to solve this straight away. I pondered for a minute and felt my phone buzzing. My heart skipped a beat of excitement when I read that it was Arianna.

"Hey, gorgeous, I've only been gone a few hours, so you've clearly had time to think. Not to hone my detective skills, but when are you coming home?"

I was met with silence.

"I know I have thought about it and I don't want to rush if you feel uncomfortable but…"

Nothing.

"Can you hear me, darling? I might have a poor signal."

I looked at my phone and noticed I had a perfect signal.

"Darling?"

Heavy breathing could be heard down the phone. The skipped beats of excitement started to slow and then speed up again for a completely different reason.

"Arianna, is everything okay?"

I could hear someone on the other end of the line.

"Detective Blackwood. You've been looking for me, haven't you?"

I closed my eyes in defeat, in despair. I knew that voice. Maniacal laughter ensued. It was Arthur and he had her. What perfect moment we shared earlier felt like a distant memory. She was in immediate danger and I was hours away from her.

"Listen here, you son of a bitch, it's me you want. Let her go and come and find me. This isn't how the game is played."

"The game, Detective? The only game we are playing is the one where I make the rules. Oh, how I envy you. You have this beautiful specimen in your life and you instead choose to hunt me. You flatter. Allow me to flatter you, Sebastian. I'll try and live the life of you for a day."

I heard him inhale loudly and heard a slight fearful whimper down the line. It had to be her.

"Arianna, if you can hear me. I'm coming. I promised to protect you; I'm going to."

"Oh, Sebastian, you fool. You shouldn't make promises you cannot keep."

"Don't hurt her. Please. I'll do anything—"

He hung up on me and I could only scream in fear. I threw the letter opener across the row of lockers and heard an almighty crash as some of the blood marked the ground. My scream echoed through the desolate bus station.

"Fuck you, Arthur, FUCK YOU!"

Be safe Arianna. I'm coming.

Chapter Six

I had already spent nearly eighteen months in Fort Rose and gotten rather close to a lot of my new family. Robert and I were like two little enforcers for Alexia. Robert was like my own personal bodyguard too. He had a real affinity for me since the day I protected his sister when I first came. I still couldn't believe we were still all together after nearly two years. I'd spent one birthday here since the incident and didn't really know how many more I would have. Birthdays were an odd, joyful celebration here, not that we really had much joy in this place, but birthdays were something that Father tried to focus on. He felt they were important because they marked another year of survival, of strength.

Father was quite a complex individual. I couldn't really pinpoint where his heart lay, or what his intentions were. A matter of weeks after I arrived, I witnessed and bore a real sympathy for him, where he spent the entire day with the kids in the back garden, overseeing a barbeque; allowing us to play and splash in a small pool. He was smiling ear to ear and showing a real love for us all. That was my birthday, and some of the other kids were clearly quite jealous. They didn't get that sort of treatment from him.

That said, it was one of the few times where there was peace in the building. The entire staffing team were present, including Mallory. Smiles were filling the place and we were generally very happy. Those times were incredibly rare and short-lived. It had been so long since we experienced a normal, joyous moment that it faded into distant memory, almost to the point we would question if it even happened. We were like a family for the first time ever.

Much like that had faded into memory, so did this myth of the cage that children would go to when we were bad. Whether real or not, there was a real fear of the cage. I'd never been in it and the last child that did go to it hadn't been seen since. We knew what rules would need to be broken to go there and made damn sure not to risk breaking them. Anything that could be viewed as insubordinate or a direct attack of the "love" Father had for us would be severely punished.

One of my sisters, Erin, once got a severe beating for writing that she hated everyone on the blackboard. We didn't take it personally, knowing she was acting out because the Gardener had shouted at her. Father was horrified to read the comment. I had never seen him so angry before. He shouted about how ungrateful we were and that we were the garbage kids of the world no one wanted. He bellowed through our room claiming we were nothing and he was making us something.

That comments were so damaging. We were already raw, separated from loving families and a part of this deranged one. That comment practically cemented any ill feelings of self-worth we may have had and more than likely made them permanent baggage we'd all carry for the rest of our lives.

Father beat Erin so much and so hard she eventually stopped crying, beaten her beyond recognition and to the proverbial pulp that could be found in the garbage. As his one free fist flew into her curled up body, his other firmly around the top of his cane, his feet would occasionally join in as he shouted abuse at her.

We all felt so powerless. I wished I could swap places with her. I wanted to take some of the beating and couldn't do anything; I was frozen and helpless. My inability to react and share the burden or the pain was my weakest point. I swore that day I would grow up and protect those that needed help. If I couldn't swap places and protect my poor sister now, maybe someday I would be able to help someone else.

Erin's weakened, youthful body ended up so battered and bruised she walked with a limp and was blind in one eye. It was clear she never got proper medical attention after the attack because it would have exposed Father and the awful people here for the beasts they were.

Screaming children, crying children, and a silent Erin caused a chain reaction of sorts. I was incredibly proud of my sister Alexia, who eventually ran to her and begged Father to stop, shielding her from further kicks. Alexia received such a slap I felt it myself, having almost shared in the feeling of the beat down Erin received.

Father's biggest mistake was assuming Robert would let that one go.

The next surge in the chain reaction was the spark that fired in his body. He just watched Father attack his biological twin sister and was rightfully furious, more so than being made to watch Erin's beating. I'd witnessed a defiance in him that actually made me proud, again, another memory I've always carried with me through life: fighting for the right reasons, to protect the weak.

Robert ripped Father's cane from his steady hand whilst he towered over my cowering sisters, one lifeless and the other shaking. An almighty crack on Father's back caused him to shout in pain; and the whole room stopped. No one cried, no one screamed, just silence. Everyone was unsure as to what was about to happen next.

No one ever physically stood up to Father before. This was a league beyond the time I took the blame for the writing on the blackboard when I first arrived eighteen months ago.

As if watching a movie, Father turned around in slow motion, in the eerily silent room. I heard his laboured breathing from the exertion depleted from Erin's pasting. Robert stood back, with the cane still in his hands, a slight tremble. I don't know if the tremble was from fear, or the sheer adrenaline coursing through his veins. Knowing how headstrong he was, I've always taken it as the latter of the two. Father bellowed across the room, with his roar stirring deep inside the hearts of all the children.

"You ungrateful little shit. How dare you bite the hand that feeds? Rabid dogs should be put down. You–"

Robert knew he had crossed a line and it sounded like a real threat. All he could do was try and hit Father again to prevent the inevitable thrashing he was going to get. He swung the cane in a vertical motion from behind his back, aiming to get Father on his head.

Father, burning with rage, caught the cane in his hand as it came down with force and didn't even flinch. He caught it like a professional baseball player would catch a ball travelling at high speed. He pulled himself up to Robert and grabbed him by the throat. He started to squeeze and as Robert's breath left his body and his eyes and skin started to go blue, Father let go of the cane. It dropped to the ground having been abandoned by Robert, who was fighting to release the grip around his throat.

Father must have sensed the fear in Robert's eyes and sudden lack of fight probably had him seconds from death, so instead he punched Robert square in the face, breaking his nose in the process. The force from the punch, and immediate release from the deathly grip, caused my brother to fall into a pile of flesh and bone. Another lifeless child hit the ground and Robert fought for air, coughing and spluttering.

"Such fire, boy. There is only one place for you."

So, the cage was real after all. Robert was dragged away in pain, coughing and wheezing, fighting for air. Erin was left in a pile. Alexia never moved from her, continually shielding her. The remainder of us looked on, disappointed with ourselves for selfishly not reacting for fear of the same. Then, the creepy old man from the garden wandered in. He never came into our room, so Father had obviously sent him. I still never knew what his name was; we always made a point of avoiding him. He was just known as the "Gardener" to us kids.

He spoke through his missing teeth, practically spitting at Alexia to move and scooped Erin up in his arms. She was still unconscious, and her head fell back to join her motionless body. He muttered about having to look after such a badly-behaved child being a disgrace to the rest of us and that he couldn't wait to teach her a lesson. He looked around the room at the children; in what I can only describe in hindsight as a seductive way. I was too young to realise the intent behind the stare.

He grinned through his single front tooth and the image of that moment has been permanently etched in my mind. Younger me had no idea what kind of predator he was, but I could still sense he was dangerous in a different way. I'd experienced it first-hand the day he threw me down and twisted my ankle, as his hands did explore me briefly before I was thrown down. Erin wasn't being taken somewhere safe to be nursed back to care. The beating was probably the least of her worries.

It was disheartening to think that all this destruction came from one mere comment spouted in anger about hating everybody. That's where I had decided to teach my brothers and sisters a few tricks from my past.

Over later weeks and months, I had gone so far as to use the blackboard in our bedroom play area as a means to teach people how to speak in code. We had a simple system where we would write a sentence and then write the previous letter in sequence in place of the one we meant, excluding vowels. Vowels were replaced with numbers. An A was a one, an E a two, and so on. For an F, we would write a D, for a Y, an X, and so on.

It was kept fairly simple, solely because some of the other kids weren't bright enough to grasp some of the other codes or ciphers I had tried to teach them originally. Alexia did enjoy the challenging codes though. We played our own games where I would create ciphers for her to break, like my real parents used to do. She said she couldn't wait to show Robert if he came back from the cage.

My heart sank for my big brother. I wished he was with us and learning the code, but we hadn't seen him in months. After all, there was little to do to entertain ourselves in Fort Rose, other than reasonably limited verbal communication, written communication through the code, and the rare occasions when we would be permitted to play in the garden. I always assumed he would have gotten a real kick out of the code breaking. There was a youthful excitement knowing we were breaking rules, but safely. It gave us a little confidence, which was something normally absent.

Whenever Father, or other members of the staff would ask what we were doing, we would say that we were practicing handwriting so we would be able to write nice letters to each other, the various numbers strewn across the board gave it a sense of youthfulness that I guess was expected from us given our age. Survival instincts even made us actually write proper letters as a cover story for the handwriting practice, where we would litter them with lies about loving our lives in the orphanage.

143

I wrote a letter to Father thanking him for saving us, to which he rewarded me with some homemade cookies. The other kids were quite jealous of the ingenuity until they realised I had always intended to save some for them, citing that Father taught me sharing was honourable. He didn't mind me sharing when I rubbed his ego.

Secret messages were the one way we knew how to talk to each other and how we really felt, without fear of reprimand, or bullying tactics deployed by the staff. In a youthful show of strength, we never uttered a word to the staff, even when pressed. It was a unified secret that gave us a sense of empowerment.

Erin finally came back to the dorm. She used to be the talkative one of the group; always acting out. She had been forced into a silence, with her new eye patch and large rimmed glasses. She often cried herself to sleep and would react when anyone would get close to her, going so far as to cry whenever she was touched. She was broken beyond repair. I'd always wondered what the Gardener had done to her but in later life, had a pretty good idea. What a shame. One angered moment portrayed in black and white with chalk would subsequently end her life in a twisted butterfly effect.

I hadn't seen Mallory in a long time. I wished she was here so she could have stopped it. She would have helped us, I'm sure of it. I told myself I had to find her and tell her what was happening and devised a plan to break out of the room and find her. The trouble was, we were always locked in at night. We had brief bursts to the garden on rare occasions and when it was time to eat, we were all marched to and from the dormitory in militant fashion.

Like a children's adventure movie, we communicated in code and talked about how we could free ourselves to find Mallory. The night we came up with the plan was one of my fondest memories. The camaraderie between the children, realising we controlled our own destinies was inspiring. We all came together, on the same page and listened to everyone's ideas respectfully. Everything from filling the lock with putty so the key didn't work, to stealing a screwdriver from the Gardener and taking the doorknob off, to the more creative of us thinking we could break the window and scale the walls like Spider-Man. The youthful exuberance from our group kept smiles on our faces, even Erin, who still hadn't spoken a word since the night she lost her eye.

We operated like a colony of ants whenever we went out for breakfast, lunch, or dinner. Everyone would report back on what they would see on the walk to the canteen. We'd keep important things written in code on the blackboard, so we had options open. The day we got let into the garden, we even got as far as procuring implements we felt could help us on our miraculous break out.

I often reflect on the thrill of knowing we were all plotting against Father. I felt alive, for the first time in a long time. There was a shred of hope amongst the constant despair. I genuinely felt as though I would never get out of Fort Rose. Every day merged into the next, wondering who would slip up next and get the next beating. But our sudden desire to try and save ourselves by letting Mallory know what was going on seemed to inspire everyone.

Then one night, we were beckoned back into our bedroom after supper and as we were shut in, I heard a distant voice shouting to the orderly tasked with taking us all to bed. They shouted back they wouldn't be long and would be there to watch shortly. Clearly, something was on television worth watching but I didn't know what.

We were so secluded from current events, that television was a pipe dream. We didn't even see so much as a newspaper. Then suddenly, silence. I didn't hear it. The almighty cranking of the lock as we are shut in didn't come. No one else seemed to notice, because it was just one of those things we'd become socially compliant in anticipating. As darkness started to dissipate and my eyes adjusted to the room, I hopped out of bed. My bare feet hit the cold floor and I felt blood pounding through my veins, creeping quietly so as to not make a sound.

I slowly meandered my way to the door and reached out to the knob, twisting gently. A glorious click had proven I was right, and the door was unlocked! Stunned silence ensued, and then panic set in. There were whispers and ushers to entice me back to the warmth of my bed from one of my sisters, but it didn't deter me. All the planning to escape and one forgetful orderly was all that was needed. At least we had fun plotting on the run up to this mishap.

I swung the door open some more and the room filled slightly with light. If I was caught out of bed, I'd be the one to take a beating, so I was already fully committed. I snuck

146

out of the bedroom and closed the door behind me. My brothers and sisters had probably written me off at that point, but I wouldn't be slowed. I had to get to the nurse's office where Mallory and I had hidden her diary and my watch. It was on the other side of the building.

I walked patiently down the hallway, creeping against the walls to minimise my shadow. I could see flashes down the hallway and blurred sounds. I crept closer, being sure not to make a sound. My movements were ever so stealthy that I envisioned myself, in my own youthful enthusiasm, as a ninja on a secret mission. As I neared the open room with the flashes, two security guards were talking over the news programme on the television. There was coverage of a story of the successful opening of the 'No Nukes' concert in Madison Square Garden, headed up by musical powerhouses. I always think back to that moment, as the date would have been September 29, 1979. I'd been in Fort Rose for almost two years, nearing my seventh birthday.

I kept myself in the shadows and moved past the two guards, my heart racing at what fate awaited me if I got caught. I had to do it though. I had to see Mallory, to talk to her about what was going on. I was venturing into practically unknown territory, lost in darkness trying to find the nurse's station. I'd only been to it once, and that was well over a year ago. The brain does some strange things when you think you know somewhere but realise you don't. It felt like I was walking into nothingness, a maze of hallways I hadn't seen before.

I tested a few doors, some were locked, some weren't. Then I heard it. The last sound in the world I wanted to hear. Tut-tut-tut. It was getting louder. That was Father's cane. I started to panic, realising I was a helpless gazelle and a lion was closing in.

I hurried back to a maintenance room I had stumbled across previously and closed the door as quietly as I could. The tutting as his cane hit the cold hard floor was deafening, amplified by the surrounding silence. He was so close. I couldn't even close the door properly out of fear he would have seen it. Tut-tut-TUT. I froze. The tutting stopped. I heard Father mumbling. He was on the other side of the door.

As if driven by sheer willpower, my eyes adjusted to the room I was in, looking for a place to hide. It was a fairly deep room, just thin. A few tall lockers stood at the side, with some shelves following the walls, loaded with various items. I didn't have time to look, but I chose a place, and committed to my hiding spot. I tried so hard to be quiet, but my breathing was laboured, and I worried I was making more noise. Terrified of the beating I would get if caught, I ran through all the scenarios. Why did I leave the room? I should have listened to my brothers and sisters. Why was I so stupid?

"Jack?" I heard Father say. I had no idea who Jack was.

"JACK," he shouted. I covered my mouth to try and silence myself further, realising I was breathing in a panicked state. I then held my breath as the door opened.

I kept saying in my head: *don't turn on the light*. I could see the outline of Father's face, as he looked in the room, curious why the door was left open.

"Jack, are you in here?"

I stayed deathly silent. I reached a zen-like state, realising I had to control my emotions. If I lost control now, I was done for. I'd be lost like Robert, in the cage, whatever and wherever that was. The tut of Father's cane matched my heartbeats as he shuffled around.

"Born in a bloody barn, Jack."

The door slammed on me and I sighed a sigh of relief. Thank God. I was safe. Then a click followed by sound of his cane on the hard floor. At least he was going. I was safe to explore again. Or did I go back to my room? That was the wise option, but I was already in too deep. I stood at the door, deciding my next course of action. Like a few years prior when I heard my Grandfather arguing with my parents, I counted to ten. Then counted to ten again. Still couldn't muster the courage.

"Two, three, four..." I felt rejuvenated. Now was the time!

I turned the knob of the door. Nothing. That's what the click was. My heart sank as I contemplated the truth of what had just happened. I was locked in. Panic started to set in again. Father had locked me in, and I was stuck. I didn't know what to say, or what to do, other than resign to my fate. I was captured. I'd be found in the morning and have to face my punishment.

The adrenaline in my body started to leave as I relaxed some more. I focussed on my breathing and calmed down. I realised just how cold it was and began to shiver. My feet were freezing, having walked sockless on the floors so I rubbed them a little, trying to generate a modicum of warmth. I sat in the corner of the room, next to the door and curled up. I eventually searched the lockers to look for something of use. I found an old coat and wrapped myself in it, finding an old chocolate bar in the pocket. I ate it without hesitation, treating it as my reward for the inevitable punishment.

I took the time to reflect on my situation as I wrapped myself in the coat, making sure to lick the residue of chocolate from my teeth and lips. My eyes had adjusted to the lack of light in the room, and I could see an array of various liquids and cleaning products. It was clearly a generic storage cupboard, likened somewhat to an indoor shed. In the faint light, I twisted my neck up to see what was above me and I could see a switch but didn't see the point in flicking it. I felt safer in the dark as no one knew I was here. If I turned the light on, I might attract the attention of anyone walking by, possibly Father.

My mind wandered. I thought back to a time when I played hide and seek with my mother. It warmed me to think about it because I sat in the dark, just like I was now. I went in my parent's study, and then hid in a large storage chest next to their antique globe. I used to love playing with the globe, spinning it and looking at all the different countries. My real father would tell me how to pronounce the countries, and if he had any interesting stories about them, would tell me.

I remembered one particular story where I pointed at the U.K. and he told me about the time he travelled to Loch Ness in Scotland. My father told me about a local legend of a monster that lived in the lake. We used to fantasise about what it would be like to go in a submarine, find the monster, and become rich and famous. I remembered re-living that story as I hid in the chest next to the globe, pretending it was our submarine. I felt incredibly safe, and incredibly secure.

I snapped awake, remembering where I was. Reminiscing of my real parents and the story of the Loch Ness Monster had sent me into a light sleep. I was exhausted. As dangerous as it was being hidden in the maintenance cupboard away from my room, there was a welcoming peace to it. I didn't have the whispers or tears of children around me. I felt quite content to the point I smirked at how I should sneak out every night to rest in my new corner. Then I heard a whirring sound, like some sort of air conditioning unit.

I had a sudden brainwave. My desire for survival and safety made me think of the vent in the nurse's office, where I'd hidden my watch with Mallory's diary. The vent was the answer. Perhaps I could escape through it and make my way back to the room? I got up from my corner and tidied away the old coat, to remove any evidence of me being here. I placed the chocolate wrapper in the adjacent locker as a practical joke in the event someone else got the blame for eating it. The staff here would deserve it for the most part, and it would remove any sense of doubt for the owner of it.

I followed the sound and just beside the locker furthest away from me, on the ground, was a vent. I lifted the latch for the vent and kneeled down. It was a tight space, full of cobwebs and incredibly dusty, with a few cigarette butts stuffed at the entryway. A secret smoker was in the midst, discarding any evidence of their vice. I felt the back of my throat start to tickle as I inhaled but managed to control my breathing to prevent bringing any attention to my whereabouts.

I shimmied in to the vent and let the latch fall down behind me. The only way was forward now. I pressed on and shuffled until I came across a split in the vent. I could go left, or right. I tried to mentally picture where I was, like I did when I played with the globe, and mapped how I had walked out of our dormitory and decided the most logical way was to go right. Whatever guided me, I continued on my claustrophobic path. I shimmied further down the vents and could see a break of light in the distance. I probably hadn't travelled too far in the grand scheme of things, but it felt exhilarating to make progress. As I neared the light, it turned off to the right ever so slightly and I was immediately met with glee on my face. There it was, my watch.

I quickly grabbed it and opened it to try and view the photo of my mother. It was so dark in the vent that I could only see the outline on her photo. I moved in to the nurse's office, grabbing Mallory's diary at the same time. It was dark, but a small rectangular window at the top of the room brought in some light to see well enough. The sky was clear and the moon visible, which helped. I looked at the photo of my mother and felt quite emotional. I'd been through a lot in the last year or so. I truly, deeply missed them.

I wished they hadn't been killed. I wished they hadn't left that day. I imagined happier times, when my mother would play the piano and sing, to the simpler times like sitting across from my real father as he read his morning newspaper. I inspired to be a better person just thinking about them and remembered why I was here. I came to find Mallory to tell her what we were going through. To tell her how much pain we were suffering at the hands of Father and his staff. If she wasn't here though, how on earth could I tell her?

Then it dawned on me to read her diary. Maybe I could leave a message in it. I flicked through the pages and the most recent entry was dated 27th September 1979. Going by the news report I sneakily witnessed, it had been two days prior. I felt ashamed for reading her private thoughts but did anyway.

Mallory wasn't as happy as she let on, clearly. There were pictures she had drawn of flowers in the diary, alongside some rather painful poems, and phrases of feeling weak and worthless. She wasn't really the strong woman I took her for. Wanting to better understand the beautiful angel I had envisioned. I flicked back to an undated entry at the beginning of the diary.

Today was another horrible day. Jack had his hands all over me again. I'm having to put more makeup on to hide the marks from the last time he got his hands on me and... raped me. There's no point saying anything. The policeman that came left with a smile on his face. Corrupt bastard. Money talks, clearly! I wish I could have left this place a long time ago. This town is my prison and I am living a life sentence. A few silly mistakes as a teenager, angered mother. I always wondered what mother's relationship is to Cyril. I heard her refer to him as a loving uncle, cuss him in one breath, then worship him in the next. He has some sort of control over her, and by proxy, me. Forced to work here now that he is paying mother's care bills. As much as I love her, I also hate her because of what I have to do.

I didn't really understand it all as a child, but upon reflection, it was obvious that Father seemed to be quite a powerful man. For years, I have wondered how he became so influential. He had clearly taken care of Mallory's mother, whatever the relationship was between them. I'm not sure I would want someone like that having a hold on me though, after all, I remember when I looked him in the eyes when he brought me to Fort Rose and thinking how there was a deep-rooted evil inside. The compendium of Father, of Cyril, would be an interesting one. Who was he? The way he even had me referring to him as Father, he was a master manipulator and had spread his virus across multiple people, multiple families. I kept reading with the moon as my nightlight. I read it over and over until I practically memorised the words.

I remember when I last tried to run away. Tried being the key word. The last time I ran away, he just found me anyway, I was dragged back, literally by the hairs on my head. I screamed. My punishment was the lowest point. He watched as I was raped on that fucking bed with the straps on each corner. Jack was one of the last. He whispered in my ear that he would have liked me more fifteen years ago. Sick. Why does Cyril protect people like this? He is a wolf in sheep's clothing.

I flicked forward a few pages.

Well, I'm pregnant. Thankfully, it can't be Jack as he can't have kids. I think that Gerry will be the father. He promised to take me away from this place. I only hope he will.

I reacted quite suddenly as I heard noise outside the door. I froze in place. Eventually the racket died down and I continued reading from a new page, having lost my original place.

I don't know if I'm lucky or unlucky, because I'm a mother to twins: a handsome boy and a beautiful girl, Robert and Alexia. I've not seen Gerry in months. Cyril has promised to keep me safe from harm now that I have kids. He knew I was being abused and let it happen; now he'll protect me? Mother took a turn for the worse. She's on the decline. Part of me can't wait until she is gone so I can try to disappear again. I write with a sarcastic smile, as that will happen... if not just for me, my kids.

Oh my God... Robert and Alexia are Mallory's children? I couldn't believe it. I didn't know whether to tell them, or to keep the secret to myself. I felt a real pang of guilt for reading and felt as though I was being too invasive. I was hooked though.

I spoke with Cyril and I know who he is. He's family all right. He was my grandfather's younger brother, the bastard child from an affair with thirty years between them. At least he isn't my father. He told me a little about my father though, and called him a dirty, meddling, pig. Talking about my father put him in a bad mood, and he told me that if I ever mention him again, I'd end up like Gerry. At least I know what happened to him now too: Cyril made him disappear. Whether dead or bribed to leave, I guess part of me knew he had a hand in it. I'm sorry Gerry. Sorry you ever met me.

I felt quite sick reading just how dangerous Father was, but I couldn't stop reading.

I spoke to mother about my father and about Cyril, but in her weakened state she didn't have

156

a whole lot to say. She did tell me about some old letters that might tell me more about them. I read some. My father never liked Cyril. I need to be careful, because if he can make policeman disappear, I'm in deep. I've got two babies now. At least working here, I stay close to them. No one has touched me or raped me since he said he would sort it out. Some kind of silver lining I guess.

I was already reading too much; I was reading Mallory's most intimate thoughts and it wasn't right. I flicked forward and was nearing the end of the diary.

Cyril told me about a little boy he brought here last night. He laughed saying the boy would be something special in life. I'd never heard him speak so highly of a child before, not even my own; and they are his own flesh and blood, to a degree. He told me the new boy, Sebastian called him Sir when they met, and then selflessly protected my Alexia when he was going to give her the belt. I'm too weak and pathetic to do anything about it. This little boy Sebastian protecting my little one makes me smile. I feel like a proud mother to him, and I've never even met him.

I felt a slight sense of pride knowing how much my actions affected Father to comment, and that Mallory was proud of me. I didn't really have anyone left in life to call me proud. For a message in a random diary that I had no right to read, it really impacted me. It taught me that honourable actions may be remembered and by what I was reading, could give hope to those that have none.

I read the most recent entry:

I have to do something. That beating little Erin received has torn me inside. I know Cyril is an evil man. Jack even had his wicked way with her. I'm a failure as a parent, as a mother, and as a responsible human. I just don't know how to do something without putting the lives of my kids in danger. I don't even know where Robert is. I wrote a letter to the nearest police station, begging for help and whoever reads it to be discreet and careful. I hope and pray someone out there will do the right thing where I couldn't.

I knew she wanted to help and felt relieved she had already to an extent, but she wasn't here. I figured I would head back to my dormitory, so I carefully placed the watch and the diary back in the vent. I felt pain for Mallory. She was as imprisoned as the rest of us here. We were all lambs in the slaughter, waiting to die. Something in me changed that night.

The bravery to leave the room, the adventure I had been on to find out Mallory's truth, and see my watch; I felt invincible, empowered. I went to the door in front of me and didn't even count to myself before trying to open it. It was locked. I chose my resting place for the night and settled on the gurney in the room. I had to hope it was only Mallory that found me.

The next morning, I awoke to a rather terrified Mallory, who quizzed me as to how I got there. I told her every single detail. She stressed about how to get away with it.

"I don't know how to explain how you got here, Sebastian. We'll both be in trouble if he finds out."

Knowing how dark and cruel Father could be, she devised a plan to explain how I got to the nurse's station. It involved smashing the glass on the cabinet full of drugs, then slashing me across the top of my head. I don't feel as though I had a say in the matter. She did it without thinking, and I gritted my teeth and winced somewhat.

"Sebastian, you brave boy," she stated as she choked up. "I'm so sorry I had to do that, I'm just as bad as them."

I reassured her that she wasn't, as I understood this was the better of any other possible outcome. I didn't want to end up like Erin. Before long, she was working on my head, stitching me up. I told her I worried about how far things would go before someone had the strength to speak up and protect us, but in a more innocent way given my age.

Mallory began to well up a little at my statement; perhaps realising she had to be the one to do something. She told me I really was incredible, and that Cyril was right, I really would grow up to be something. It was only a compliment because she was the one saying it. We talked and joked a little bit, before she cautiously asked me if I read her diary. I stayed silent, and she told me she promised not to be angry if I was honest with her.

159

I came clean and said I knew she was Robert and Alexia's mother. She wept at the revelation, almost as though I was a trusted friend sharing a secret. She begged me to keep it secret for the sake of the kids, as they didn't know. She was worried Father would use it against her, or the children if they ever found out; not to mention, she was worried other children might treat them differently if their mother was part of the staff. Something hit home with that one, as I knew from our coded messages just how much we felt disdain towards the orphanage staff, excluding Mallory though.

I couldn't predict how people would react, and I was playing with a big secret, so didn't want to do anything that might harm someone else. I asked her why she hadn't left with the kids already and she merely responded it was complicated and patronised me a little by saying that was an 'adult' conversation.

Strange considering how we had opened up so much already. She probably realised she was crazy for talking to a child about it all. I certainly didn't feel like a child. The last couple years made me grow from a child to a teenager. I was nearly seven, going on seventeen, and had the mental capacity and intellect of someone even older, courtesy of my real parents, intuition, and empathy I picked up along the way.

Mallory flustered a little more as she finished patching me up and put a plaster on. She told me to say that I tripped and banged my head on the end of my bed, which was a weak lie in itself, but she beefed it up a bit by saying she came to the dormitory after hearing crying, then noticed I was bleeding so tended to me before breakfast. I bought into it and that was enough for her to escort me back to the canteen where my brothers and sisters were having breakfast.

The other kids looked on in amazement to see me join them at the table. Mallory announced I was silly and that'll teach me to run in the bedroom and bang my head. The other kids accepted the lie and before disappearing into the building, Mallory whispered in my ear and told me to be patient, she'd see what she could do.

The military march back to our dormitory was swift, and when the door closed behind us, the other children were quick to quiz me on where I had been all night, surrounding me until I came clean. Some of them said they hadn't slept because they had been so scared. I told them all what happened, minus a few details, and they laughed when I said about the chocolate bar in the maintenance room. That's when I realised Alexia wasn't there. I asked the others where she was, and they said when I didn't come back for a few hours, she went out looking for me and hadn't come back.

I felt genuine fear. I climbed in my bed, went under the covers, and cried real tears for the first time in nearly two years.

It seemed like anyone I got close to in life ended up missing.

I felt alone.

Chapter Seven

Thoughts of impending doom circulated in my mind. I was screaming a silent scream, full of panic and dread because the love of my life was in danger. Why did this always happen to me?

Thoughts flew back to my childhood where I felt worthless, where I felt conscious of my loneliness. It really was true. Any time I fucking got close to someone, something bad happened. I was a walking nightmare. I felt as though I had broken one hundred mirrors, had a herd of black cats walk in front of me. I felt like the unluckiest man on the planet. Destined to be unhappy.

Arthur Henderson, I will fucking kill you if you hurt her. That bastard laughed down the phone. I've been playing his stupid fucking game, almost admiring him for getting my brain ticking, admiring him for almost making it fun. I felt sick. I felt my stomach churning at the fact I had enjoyed our chase up to this point.

He had just taken something from me. I wasn't thinking clearly. Then it happened. I vomited on the bus station floor. I vomited some more until I was dry heaving, trying to will something up. I pulled myself to my feet and worked my way over to my mobile phone I had thrown across the room. It still worked, thankfully. I curled up in the corner of the lockers and pulled my phone to my ear, in a startling resemblance to my younger self in the maintenance room when I escaped my dormitory.

I tried calling Arianna. Straight to voicemail. No doubt the bastard had discarded the phone as well. I called Michael.

"Hello?"

"I need you, mate. I really fucking need you."

Realising the desperation in my voice, and that I couldn't speak, Michael flipped that switch in his brain which almost brought him back to military mode.

"What is it, Sebastian? Talk to me. Slowly."

I struggled to find the words. "He has her."

"Whoa, what? Who has who?"

I was fighting back tears of desperation.

"He has Arianna, Michael. Arthur-fucking-Henderson has my wife."

Michael didn't know what to say. He was stunned. His words of reassurance fell on deaf ears because I knew there was nothing that could be said or done to make me feel better.

Arthur had been taunting me since the beginning of this case and decided to make his coup-de-grâce a stinging stab to my heart, by taking the person that means the most to me in the world. If anyone ever wanted to hurt me, they'd only need to take away the person that matters most to me or destroy my father's watch. I clutched on to the latter as tight as I could, whilst listening to Michael ask questions.

"Where are you? I'm coming to you."

"Don't."

"Don't shut down. Focus, Sebastian. Get your head in the game."

"I'm going to head home. Do me a favour, grab everything you can out of the situation room and bring it to my house. I'm going to find this fucking creep. I won't catch him if I'm chasing from behind. I need to fucking get in front of him. I'm going to kill him, Michael. I'm going to fucking kill him!"

"I know how you feel. I've felt helpless before. Just don't do anything stupid. As for the evidence, I'll make it happen. I can be there in about an hour given the detour to the station."

"I don't have an hour, Michael."

He paused. I felt my voice shaking and screamed again.

"Give me forty-five minutes."

I ended the call. The nice, friendly gentleman for the bus station staff poked his head around the corner having followed the latest scream. He took his crown back. He was once again the happiest person in the place after I foolishly chose to boast about besting him. He could see I was in crisis and offered to help before assessing the vomit and look on my face.

I briefly apologised for the mess I left on the floor and flashed my badge, so he didn't feel the need to call the police, or an ambulance. I walked away from the lockers with my mind spinning. I was reliving that moment when Arianna left me again and again, only this time felt worse because of the obvious risk factor. I felt as though she was

164

gone, forever. I was giving up hope of seeing her again. My heart twisted, my stomach churned, I felt genuine pain like I had never felt before.

Stop! Just STOP! You are better than Arthur, Sebastian, you can find him.

My walk turned into more of a jog; I had to meet up with Michael and figure this out. I kept my phone handy just in case Arthur called back. He'd crossed a line. Whatever game we were playing before, the rules had just changed. He crossed a line that no one had ever crossed. I was going to find him and be the one to put him down. Not for Jessica, not for little Sebastian, not even for Arianna... I was going to put him down for me.

Fire filled my heart. I felt a deep-seeded rage inside me. Throughout my entire life, I had managed to keep evil thoughts and feelings suppressed. The good in me was enough to rise above. God knows I had every right to have turned into someone like Arthur because of the loss, the pain, the beatings, the abuse, and the loneliness. I let it shape me, but I grew from it. Arthur's act, taking Arianna, was enough to let the beast inside me out. I felt conflicted as I was thinking dark thoughts that I never knew were inside me.

The drive to my house was quick. I broke a few laws, not caring if I was stopped. I'd have just flashed a badge if I were. I pulled up against my house, seething with anger and brimming with pain.

"Hi, Seb! Thanks for the drink the other day," said the kind mechanic that fixed my vehicle.

I rudely walked right past him, bumping into him as I stormed by. I said my thank you in the pub, don't try and be my friend. I turned the key to get in my house and looked out to the world as I stood at the door. The kind mechanic, Al, I think his name was... he looked at me quite flabbergasted. I had obviously offended him, though he did have a slight look of concern given my obvious demeanour. I gave a weak nod of acknowledgement as I closed the door on him, on the world.

I paced up and down the hallway, waiting for Michael. I heard the ticking of the clock as my pacing matched every long, painful tick.

I moved to the dining table, littered with old newspapers, magazines, and letters. There were some envelopes stamped with 'urgent,' probably bills but nothing mattered quite like what was going on. I lay across it; arms outstretched and then pushed everything off the table in one fell swoop. The noise of the papers flying everywhere, loose pages gliding in the wind as I'd given them a boost.

I stomped through to my old, unused office and dragged out a whiteboard. The clicking of the wheels as I dragged it through to the dining room and the sudden bang as it hit the doorframe altered me to my current whereabouts. Realising I had jammed it in the door and appreciating my recklessness, I readjusted the whiteboard to manoeuvre it through the door frame.

I looked at some old pictures on the wall, pointless frames with stock photographs of landscapes in them just to fill out the room. She chose them. She felt the wall was too bare and required some colour. I threw them across the room, clearing some wall space, and then stopped suddenly at a photograph of us. She was so beautiful, her bright teeth and smile grinning from ear to ear.

That was the day I proposed. I had taken her to the top of Eidolon Hill, a neighbouring hill surrounded by nature overlooking the city. It was where she would often sit and think, then do her writing. It was incredibly peaceful and high enough to negate the hustle and bustle of the city, replacing the sounds of the city with the sounds of the birds. I asked her to marry me that day and she was so happy she cried tears of joy and hugged me so tightly her makeup ran on to my shirt.

I felt a tear in my eye as I looked at the photo. It calmed me but didn't shake off how real this was. As much as I looked into Arianna's eyes, I knew what was at stake. I had to find her. I had to save her, or I'd only ever be looking at them again in a picture.

The door crashed open.

"Sebastian?"

I didn't respond, as I was looking at the photo.

"Sebastian!" Michael stumbled into the dining room. He looked right at me, frozen in place with a lost gaze. He scanned the room, witnessing the upheaval; as though my house had been robbed.

"Whatever you need, my friend. Let's find her."

I couldn't say anything. I kept looking at her face, the tear that built up in my eye started to roll down my face. The day she made me the happiest man in the world was right in front of me, framed beautifully on the wall like a window to the past. I wished I could jump into the frame just to hold her one last time. I felt as though I could still smell her from our liaison.

"She didn't deserve this, Michael. She didn't…"

Michael listened, without saying a word.

"If I knew what she would go through by saying yes to that question. If I knew the pain and the hurt this day would cause, I would have run a mile, saved her from it. From me."

Michael placed his hand on my shoulder reassuringly, adjusting his stance to face me, his back to the photo I was gazing into.

"I can't bear the thought of losing her again, Michael. Arthur Henderson is as good as dead. Why the fuck didn't you shoot him? Why didn't you put that beast down?"

Michael looked at me with a slightly defeated face. I knew it wasn't his fault, but I was projecting my pain. I was projecting my anger.

"I…"

He turned to me.

"I didn't mean that, Michael. I just wish that bastard was dead. She doesn't deserve this. I dread to think what that fucking animal is doing to her. It kills me. My heart is sinking so fucking low that I don't know what to feel. I need to save her. I need to save her to save myself. If I lose her."

I stammered, unable to find the words. Michael's hand tightened on my shoulder, as impishly comforting as it was. My gaze hadn't left Arianna's eyes in the photograph.

"If I find him, Michael, I'm not sure what I'm capable of doing. I want to kill him myself."

I snorted, as though accepting my fate and the path laid out in front of me.

"You have to help me find him."

The angel on my shoulder was starting to contend with the demon on the other.

"Michael, just promise me that if we do find him and she's not–"

"Don't think like that, Sebastian," he scolded me.

"Just promise me you'll save me from myself."

Michael nodded silently. He knew the stakes. He knew how serious I was. I probably had the same look in my eye he was used to seeing when he served in the military. I had entered a battleground, and for once, I was happy with the company. Michael would likely save me from myself.

The angel on my shoulder didn't want me to lose myself in the process. The smallest part of me thought about what Arianna would think and want. I was already thinking as though she was dead. I knew what Arthur Henderson was capable of. I knew what he could do to her and part of me hoped that if death was fated for her, it would be swift and painless.

That single thought that entered my mind was enough for the devil on my shoulder to silence the angel once again. The single tear that had rolled down my face dropped and the newfound silence in the room allowed it to be heard as it crashed against a loose newspaper page from my earlier manhandling of the room.

Michael let go of my shoulder and turned away. He started heading towards the exit and swung the door open. I finally broke my gaze from the photograph. Fuck him then. If he doesn't want to help, I'll do this myself. As I pictured how it looked, he stormed out. Thoughts of when Arianna left caused me to switch my gaze back to the photograph. I exhaled deeply, only this time as I looked into the past, I didn't look at Arianna, and I looked at me. I looked at the man I was, and who she helped me become. All the pain growing up, the way I was made to feel in Fort Rose, to the panic attacks and anxiety I had felt throughout the years; I felt alone.

That's when Michael walked back in the room, clutching a box.

"I grabbed everything I could from the situation room," he said as he kicked the front door shut.

I smiled, realising that I hadn't lost my partner after all. I was quite taken aback with my negative thoughts. Interestingly, I also just referred to him as my partner. Maybe I was okay with the idea of it. I mentally scolded myself for assuming he was leaving, though appreciated its just that I was used to being left alone.

The box was thrown on to the dining table and we emptied the contents, inanely chatting about what our strategy would be.

"What do you think you'll find in all this stuff? It's just crime scene photos, riddles, and red herrings. He taunted you, Sebastian. You can't expect to see much, surely?"

I walked over to the whiteboard and flipped it over to reveal what was on the back. I had left images, Polaroid photographs, and theories regarding Arthur. Michael assessed them jaw-dropped, picking up one of the photographs of Arthur outside his house, smiling. He then grabbed a second photo, one of Arianna casually shopping.

"What the...?"

"He's been taunting me for a long time, Michael. It almost became a game. A game I enjoyed playing. It seemed that whenever I started to get close, he'd send a new photo, which is what would make me get lost in the chase. I'd look back at crime scenes, but, I've been going stir crazy trying to make the pieces fit. I've been going mad."

Michael was stunned. He looked at the wall of images and theories on the board. I started to unpack what he had taken from the station. Every piece of the case brought back memories.

I felt myself snapping back to the crime scenes, the bloodied hotel room with the lamb head crown. That was just a gory tribute to his testament to kill without thought or

171

feeling. The lamb head, perhaps that was a message in itself. The UV light with the message and the riddle.

I reached further into the box. Little Sebastian. My God, the scene that started the hunt. I mean, I knew about Arthur from the rape case. The one thing that finally had us catch the bastard, yet the weak jury and piss poor prosecution couldn't make anything else stick against him. We were reaching though. He was as slippery as he was smug.

Everyone in this city knew about Arthur. He was feared amongst the criminal underworld. I proudly thought of how Jessica captured him and gave us what we needed.

I couldn't forget that scene with his own son though; his own boy, damned by the devil himself. I felt a lump in my throat as I thought about what he could be doing to my beautiful wife. Michael sensed it when he realised I stopped moving and had the photo of that scene in front of me. He didn't say anything, instead helped unpack more of the box.

I started to stick things up on the wall, now free of photographs, except the one of me with Arianna on our engagement day. It felt fitting to leave it up there with the crime scenes around us, a constant motivation for what I had to do.

The phone rang. My heart started racing. Michael urged me to get it out and I placed the phone on the table. I answered and put it on speakerphone.

His twisted, malicious voice was silenced, behind a laugh. I punched the table and I know he heard.

He mocked me. "Feeling helpless yet, Detective? Do you feel that sense of impending doom?"

I shouted back a wealth of obscenities, met by breathing.

"You are probably looking back at some of my photos. The ones I sent you? I'd be lying if I didn't say I felt some dark urges when I looked at your wife. I fully intended to hunt you down. I fully intended to inflict pain on you. Then, like a fine-looking angel, your wife walked out the door. I had to have her. Only, every time I got close; your rat colleagues were watching her. She was tough to get a hold of."

At least my paranoia wasn't too unreasonable at the time. My paranoia had ironically kept her safe from harm.

"Then, one day... she was gone and nowhere to be found. It angered me."

The line went dead.

"No, no, no, no, no," I screamed. "Fuck!"

Michael tried to talk me down as I punched the table some more. The phone started to ring again. I answered without hesitation.

"Just in the event you somehow managed to track me. Now, where were we?" Arthur cockily spouted with his serpent tongue.

"You were just telling me about how I'm going to fucking kill you if you hurt my wife."

"Ah, your wife. Yes... she was suddenly gone one day. The woman I had to have, gone. That angered me. She wasn't at work, wasn't at home, and your lackeys didn't lead me to her. But guess what? You finally did. Oh, the relief, the excitement. Patience paid off, Sebastian."

I closed my eyes and held my head in my hands. I brought this on her. She would have been safe without me. I inflicted this fate on Arianna. I felt an incredible amount of shame at the prospect.

"Why don't you tell me where you are, and we'll trade. Me for her."

"Don't you fucking dare try to treat me like an idiot!"

I started to calm him by saying I was an idiot. I was baiting him, and I had no idea where he was.

Assessing my silence, he piped up some more, "Sebastian, Sebastian. I will have my way with this beautiful specimen."

He was talking in a way as though he was looking at her. I felt relief. She was okay for now, hopefully unharmed, but in danger. I tried to take out the slightest positive given the circumstances.

"I envy you, detective. One of the seven sins and believe me, I'll do many more with her. I will desecrate your wife like I did that cunt Jessica."

His lips smacked as he spoke seductively about Arianna. I tried to respond but was immediately shot down with Arthur's retort. "Don't interrupt me! You want to play silly cat and mouse games with me? You can be a part of the game I play with your wife. You are going to hear every painful second of what I do to her."

174

My heart sank at the suggestion. The sick fuck. My desire to kill him grew, as flashes of the statue in the station entered my mind with the proud justice and equality plaque. The image of me walking through the station, echoes in the hallway as my brogues hit the floor were fleeting memories and felt distant now. The game I would play if I caught up to him would be simple: involving one bullet.

My thoughts were interrupted by his gravelly voice. "You are going to listen to me have my way with the love of your life, Sebastian. She's going to tell you how much she loves it too. If you don't listen, or if you hang up, I'll kill her. If she doesn't tell you she loved it, and I don't hear your pain, I'll kill her."

He laughed. He laughed harder than ever before and must have waved the phone in front of my wife as I heard her crying and whimpering.

"Do you hear that? That's the same sound Jessica made as I ran the knife up her son, our son."

"You sick fuck," Michael screamed.

"Oh, do we have an audience? How fortuitous that we get to share the moment with a crowd. It won't be our dirty little secret. AH!"

A sudden crack met with his recoiling in pain made me silently snigger at the escapade down the phone. That's my girl. She had some fighting spirit in her. I hoped she had snapped his neck, much less broken his nose but I took great pleasure in hearing his bones snap. As my stomach churned

175

at his threat of raping my wife as I listened, it jumped with joy knowing she'd gotten a hit on the bastard.

"You have a fiery one here. I think the bitch has broken my nose."

I heard Arianna's muffled scream. She'd obviously just been struck. Oddly, through it all, Arthur seemed to find the whole situation amusing. Further maniacal laughter ensued with some strange noises and boasting, he was obviously enjoying the moment of power he had over us both. He was a prize bastard.

"I'll let her calm down before the main event. Expect to hear from me soon, Detective Blackwood."

The line went dead. At least she was alive, and she had bought us some time. My heart was racing with fear. I felt sick knowing that he wanted me to listen to my wife get raped by him. He was a sadistic bastard, the lowest of the low. If I didn't find her, I could only hope he would let her live after it. I couldn't risk hanging up on him, as he'd do it to her anyway, and I'd only risk her life in the process.

I regretted every single second of the chase, every single second of the game, and every single second of my time protecting, serving, and upholding the law. I regretted life, because every second of it culminated into this horrific moment of helplessness where the most beautiful, caring woman was at risk. Why? It was all because of me.

I felt horrible. Michael didn't know what to say. He didn't say a word, clearly waiting for me to break the silence. I collapsed on the floor, unable to find anywhere else more appropriate.

"What do I do, Michael? What the fuck can I do?"

The room was silent. I felt a twisting in my stomach. I felt a pain I've never felt before. I continued to set up the display of images, crime scenes, and riddles. I started to write up the latest riddles in sickening silence.

Formed in an instant, lasting a lifetime; I draw you back to where it began.

A bare-faced lie; he carried something new, weightless unlike the guilt of the past.

Deities Apollo and Artemis protect us, he defiles us.

Chronos mistaken affiliation, despite devouring his own, puts reflection on who the victim may be.

Michael looked on confused. He didn't recognise it. I explained I had taken the bus key card from the Xander Hardiman scene and found the clue in the locker.

I added the second riddle, which I believed I had figured out before anyway.

Sebastian, Before you doth see, the Head of a Lamb,

Desecrated and carved is the Middle of a Pig,

With her Serpent Tongue, remains the Hind and Tail of a Dragon,

*Remember, and brand this bitch the animal that
she is? For she does the same.*

A weak, older woman branded a bitch and gutted with an 'X' in her stomach to reveal the UV light.

I started to log the types of flowers found at the scenes:

Carnations – an array of colours – Jane Doe

White, Pink, Purple, Yellow

Chrysanthemums – white – Xander Hardiman

I noted every shred of detail I could think of from any of the scenes and the possible relevance to Arthur's motive or where I could find him:

Satanic symbolism – Jessica/Sebastian

Belief in greater beings, devils, gods?

Bodies disembowelled

Ceremonial dagger – warehouse attack on me

Vines/Ivy on dagger – symbolism? Flowers?

'X' marks the spot

Removal of identifiable marks, teeth, and fingerprints – Jane Doe

Faceless man – Hardiman

Both victims, removal of identity, playing God?

Lamb head – the lamb of God?

Victims watching – Jessica/Sebastian McColm case – Power play

Victims listening – Me/Arianna – Power play

178

Feelings of grandeur – the 'right' to kill his own son.

Why take my wife? Why take Arianna? I'll save you.

I underlined those last three words numerous times. I then drew some of the notable symbols that had been littered over various crime scenes and what they could mean. Somehow, if I could piece together the motive, or the link behind the killings, could I get ahead of him? Could I figure out his next move?

Time passed quickly, and before long it was getting into the late hours of the evening. Michael had left hours before, promising he would be back shortly, he just wanted to see his daughter and kiss her goodnight.

I think the photos of the Sebastian crime scene were enough to make him miss her more. He didn't want to leave me, but it was important, so I didn't try to stop him. The fact he was there for me and had brought all the files meant a lot. If the Chief knew Arthur had taken my wife, he'd have likely removed me from the case, as it would have been too close to me. At least Michael understood; he had the balls to help. He did suggest I involve the force, but I swore him to silence. For now.

I scanned every shred, every clue again and again. I couldn't make it fit. My mind was wandering and in the wrong places. Feelings of hopelessness and dread filled my mind. I was waiting for the phone to ring every few minutes. Sharp pains ran up my arm, a knock-on effect of me emotionally reacting to the situation and punching the table and the walls. What was I doing?

I started to doodle on a piece of paper, with a slight tremble in my hand from punching the table. I had, in my rage, pictured Arthur's face and how much I wanted to, no, needed to beat the shit out of him. Then, I thought about her smile… I scratched her name into the paper with a pen before ejecting it across the room and filling the room with my screams. Tears were running down my face. I couldn't remember the last time I had cried. I always promised myself I'd never get this weak.

I had to snap out of it, I had to calm down or she'd never be saved. Then, out the corner of my eye, in the dark night sky, a silhouette. I was being watched. The tears stopped and my mind began to focus. I wasn't armed right now. I didn't have what I needed. Was it him? Taunting me?

I slowly started to turn my head towards the window, and then there was movement. The shadow was running. I fought myself out of the slump I was in, banging my legs against the table in the process. Fighting through the pain, grimacing at the sharpness jolting up my leg, I ran. Every second felt like slow motion as I ran to the door. The rage, the excitement, knowing I would catch him. You are mine, you fucking bastard.

I swung the door open and started to chase the shadow, not thinking about my safety whatsoever. He could have been armed. He could have been holding another knife. The shadow was quick; it already managed to separate itself from me. The sound of hurried footsteps banging in the night echoed down the street. Then suddenly, the storm that had been overshadowing the town for the last few weeks crashed an almighty crash.

The night sky lit up with lightning, raindrops pouring. The sound of thunder resonated in my soul as I pictured Arianna's face and my pace quickened. The lightning began to illuminate the shadow's figure. A black beanie hat and hooded top concealed him. Adrenaline pumping through my veins, I focussed on the slippery bastard with the tunnelled vision of a lion hunting a gazelle. It was the quickest I had ever run, and I wasn't about to let up.

The assailant turned to a nearby house and started to scale the fence. I was closing in on him, mere seconds away and he jumped quickly, hurriedly, appreciating he was close to being in my grasp. Without even thinking about the ramifications, fuelled with adrenaline, I didn't even steady my pace to leap the fence, I ran through it. The rotted wood crumbled as I steamrollered my way through it.

The assailant, unexpectantly recovering from the drop of the climb was inches in front of me. My pace didn't even waver and I ran into him as quickly as I ran down the street and forced him into a tackle. Without thinking, in a blackened haze, I started throwing my fists into the back of his head, to hear weakened screams. The assailant's hands rushed to protect his head and his body retreated into the foetal position as best it could with me on top. My fists, renewed with energy kept flailing at the shadow, rotted wood chippings from my altercation with the fence dropping off me.

"Stop, stop, please!"

My fists started to slow; it wasn't him. I spun him round to look in his face, and a frightened young man, probably no more than eighteen years old was looking back at me. I lifted his head up to mine, the heavens opening on us, rain hitting our slumped bodies.

"Who the fuck are you and why were you spying on me?"

He responded weakly, whimpering from the pain of the beating I had laid upon him.

"Speak!" I shouted, alarming the resident of the property whose fence I had just ruined. A porch light lit up and the resident wandered around to see what the commotion was. A curvaceous lady, scantily dressed in eveningwear and slip on shoes emerged from the light, brandishing an umbrella.

"Hey, get off my property you two! You!" She pointed at me. "Get off him!"

"I'm a police officer."

"I don't care who you are, you shouldn't be doing that to him," she chastised, recognising the position I was in and that I'd obviously inflicted harm on the teenager.

"Who are you?" I demanded from the boy.

Weakened by my flurry of punches, he replied he was no one and was just curious what the screams were from the property.

I shouted at him, calling him a liar, not believing the story.

He pleaded his innocence, advising he was genuinely curious what the commotion was.

I punched him again, not accepting his tall tale.

"You! What is your badge number?" The woman hurried towards me. "Are you even a police officer?" she questioned, worriedly.

I admired her willingness to challenge me, having broken her fence and beating on a young man in her presence.

The realisation of my actions suddenly dawned on me. I had just committed a felony. I'd committed assault, in front of a witness, committing property damage at the same time. I was losing my mind.

"My name is Sebastian Blackwood. Detective Sebastian Blackwood," I uttered in shame, recognising the weakness in my voice. "My wife was just kidnapped by the man I have been hunting, this young man was spying on me, looking in my window and I thought it was him. The man I was chasing."

The woman offered me her two cents on the matter, citing that it didn't make my actions permissible. I felt ashamed. I acted without thinking.

"So, that's why you were screaming?" the boy interjected with a hint of empathy. I could feel how terrified he was. I'd chased him down the street, rammed through a fence and started beating on him, largely unprovoked. I climbed off the boy and started to weep.

I stumbled to the woman's house, leaning up against the wall in the garden, rain snapping on my face. The boy I had been chasing acknowledged he genuinely had nothing to do with what I was crying about, threatened to report me, and ran off into the night through the new gap in the fence.

If not for how I felt, I'd have been quite proud about how I had bowled through the thing. Maybe I could tell Arianna one day. Gloriously show off how macho I was in my quest to save her. Or maybe I'd look back on how I'd lost control. My anxiety was starting to flare up. I felt my heart sting.

My head fell into my soaking wet hands, shaking from rage and fear, my whole body was left soaking in the elements. Nature truly was beautiful, and I was its joke tonight. I was useless. I'd beaten a young man, out of frustration. I had lost control of myself, my emotions. I never acted without thinking, yet this evening, my own beast was unleashed. Eyes closed and feeling the rain on the back of my neck as I held my head up, suddenly, I could hear the rain, but the drops weren't hitting me.

The woman who had chastised me had sheltered me, trying to console me in my desperation. She offered basic verbal nods to try and reassure me, but I wasn't hearing her. Then she lifted my head out of my hands and smiled. She had a smile like my mother. The stranger's smile eased me slightly, putting a stop to the panic attack building up inside of me.

She offered me a hand, and then pulled me up from my slumped position. She ushered me to her back door, before inviting me in from the rain. I followed, numbed by her sudden kindness. She flicked the switch on her kettle and hit me with a flurry of inane questions about whether I took milk or sugar, whether I would be replacing the fence, what my badge number was.

Truthfully, I've no idea what I responded with but the beverage she did produce hit the spot to my tastes and I might have offered to personally fix it. The kindness of the woman brought me down a little. There was good in the world, untouched by sadness, pain, or Arthur-fucking-Henderson.

We parted ways, and I started to head home. Flurries of apologies were thrown into the direction of the lady, whom I didn't even ask her name. The walk home with my body soaking, my clothes sticking to my body was long. I wished that the person I had caught was Arthur, just so I was a step closer to Arianna.

I arrived at my house with the door still wide open from when I had bolted out after the young man. Worryingly, as I got up to the door, I could see wet footprints on the wooden floor. It hadn't been raining when I dashed off, so I immediately knew someone had been in my house since I had given chase.

Thinking it could be Michael; I pulled out my phone and dialled his number. It rang a few times, but I didn't hear so much as a vibration or a ring in the house, so ended the call.

I walked patiently into the hallway, following the footsteps. They led back into the main room to my new base of operations. I picked up an umbrella, the best weapon I could find as I crept to the doorway. I emerged into the dining area, where nothing seemed to be disturbed. I cleared the room, making sure to check any of the corners.

As I made my way back to the hallway, the footsteps had been and gone, just from the main room. They hadn't led anywhere else, so I halted my search and returned back to the dining room and the whiteboard. Whoever was in here probably witnessed some of the images and thought twice about doing anything or taking anything. Who could it have been? Nothing had been touched, just observed. It could have been Michael I suppose, maybe he's checking in at the bar?

I sat at the dining table, thinking intently, but not connecting any dots. I was too tired and emotionally scarred to think clearly, so I dropped my head and slept.

The dreams I dreamt were the most disturbing I had experienced in a long time. The same crippling thoughts of losing Arianna cycled around my mind. I dreamt that Arthur violated her, and I was made to watch, not hear. I wanted to wake up but couldn't. The thought of him running his filthy hands over her made me feel sick. That such a disgusting man could have his way with her, against her will, and I was powerless to do anything.

I hated having anxiety; I hated that feeling of the world swallowing me. I hated it more when my body was so fatigued that I needed sleep and I was trapped in my dreams, forced to relive distant memories, or forced into made-up scenarios that had me powerless. I screamed silent screams at Arthur in the dream. Then, in typical dream fashion, it became twisted. Horns formed from his head like the devil he was, and as he danced around a bound and gagged Arianna, he laughed. His laughter filled the room and drowned out my screams.

The small shreds of hope in my heart started to contend with the defeat in my mind, as the dream took a turn for the better. A devil, in the form of Cyril came forward, the tut of his walking stick drowning out Arthur's laughter. The tutting got louder and louder, and suddenly an almighty crack over Arthur's head sent it flying from his body. The devil of my past bested the devil in the present.

My screams stayed silent as I watched a helpless, now naked, Arianna fighting to escape from Cyril. As I got closer, he and Arianna got bigger, and I faded into nothingness. The dream felt ever so real.

"Don't you dare come at me, boy! You are weak and pathetic! You would be nothing without your father! You are fucking useless," Cyril said.

Appreciating that I had morphed into my younger self in the dream, Arianna had turned into Alexia, the young girl I considered my sister. Like a time machine, my mind was flicking between people I knew and cared about. The helpless victim in front of Cyril was another person I had failed to protect.

"Don't worry about me, little brother, I'm safe," Alexia softly said before my dream changed her back into Arianna. I wasn't her younger brother, that's what Robert used to call me.

Arianna then laughed at me, bound and naked like before. Arthur's newly decapitated head laughed and whispered he was miles away and would never be caught by someone so worthless.

Suddenly, I started to fall. As I was falling, I could see lots of eyes on me like the night I walked into my room at the orphanage. I landed in a pool of blood like the hotel crime scene, where the Gardener stood up from the bed, covered in flowers. His slippery hands started exploring me; he whispered about how many children he had claimed in Fort Rose. Robert appeared and hit the Gardener like he hit Cyril when he beat Erin. "Run, little brother, don't let him touch you too," Robert screamed.

My stomach kept churning at the thought of what actually happened at Fort Rose. Why couldn't I wake up? The night terror continued with Mallory and Miss Battersby each taking me by the hand, my adult self. As they led me away, Miss Battersby crumbled to dust. My grandfather, who I hadn't thought about since that day he argued with my father demanded I look into the mirror and see the truth. I felt the heat of fire and flames surrounding me to the point I couldn't breathe.

I was gasping in the dream and Cyril's stick was tutting. His words became deafeningly loud. "I thought you would be one of the stronger ones, Sebastian. You've let me down. Make me proud. Make your FATHER proud."

The whole room had turned into a mirror, with invisible hands writing some of the code I taught the children back at the orphanage. As I was gasping for air, struggling to breathe, I focussed on the writing in the mirror. It read: *J3FF2M*. All of the writing changed to *J3FF2M*, then the mirrored walls shattered and revealed the spot where I asked Arianna to marry me.

Suddenly, I could breathe again, my mind entering a safe place. Arianna could be heard. Her laughter was distant but resonated in my soul. Arthur's voice followed with creeping doubt. "Detective, 'X' marks the spot."

The spot that I proposed to Arianna. Was that the spot? Was that 'X'?

My mother appeared and then started to stroke my head like she did when I was a child. She told me the answer was in front of me. She told me the code was the truth, then whispered every painful letter and number: *J, three, F, F, two, M.* She kept repeating it, and my wife echoing in the distance, saying she was fine, and the answer was there. What answer?

Suddenly, the bright sky darkened. Cyril's ice blue eyes acted like a frozen sun, looking at my mother and me and getting larger, until I was engulfed in blue flame. The eye got closer and closer. I looked back into the giant dream-weaved eye and my mother started to shake me violently, and through sheer panic started to shield my head.

"Wake up, son, please," she bellowed until she devolved into screams. Cyril's eye so large I couldn't see anything but the ice-like iris and the blackened, soulless void in the centre of his eye. My mother finally succeeded through her screams. "WAKE UP!"

I jolted awake, sweat pouring down my head. My mind was playing tricks on me. I couldn't escape them sometimes, my thoughts. I try to suppress them, I try to fight them, but they are there, and they don't leave. They stay loud, but unlike my screams, they don't stay silent.

The sounds inside my head sadly weren't as quiet as my surroundings. Peace. Reality. Tranquillity. For a split second, I seemed to forget it all. I exhaled deeply. I jerked my body around slightly and started to feel life. I tried to sit up, lifting my head from the wooden table. That dream felt eerily real. I'd had nightmares before and could usually force myself awake. My mind was taunting me with villains and angels from my past and this one felt real. I reflected on the dream, feeling that this one was different.

I grabbed my pen and went to the board, adding a new line to my shreds of clues:

J3FF2M

The code. What was it again? Every consonant had to be rolled back excluding vowels, and every number coincided with each of the vowels. J = H, 3 = I.

I started to write the answer on the white board. Why was my mother, my true mother, whispering this in my ear? Why was I seeing it in a mirror in my dream? F = D, 2 = E, M = N. J3FF2M = HIDDEN.

I'd never had that before. I sometimes documented my dreams as part of my therapy growing up but nothing quite so blatant and obvious had ever happened. There was always a meaning behind certain events, as my therapist would say. She'd provided me with a book of dreams once.

How intriguing that my mind would take me back to the code though? I didn't need a dictionary on dreams for this. What was hidden? My mind racked up numerous scenarios and possibilities, but I couldn't figure it out. I think I was still in shock from how real the dream felt, coupled with the fact an actual message had come out. The answer to finding Arthur is hidden in the clues? How?

My sub-consciousness was clearly joining some dots, but my conscious self was blinded by emotion. I was too tired and groggy to make any sense of it. Still wearing the rain-soaked clothes from the night before and sweat now dripping down my cold body from the night terror, I opted for a shower.

I loved the shower, as by contrast I had warm water hitting me, contrary to the previous evening.

What was I thinking, beating down that kid? Maybe that's why I dreamt of Father. If that kid had been Arthur, I'd have punched him, beaten him, and killed him like Father did Erin back in the orphanage. I felt awful. I'd accepted that I was losing control of myself by allowing myself to get caught up in pure emotion.

Whatever it was, I knew it wasn't going to help me find my wife. I needed a clear head, some element of tranquillity like those precious seconds after waking up. I genuinely felt like I was living in a nightmare. That's when a penny dropped. I had a book on dreams. I needed to get some books on gods, deities, flowers, and decipher the hidden messages within the items and the scripture left behind.

I gave myself a shake, as under normal circumstances, Detective Blackwood would have followed through with that. Only this time, I was Sebastian. A scorned, worried husband and like the dream, a frightened child. I felt out of my depth. I'd hunted beasts successfully, numerous times before; only none of them had ever turned the hunt back on me like Arthur. With reinvigorated pride, I shut the shower off and restarted my mission.

As I was drying off from the shower, I heard loud banging at the door. Thud, Thud, Thud.

"Calm down, I'll be just a minute!"

I figured it would be Michael but there was no need for the stupidly loud banging. I dried off and quickly threw some clothes on. As I fumbled into some socks, I shouted back at the door to say it was open. It didn't swing open, so it definitely wasn't Michael.

The door swung open and I was greeted with daylight. The faint sun blinded me at first as I'd been so used to overcast skies and the comfort of the night. No one was there. I walked onto the porch and looked both ways up and down the street. No movement; pedestrian or vehicle. I turned my back to the door and there it was. I hadn't seen it before because I'd been blinded by the sunlight. It also explained the incredibly inappropriate banging. A polaroid photograph of my wife, bloodied and bruised, practically naked, almost like the dream, had been nailed to the door. I ripped it off and on the back of it, read a note: *Missing you loads babe xxx.*

She never called me babe. We hated that kids and youth referred to themselves as babe or baby. In fact, we used to joke about it as we had some friends that used the term in an incredibly cringeworthy fashion given they were in their late forties. It was an obvious taunt. The kisses on the message, was that another 'x'? Or just Arthur's piss taking?

I ran back out to the road, looking for the remains of a trail. He had to be close, in fact, he was probably watching.

"I'll fucking find you!"

I collapsed on the pavement and as I fell to my knees, the sound of a car could be heard. Looking up, hoping it to be a getaway vehicle and a new clue, it wasn't; it was Michael. He apologised profusely for leaving me, and that his daughter was unwell. I didn't care. I'd rather he'd have stayed with his family, because if Arthur was watching, they were probably in as much danger as my wife.

A photograph was all I had of her, though the only shred of hope was that it obviously had to be quite new and it had been taken in the last twenty-four hours. I heard my phone ringing from the pavement outside the house and dashed back in the door. I answered, carefully doing my utmost not to roll off a load of expletives to my deserved captor.

"Blackwood." It was the Chief. Just as well I hadn't answered with what I was going to.

"Chief?"

"Care to explain how I've come in this morning to a complaint from a young man who said that a detective Blackwood beat seven shades out of him?"

"It's a long story, but I won't make it in today, I need a personal day."

"You don't just get to take a personal day, Blackwood. This isn't a Hollywood movie. Get your ass in the office, my desk. Fifteen minutes."

"I said, I am taking a personal day, Chief."

"Don't you dare backchat me, Blackwood. You either get in here and explain yourself and put this alleged assault to bed, or I'll come and drag you in myself. Which is it?"

"Chief, I've never asked for you to trust me before. But I am begging you to trust me, that shit last night was me hunting down Henderson. Collateral damage. I'm close. I'm inches away. I turn a few more rocks and that bastard will be mine. Please, just give me twenty-four hours."

I knew I was on borrowed time. The Chief wasn't going to bend, and I could hear it in his voice. The scales from that statue were clearly swaying in his head. Did he let me follow the lead I didn't have, or did he drag me in to the office? Either way, I was going to be looking for my wife.

The line went dead. I had my answer. A text from the Chief said he had no choice but to suspend me, pending investigation. The fact he hung up meant a lot. At least he had my back. Suddenly, and unexpectedly, the phone rang again with Arianna's number displayed.

"Yeah?"

194

"Did you like my gift, Detective?" The bastard was taunting me. I heard the background noise as though he was driving; clearly he'd been the one to stick that photo on my door.

"I hope she breaks your neck next time, not just your nose," I scoffed, proud of my wife's defiance.

"She does have some fire in her. I admire that. I also love that my encore to our game of cat and mouse is that I get two for the price of one."

"What do you mean, you son of a bitch?"

"Now, now, Sebastian. Beloved Sebastian, who is going to kill me. Ha! Can you believe that? She thinks you're going to save the day. You don't stand a chance of finding her, or me."

I didn't answer.

"And the real beauty is that when I kill your wife, because I will, Detective."

My heart sank; I really was beginning to give up hope. Knowing what this animal was like, I didn't see the point in taunting him and expediting the inevitable. He really would kill her, and he wouldn't think twice.

"The beauty is that when I kill your wife, I inadvertently kill you."

"Fuck you!" I retorted, anger building up inside me.

"It'll be the perfect crime. I kill someone without even touching him or her. I'll kill someone by breaking their spirit, their will, and their soul. I will be your end. Arthur

Henderson will have bested the decorated Sebastian Blackwood."

Silence. I was at a loss for words at this point. He had already broken my spirit and my will.

"Nothing to add? Oh well. Keep your phone handy, I'm going to call tonight and that little game we played last night? You'll get to hear me defile her one way or another."

In the space of a day, I had reconciled with my wife, and then lost her. Likely forever.

I had become suspended from duties because of a beating I gave a kid.

I had no real leads other than a lucid dream subconsciously pointing to hidden messages.

That bastard still had my wife.

I needed a lifeline because like my heart, the phone line went dead.

Chapter Eight

Every hair stood up on my body. I could feel a cold sweat running down my forehead. I was so used to anxiety attacks but this one was different.

"Sebastian!" a rough voice echoed down the hallway.

I was shaking. I looked at my hands trembling and placed one of them on my chest to feel my heart racing. Even it was afraid. Thumping like a jungle drum, resonating in my fingertips. I paced up and down the room until I found myself staring in the mirror. I studied my petrified face, then tightened up my tie as best I could.

"One, two, three, four." I tried counting to ten doing my mental preparedness ritual I'd adopted since I was a child. I heard my name being shouted again. The door handle was being man-handled by the figure on the other side, the outline of his feet shadowing at the bottom of the door, cracks of light breaking in. The figure protested at my stupidity, then chuckled at the thought of me locking myself away. Weddings. I had never been to one before, never mind taken centre stage with all eyes on me.

The people here wanted to be though. It was a happy moment, or so I thought. How could such a joyous moment be fraught with feelings of impending doom. My demons were sitting on my shoulder enjoying my internal destruction. I was beyond nervous. Then I thought of her, Arianna. How did I get so lucky? I had the most amazing woman in the world, and she agreed to marry me. I'd won the lottery of life.

"If you don't hurry up, she'll think you have cold feet," was what I heard as the door was expertly kicked open. It was my adoptive father, Henry Galleta. We'd become remarkably close as I was growing up and there was no better person to be my best man.

He spun me around, breaking my gaze with the mirror, and sorted my tie properly.

"Son, you look horrible. I wouldn't worry though, I think all good men experience this pre-wedding nervousness. Been there, done it myself," Henry stated, filling me with reassurance.

"How do I look?" I stammered.

"You look incredibly handsome, my boy. I am so bloody proud of you, you know that?" He hugged me and I felt a sense of calm wash over me. I was always comfortable around Henry. He was a rock in my formative years, helping erase the memories of the past.

He ushered me out of the room and the clicking of our shoes created a symphony down the hall. The inane chatter of the wedding guests buzzed in the air like a busy restaurant. I looked at the clock and we were minutes away from the rest of my life; between me and some large wooden doors.

I pulled at them to hear an almighty creaking sound, the echo of the rusted hinges breaking everyone into silence. I walked through the doors with Henry closely by my side and the guests turned their heads to see what the disturbance was. Eyes were fixated on me and I scanned the room. I felt like I was a child again, walking into my dormitory when I first went to the orphanage. The comparative thought caused me to inhale sharply.

"Stay alive, son, stay with me," Henry chirped in, sensing my discomfort. I looked down the pews at the guests and my adoptive mother, Isabella. She was beautifully turned out and had a tear in her eye as she watched her husband and son walking down the aisle. She smiled and blew me a kiss, which only served to make me smile back in return, weakly.

As I stood next to the priest with Henry, the guests fell silent, except for the occasional whispers anticipating the stereotypical wedding bells to chime with *Here Comes the Bride* filling the room.

Time felt so slow as I stood waiting; I felt as though I was the hangman being led to the gallows and waiting for the executioner to just get on with it already. I was still so nervous, but joyful. It was an awkward nervousness because it was all borne from a positive place. Realising how stupid I was being, and following a fatherly stare from Henry, I gave myself a shake and exhaled. At the end of the day, I was going to marry the woman I loved and nothing, not even the demons on my shoulders were going to get me down.

The first note from the song hit the room like a freight train. The melodies filled the air and emerging from the hallway and coming into view through the wooden doors, was Arianna. She was beyond beautiful. I was so awestruck by her that I felt a tear forming in the corner of my eye.

She wore a classy bridal gown, nothing too ornate, nothing too fancy; it was flawless. Her figure was complimented perfectly with the colour of the pure white dress gleaming in the room, radiating her angelic beauty. Whatever demons that followed me were surely scuttling away, incapable of laying their eyes upon her.

Every footstep she took towards centre stage made my heart thump, every note from the bridal song pulsing through my body as I stood awaiting her. My heart was beating out of my chest because the love I had for that woman was so pure and it was itching to come out. I honestly wanted to ignore everyone in the room, run up to her and just embrace her but obviously couldn't. This was her moment; it was her special day and every eye was rightfully on her.

Flattered beyond reason, her eyes didn't leave mine. I could feel the love in return.

My jaw dropped slightly, and my lips pursed as though I was trying to form some words. Obviously breath-taking beyond reason as nothing would come out. I mouthed the word beautiful to her, forcing her to smile. Our connection across the room of people and loved ones was infallible and unbroken. I smiled like a Cheshire cat, knowing that the feelings I was feeling were mutual. Our relationship was beyond words that a simple smile said it all.

Her father released her, and she stood opposite me in all of her glory, smiling from ear to ear. We wrote our own vows, to make them even more special. Any fears I had dissipated swiftly, as I was surrounded by the best people I had in my life and looking into the eyes of the woman I loved unconditionally. My big moment came when I read my vows.

"Arianna, I love you more than these words can ever express. You are my best friend, you are my rock, you are my everything. I've always been in awe of you. You are the most beautiful, intelligent, and generous person I've ever met. Your heart is so pure that you would give away everything you had if it would help someone else. I admire that more than you will ever know, because I know that you will share your life completely with me. The ultimate gift you could ever share, and I will be as true to that as I can be. Since the day I first set my eyes on you, you have made me smile. Your incredible kindness, unselfishness, and trust is cherished in the highest regard. I promise to remain true to you, to love you, and to protect you. There is nothing we cannot face if we stand together. I promise to be your partner in everything. Know that I also see my promises as privileges, as I get to laugh with you, cry with you, care with you, and hopefully build a family with you. I get to walk, run, and build the best life I can with you, as the luckiest man in the world. I said my words couldn't express how much you mean to me, so let my actions show it, for the rest of our lives, for as long as we both shall live."

Her tearful eyes welcomed the words I had written, perfected, and learnt off by heart. The truest words I had ever spoken. Arianna was very emotional and full of joy, only breaking the moment to speak her vows back to me.

"Sebastian, my ever-handsome man. The love of my life. I feel as though I have found my best friend, my mentor, my confidant, and my greatest challenge." The room laughed with us. "But no challenge is too great if we remain true. You are loved so much, more than I ever thought possible to love someone. You make me a better person and I am so lucky to be a part of your life, which from today becomes our life together. I promise to walk with you hand in hand, living, learning and loving. I promise to believe in you, the person you will grow to be, and the couple we will be together. Together, forever."

The room erupted into cheers as I was told to kiss the bride and our coupling was complete. It was a very passionate kiss in front of friends and family, but we didn't care, it amplified the power of our words and our promises. Promises so meaningful it had brought our respective families to tears.

We became one that day; until death do us part.

Chapter Nine

I hadn't seen Robert in about three weeks, and Alexia was nowhere to be found either. She hadn't been seen in about four days. Father wasn't an idiot; he knew exactly what had been going on as he kept looking at me with a wry smile whenever he was around the kids. The cut that Mallory gave me as a cover story was wearing thin and not really believed, perhaps the reason she was sporting a busted lip. The kids hadn't really talked at all over the last few days, not even in code, or on the blackboard; purely out of fear. I was truly starting to hate my life in Fort Rose.

We constantly lived in fear, walking on eggshells and afraid to make a small wave. I reflected on my journey out of the dormitory and tried to tap into that newfound strength. I got on with the other kids, but Robert and Alexia were the two people I was sincerely closest to. I'd sort of taken Erin under my wing since Father beat her to a pulp, though it's not as if she was prone to conversation having had the words beaten out of her.

Suddenly, the tapping of Father's walking stick could be heard. The kids were so silent the echo was so great. Kids around me started to retreat to their bedside, masking any shred of fun or joy that might have been going on in the room. For children, we were demoralised, defeated, and alone; we weren't children, we were empty husks masquerading as children.

The door swung open and I didn't even react in fear, I barely reacted at all, numbed by the same old futile existence. Father walked up and down the room, stopping at Erin who was cowering on the floor. This was when I realised just how much Father desired power and control over people. He towered over her, spouting nonsense about how he could have put an end to her snivelling.

"Where are they?" I shouted at him. "You can't keep taking people or hurting them. You're a monster."

Father turned around, infuriated by my act of defiance. He lowered himself to my height and we stared each other in the eyes. I head-butted him and he fell over, his walking stick crashing to the ground.

"Boy, you exist because I allow it. You'll die if I demand it," he snapped at me as he slapped me across the face. He licked his lips, excited with the pain he was inflicting. I protested weakly.

"Why are none of you grateful? None of you respect me."

He grabbed me by the neck and squeezed harder than normal, I was struggling to breathe. I felt the air leaving my body as I punched and scratched his face, trying to get him to release his grip. Other children looked on, fearful for my life but did nothing to help. I started to panic, feeling the air leave my body and life start to dissipate. I felt myself losing consciousness, thinking I was dying and the last I heard was Father telling me I was off to the cage.

I regained consciousness being dragged by my leg down the hallway, the sound of the tapping of the walking stick banging like a jungle drum against the floor. Father was pulling hard. I recognised the hallway, where the maintenance cupboard was. Father led me further than I had gone before, to an ornate door with a plaque above it. It read: *Chapel*. I thought this place was devoid of any sense of joy, or God-like omnipotence.

I was dragged through the door, hitting my head on the wooden doorframe jutting out. A few rows of benches, dusted and untouched for a while, lay there. Father threw me into the corner, groggy and dazed from the previous happenings, I just watched. He pushed a long oak table aside and revealed a hatch. He raised the hatch door and motioned for me to go down some stone stairs.

The hatch had obviously been built over the entryway to a basement. I stood atop the stairs and arched my head down to see a light in the distance. The stairs were dimly lit from a distant light and daylight creeping through the windows.

I started to walk down the stairs and Father followed. He closed the hatch behind him, and the dim lights were the only way forward now. He pushed me with his walking stick, if I defied him here; there was no going back, no witnesses. I genuinely felt fear.

The dim basement corridor weaved around a few corners until I found myself in an open-planned wine cellar. It wasn't stocked, aside from an old, rusted water tank. Was that the infamous cage? Where were my brother and sister? Father approached a giant bookcase with a solid panel back. He stood and played with it, revealing the shelves were hinged. A small opening concealed a hidden room. I was ushered through the opening in the fake wall, and that's when the truth unfolded. Rows of cages lined against the wall. Torture tools were pinned to the wall, almost like a shrine for inflicting pain.

My brother and sister were in cages, unresponsive. I didn't know if they were dead, or sleeping, or unconscious, or weak from whatever they'd gone through. Robert was leaning up against his cell, his hand reaching through the cage, holding Alexia's hand. It was hard to watch, but I loved that even what they had gone through, they were together, united.

As I was taking in the scene, and before I could open my mouth to call their names, Father cracked me over the head with his stick, sending me down to the floor. He watched me recoil in pain, but I didn't cry. I refused to cry because he wasn't worth my tears. I was standing strong.

"You think I am fucking stupid, boy? I know what you kids do, with your coded little messages. I wasn't born yesterday. I admire that you were quite ingenious, but I despise the fact that you all breathe my air, eat my food, and take my shelter. You will learn to be obedient down here. You will learn to fall in line and respect me."

He threw me into an adjacent cage, with my brother and sister still lifeless. I was immediately hit by the smell from buckets littered around the cages; our obvious latrines given the lack of noticeable plumbing.

"What have you done to them?"

"*Father.* What have I done to them, *Father*? Nothing, boy. Until they learn respect, they won't get what they need to survive. Same goes for you."

"Yes, Father," I responded, accepting the terms of the game. He paused for a second, then laughed and threw me a bottle of water. Smirking, he left, closing the fake door behind him. A dim light stayed on in the room. There were no windows, just an air conditioning unit, and a small vent in the wall. I clutched the bottle in my hands.

"Alexia. Robert."

There was the slightest stir from Alexia. She turned to face me, letting go of Robert's hand in the process. It was enough to make his survival instinct kick in and wake up. He was exhausted. He was beaten. He'd been bruised, he'd bled, and he was battle scarred. It wasn't right. We needed to get out.

"Seb," Alexia said, excited to see me. "I thought you were gone. I left to find you but couldn't."

She started sobbing out of sheer elation. She was genuinely so happy to see me. She was like my little soul mate, as I was as equally happy to see her.

"I'm sorry I didn't come back. I tried to find Mallory. I tried to get someone, anyone to save us."

My sister looked on quite proud of my attempted heroics. She smiled, and it was the most amazing thing I had seen in weeks. Recounting the story of how that night went made her laugh, something that made Robert stir.

"Is Robert okay? I haven't seen him in ages," I pleaded. "Is anyone else down here?"

"Not that I know of. He's not good, Seb. He barely speaks."

Robert weakly turned his head, I looked him in his eyes. Void of any sense of joy, or the sprightliness I was used to seeing from him. Despite our surroundings, we were a unit together, and seeing him this way was heart-breaking. He had bags under his eyes, the kind that you would never expect to see on a child. His lips were so dried and chapped. I opened the bottle of water and took a small sip before motioning to my sister to get it to Robert.

He could barely lift his arm, but weakly lifted the bottle to his mouth and sipped gently. Eventually, realising it was good for him; he started to gulp then coughed a little. What really surprised me was that he put the cap back on the bottle then started to drink from a puddle on the floor.

"Robert. That is disgusting," his sister blurted out. He stated that not a drop could be wasted where we were, before returning to the puddle and slurping it up.

I shuddered at the thought of what awaited us. This was the legendary cage we were always threatened with, only now it was the axiomatic truth behind the words. It was an actual cage where unruly children were kept. It never was an empty threat; it was a promise.

The concept of time was forgotten in there. Minutes felt like hours; hours felt like days. It didn't matter how much noise we made, because we were sure no one could hear us.

I tried to get an understanding of what happened down here.

"Does Father bring down food or water?" I asked innocently.

"Don't fucking call him that," Robert snapped. I'd never seen him so incensed and couldn't recall him ever using the 'f-word.' I was surprised that he swore at me. Robert's sheer annoyance at my comment upset Alexia and she retreated to the back wall of her cage. She curled up and hugged her legs, resting her head on her knees. Robert tiredly rolled his eyes.

"Why do you call him that, Seb? He hates us," Robert stated.

"That's why," I said as I pointed at the bottle of water.

"I might hate him too, but you know what? I'll play along. I'll play the game he wants us to play to make sure he doesn't hurt us. Think, Robert! Acting out all the time gets you nowhere."

Robert sat in silence, frustrated with himself by being led by his emotions. He nodded in agreement.

The one thing I knew about Father was that he needed to be validated, he needed that respect. Robert's acting up, or all of ours considering we all ended up here, was out of sheer frustration. Father lost control of us and put us away to think about it. To show his dominance to the remaining children, or staff given what I had read in Mallory's diary.

"You are clever, little brother." Robert laughed weakly, to the point he started to cough uncontrollably following the exertion.

"You really are clever, Seb. Amazing," Alexia said, infatuated with my mild, childlike intellect.

Robert looked up at her and smiled at her smiling towards me.

"We need to get out of here. I promise, I'll do what I can," I said to Alexia.

It made her so happy to know I was looking out for her and it made Robert calm somewhat, knowing he had some support. Seeing himself locked up, with his helpless sister, broken and unable to do anything probably angered him. He couldn't be the brother to his sister as he was caged, trapped, and before we had arrived, lonely.

"Robert?"

A weak nod followed.

"What have they done to you down here?"

Silence followed, so I chose not to press the issue. Faint footsteps could be heard on the other side of the fake door. We all reacted, looking towards the door, as it swung open. I was expecting to see Father but was greeted by the Gardener.

Like lambs to the slaughter, he paced up and down the cages, eyeing us up. He stopped at the middle cage, which my innocent sister was in. She had retreated back into a position where she was curled up, trying to protect herself.

"Now, now. Don't you want to see what daddy has for you, little one?" the Gardener asked, pressed up to the cage.

"Fuck you, you bastard." Robert spat at him. It infuriated him, knowing this predator was eyeing up his sister. What little energy he had; he was dwindling it away to bark at the monster on the other side of the cage.

He was laughed at and taunted.

"You know what happens when you disrespect me, boy?" The door to his cage had an almighty click as the cylinder of the locking mechanism was breached. The Gardener angrily reached out at Robert, who punched him in the face.

This caused him to fall back and drop the keys he had in his hand. Riled by the actions of a child, he hadn't noticed and instead retorted with his own fist. Robert was already too weak to fight back and fell down quickly. Dragged by his feet, that he was flailing in a bid to kick his way free, he was pulled out of the fake door, banging his head in the process. The Gardener grabbed a baton off the shelf as he passed it. The door slammed, leaving a frightened Alexia and me in the room.

I heard the faint words through the door from our captor. "I'll teach you not to mess with daddy, boy. I'm going to fuck you... up," he said with a sneer and an eerily long pause.

The noises dissipated as Robert was pulled away from the cage.

"Get the keys," I ordered Alexia. She didn't react, not knowing what was happening to her brother, terrified of what was going on.

"Alexia, please. Listen to me. I need the keys."

She came to life, somewhat, and reached over to the keys and handed them through the bars. I grabbed her by the hand to her surprise, looked her dead in the eye and promised that I would get us out. She nodded, tears in her eyes.

Something told me in that moment she knew what was going to happen to our brother, and what he had probably just saved her from. I fumbled with the keys and tried to unlock my own cage, eventually succeeding.

It's amazing what you learn when you've spent so much time in the dark. My eyes were attuning to the smallest details in the room, assessing what could and couldn't be used. I didn't unlock my sister's cage, but she begged me to.

"I can't, not yet. I need to figure out what we are going to do. If we blow it now, we'll never get out. Please, trust me. I'll keep you safe. I promise."

It was a promise I was determined to keep but was probably not in the best position to offer. A small bag of sawdust was in the corner, so I quickly grabbed it, moving it into my cell to consider as a makeshift pillow. I moved to the shelves, laden with tools, some sharp, some blunt. Dried blood was on the end of some of them. I dreaded to think how they had been used. I took a star screwdriver and put it in my pocket. I looked at the fake door and realised I was going to have to see what was on the other side, properly.

I turned to the door and as I was pressed against it, revealing the smallest light on the other side.

"Please don't go. Please don't leave me alone here," Alexia pleaded.

"I promise I'll be back. Trust me."

She nodded, through tears and it was the last thing I saw as I closed the fake door, leaving it only slightly ajar. My focus shifted around the room, and I struggled to find anything of use. Empty barrels were in the room, which I figured might make for a good makeshift ladder to reach the vent but decided to leave them in place.

I could hear distant slapping sounds, coming from a small hallway that I hadn't recognised. It wasn't the way I was brought in. I tiptoed into the shrouded corner of the room to see where it led. I heard my brother whimpering at the beating he was receiving. I took the screwdriver out of my pocket, wielding it in an upright fashion, knowing I may be forced to use it.

I crept closer and snapped my view to some useful items: a container of oil, old pieces of wood, and general maintenance items. This basement must have been a storage area. I scanned the area until the sound of my brother refocussed me. I kept moving towards the sound, pressing firmly against the wall in the process.

I peeked around the corner to another opening, much like the area with the barrels; only this one had a bed, and an old fashioned, massive camera. It was like a film set, with lights, cameras, and a white sheet.

Youthful naivety couldn't comprehend exactly what it was used for at first, but I could sense that it wasn't for anything innocent. I looked closer at the bed to see a number of straps on each of the corners, evidently used to restrain whoever had the misfortune to lying on it. With hindsight, I often think back to reading Mallory's diary and her unfortunate experience; presuming this was the place it happened.

I slowly edged forward. The noises were coming from behind a small area of the room, shielded by a curtain. I hid behind the large camera and peeked forward, to see the Gardener, who by this point having thought about Mallory's diary, figured was the infamous Jack. He had a name, though beasts didn't deserve one and I certainly wasn't about to use it, as that would suggest I had a modicum of respect for the fact he was an adult and I was a child. He was beating Robert across his bare back, his shirt ripped off; blood was seeping from the newly formed cuts.

The Gardener opened his mouth, undoing his belt. "Remember what happened last time? You are my property. You are all mine." His trousers had fallen to his ankles and he was working his slimy hands down Robert's back. I knew I had to act quickly. I knew I had to stop what was about to happen.

Robert was struggling to keep himself upright, struggling to form any sort of protest in response. I had my screwdriver but didn't want to risk blowing any attempt at escape, or either of our lives, as that would leave Alexia alone. I picked up a small piece of metal, a solid rebar that was at my feet; not knowing if it was a part of the set, or a weapon used to beat someone else.

Without a second thought, I backed up slowly so I could make my retreat, and then launched the piece of metal into the corner of the room, opposite Robert. It bashed off the wall and landed beside some tattered old boxes. The noise of the clattering was alarming in the echoey room.

"Who the fuck is there? Cyril?" the beast demanded. I could hear him fumbling with his trousers, as though he had a shred of guilt and didn't want to be found by anyone else. I ran away, tiptoeing back to the cells for fear of being caught. Armed with a screwdriver, I moved like a ninja, soft-footed and carefully back to the room.

As I opened the fake door that I'd left slightly ajar, I put my finger to my mouth and tried to hush my sister, who was quizzing what had happened and where I had been. I closed my cell door, not snapping the lock back into place, hoping I wouldn't be caught out.

Hearing footsteps in the distance, I knew it was him. I knew he was investigating the noise in the event it was one of us. How on earth he could have thought it was us, I don't know but before he could get close, I tossed his keys to the other side of the room, out of reach.

The door flew open, and Robert was with him. He dragged him into the room and ushered him back to his cell. I felt a minor victory knowing I had prevented any further assault. The Gardener noticed the keys on the floor. He fumbled and felt both of his pockets, realising they were his. He muttered to himself about how they ended up there and then put them back in his pocket. He scanned the room, looking to see if there was anything amiss.

My heart was racing, hoping he wouldn't see that my lock was undone. He looked at the cells and to his pocket, like a tennis match going on between them. He snapped the lock back in place on Robert's cell and Robert foolishly retorted, "Is that all you got?"

I admired Robert's bravery considering what he had just been through, but it clearly only served to anger our twisted host. He sneered and left the room, sexually unfulfilled and incredibly pissed off. The fake door slammed and all I heard was Robert's whimpering. He was in pain and there was nothing I could do right now.

We sat in silence, taking in the happenings. Unaware of the time, or what was going on; I lay there thinking, constantly. The only thing going through my head was what the hell we could do. I was thinking, feeling the call of the void, and playing out numerous scenarios that could end in one of us being seriously hurt, or worse.

I must have fallen asleep as I jerked awake, my brother and sister also hadn't moved. I truly wasn't sure how long I had been out, but I knew that doing nothing was the wrong thing to do. I got up, opened my cell to my brother's surprise, and made my way out of the room. I left the door open and worked one of the barrels into the room, setting it discreetly in the corner of our celled room. I was going to use it to get up into the ventilation shaft later.

My sister was watching me intently and had worked her way up from her protective stance. She stood at the cells with a huge smile of admiration on her face. I looked back at her proud and said two words to her. "I promised."

She smiled, saying she was lucky to have me as a brother. That they both were. Robert was so pained by his latest beating he was in and out of consciousness. I pulled at a small piece of the barrel and got some of the wood together and peeled it into small stands, getting a splinter in the process. I sucked in air through my teeth at the same moment the wood slid into my skin. I pulled at it and thankfully, managed to get it out so as to not live with the discomfort, not that it would have made my current residence much worse. I gathered some of the wood strips and stuffed them into the keyhole of my cell. It was the only way I could safely ensure my cell would remain unlocked.

"You really are clever, brother," Alexia said to me, practically infatuated with me. Truth be told, I didn't really know what brought it all on. I like to think that it was my intellect, perhaps combined with the sheer will to survive. My entire time in this God forsaken place was a trial, a test of endurance and stamina. As I was assessing the vent above the barrel, the thoughts of how long I had been here made me snap into the memory of my arrival.

It suddenly dawned on me that there was a boy when I arrived at Fort Rose. He was nowhere to be found after going to the proverbial cage. He wasn't here. Where the hell was he? Something in me switched right then. It was obvious we weren't safe and that we were in danger, hell, I watched my brother get a beating earlier. The risk of being beaten and hurt I understood, but death? Was that other boy killed? Did someone take him away? His personal effects weren't taken from the dormitory when I thought about it. I had forgotten his name and given that I had barely seen him in the fleeting seconds of that night; he was faceless in my mind's eye. What happened to this poor kid?

"Robert?" I quizzed, knowing my brother was not really in a fit state of repair and probably not eager to chat.

"Yeah?" he responded through sheer willpower.

"Was anyone else down here when you got here?"

"Just George." Robert started weeping. He was inconsolable. He was so dehydrated that his tears were struggling to leave his body. I thought better against asking where George was, or what had happened to spark that reaction.

"That bastard," he said, as I smiled to myself thinking what one, as we were amongst many.

"The bastard that did this to me, killed him. I couldn't do anything to help." His tears getting beyond comfort. They echoed in our new bedroom, destitute of any sense of security. Part of me was expecting it. Part of me wasn't even shocked, but I still stood there in disbelief.

I wanted the ground to swallow me whole knowing that one of the kids had actually been killed. It motivated me to do something to help us all, to help us get out. I was praying that Mallory's letter had reached the right person.

"You couldn't have known what would happen, Robert," Alexia said softly.

It didn't console him. I felt helpless. He was right in front of me and I couldn't get to him. I felt a wave of empathy wash over me, the kind I have never experienced before. My brother was broken, mentally and physically. It brought Alexia to tears as well. All I could do was to stay strong for him, my sister, and figure a way out.

I left the room, determined and driven to make a change, to get to my brother. I searched the maintenance shelves and didn't find anything then it hit me. Of course! The piece of metal I threw. I snuck down the hallway and was met with a comforting silence, knowing that no one else was there. I walked around the corner and froze in place. There he was.

The Gardener was resting on the bed, with a television and a Betamax player at the foot of it on a small stand. He was sleeping, with his trousers at his ankles, exposing his penis. Playing on the television was a video of Erin, unconscious and battered, as the beast resting in front of me took away her innocence. This was recent.

I snuck up behind him, armed with a screwdriver and fought the urge not to hurt him back. I raised my hand in the air, with the blade of the screwdriver glistening against the light from the television. The sounds and grunting of pleasure emanating from the video awoke a demon inside me, as I knew I could enact swift vengeance on the son of a

219

bitch in front of me. Erin... I wish I could have been where I was now, before you got hurt. I could have stopped him. I could have saved you.

That very thought of saving Erin was enough to make me lower my hand. Doing what I was thinking of doing now wouldn't help anybody. I'd be endangering myself, and my other brothers and sisters. I looked down at the sexually exhausted cretin in front of me, knowing I had the power of his life in my hands and I had chosen to spare him. Truth be told, I knew then and there that that decision, that moment, would forever define me. My life reached a crossroads and I had taken a path, completely different to the possible alternative.

I continued to sneak into the corner, looking for the metal rebar that I had tossed earlier. I had to sneak in front of Jack, the Gardener, in order to get to it. Dammit! It was now or never. All of the courage I could muster, I counted silently. *Two, three, four.* I crept quietly to the rebar, looked over my shoulder and could see that bastard snoozing softly. I kept edging forward and was jolted upright, startled by a loud snore of sorts. Staying true to my mission, knowing I was right under his watchful gaze if he opened his eyes, I crept up like a ninja and grabbed the rebar. It scraped quietly across the ground, which sent shivers down my own spine. I quickly hid behind the tatty boxes piled up, carefully concealing myself from the bastard on the bed.

That scrape had obviously altered him as he was beginning to stir. Sheer panic washed through my body. I was struggling to breathe at the thought of being caught.

One of the scenarios I had conjured in my brain moments before as I was stuffing my lock with wooden chips felt as though it was becoming real. What would happen to me if I was caught? Would I get a beating like Robert? Or worse, would he do to me what he alluded to doing with Robert? Or worse yet, what I had seen him do to Erin on that video. That was the one moment in my short life that I had felt completely and utterly powerless. I was a wounded gazelle in the den of a lion, hiding and praying he couldn't sense my fear.

"Cyril?" I heard amidst the sound of his grunting on the video. The sound of skin on skin echoing through the room from the video was sickening. Thankfully, from my current position, I couldn't see the screen, just the back of the television.

"You are a fucking animal, Jack," I heard. Oh my God... Father was here. Now I was really in trouble. He probably knew I was out of my cell. I'd left the door ajar again. Dammit! If he knew I was out of my cell, they'd probably punish the others to find me.

"I learnt from the best," I heard him say back.

"You didn't learn this from me, you sick fuck. I don't do... this... to the children," I heard Father retort in a disgusted voice.

Part of me was mildly grateful, as Father might consider me quite resourceful and take pity on me if I was found. The room became silent as the background noise and grunting stopped.

I heard the television get powered down, alongside the Betamax player. I heard, through gritted teeth. "But you're happy to make the fucking money from these videos. Hypocritical cunt."

Then it dawned on me and I edged my head out to scan the room, Father wasn't there. It was him on the end of the video. So, these sorts of videos were one of Father's cash streams... disgusting.

Suddenly, I felt slightly more at ease that there was only one devil in the room, not two. It didn't change the fact I was still in danger. At least I knew my brother and sister were okay for now, that no one knew I was out of my cell. It was getting back without being found. The dimly lit room was enough to make me think it was possible to make it out somehow. It was the most terrifying, exhilarating feeling I'd ever felt. I was about to dance with a devil in his own version of hell.

I gazed around the room, trying to plan my route back. The white cover behind the bed seemed like one possible route. The safer of the many routes from the boxes to the hallway back to my cell. The irony of a prisoner wanting to get back to their cell wasn't lost on me, even at that age.

It hadn't dawned on me that I was actually in the presence of a killer. Robert said that the man in the same room as me killed George. I almost tricked myself into another anxiety attack just thinking about it. My heart thumping, I figured I had three choices. The sneaky route behind the white backdrop was where I was most likely to elude the Gardener. The bolshy, direct route sneaking

222

around the various camera equipment, largely exposed to a watchful gaze with one wrong step leading to me being another victim, or the suicidal approach of running right at him, sticking the screwdriver in his neck and rushing back to my cell; a fitting end for a child killer.

I sniggered at the fact the devil on my own shoulder was trying to force direct combat and murder as an option, before electing for the safer approach behind the backdrop. There were greater forces at work, and I had to get back in one piece. I could fantasise about the other options when I was back in the slightly safer territory.

I counted in my head again, willing myself to make my first move. I heard my captor readjusting his belt, so I peeked out the corner, conscious that he would be looking at the ground. This was it; I snuck up and moved slowly behind the white backdrop. I felt alive. I felt as though I was a secret agent, on a mission to save the sorry souls that had also found their way to this hell hole.

He was moving around, clearly readjusted. I could hear his footsteps edging towards me from my right-hand side, from the location of the boxes that I had just been hiding behind. His back turned to me; he fumbled with the top of the box, moving the flaps. I heard the clash of plastic cases, assuming it was him returning the video to his warped collection. A heart attack right now would be a just end for such a person. I crept out from behind the backdrop and as lightly footed as I entered the room, I glided back out into the hallway. It felt as though my heart was beating louder than anything else I was doing. As terrified and alive as I felt sneaking back to my cell, I felt nauseous from the adrenaline pumping through me. The swift, fleeting dance across the room where I was undetected worked wonders for my self-esteem. I felt invincible.

Rebar in one hand, screwdriver in the other, I combined the two items into one hand, then pulled the fake door closed. My brother and sister were silent, almost in awe with me and I felt incredible as a result. I hurried back into my cell, using the screwdriver to pierce the bag of sawdust that I'd put in there as my pillow. I stuffed the rebar and the screwdriver in the bag, concealing them in the interim.

I turned back to my cell door, closing it behind me, and uttered silencing words for my cellmates. "I'll explain later. Trust me. He's close."

They did. The room was met with silence. I was reluctant to make a move for now, taking in the recent events that left my heart pounding. Minutes once again felt like hours, my heart still racing. I couldn't tell what was causing it. Fear, excitement, being so close to danger but coming out unscathed? I felt on top of the world.

I felt sorry for Robert mainly. He was moaning out of pain the entire time we lay there, helpless and waiting. Alexia was snoring lightly. Then the distant sound from the thudding of a walking stick could be heard. There was only one person that could be, and I stood up, patiently waiting for him. My only real concern was that I wanted to conceal the tampered lock. I hung my arms out the door, letting them hang loosely over the lock.

The door opened and Father stood there, gazing at us. He looked at a weakened Robert, a frightened Alexia, and a confident me.

"Sebastian, my boy, how good to see you." He laughed.

I smiled at him. He turned back to the door, dragging in a trolley with food and drinks. I was surprised he was going to feed and water us. However, that was not his intention. It was to taunt us.

"This is what you get when you start to show me some respect."

He set the trolley just beyond my reach and let it sit there.

"Anyway, it's late. Sleep well, kids. I'll see you in the morning."

He left, but I had two advantages. I knew it was late, and I had a few helpful implements that could help me get us the spoils of war. I could reach out with the rebar and... just open my cell door to get at them. I went for the trolley and my sister giggled.

There was plenty of water on the table, so I told Robert to position himself at the edge of his cell, ripped my shirt off and started to wash his cuts. He grimaced and gritted his teeth.

"Thank you, little brother," he said, mildly rejuvenated from the care he was receiving. I think most of it was mental, as I wasn't doing anything to treat the cuts, merely washing them out.

225

I passed a bottle of water through to him, as well as some of the food from the trolley. Before I passed some to my sister, I dropped some of it on the floor.

"What are you doing?" my sister chastised through the bars.

"I'm making it seem as though we struggled to get to the food. Like I've had to use my shirt as a lasso to grab it, with mildly unfortunate results."

"This is why I love you," Alexia exclaimed, to the surprise of both of us.

I was quite taken aback with the compliment I received and proceeded to pass through more bottles of water and food to my sister. It was an interesting concept: that she loved me. Being united in our miseries did bring us close, but it made me feel great. It made me more motivated than ever to help get us out.

I partook in some of the spoils before climbing up, bare chested to the vent, using the barrel as a stepping-stone. It was large enough to fit in and was screwed down. Thankfully, like the fates were aligning, I had the tools to do the job. I removed the vent cover and hoisted myself up. I shimmied through the vent, promising to come back for them shortly.

The vent was quite spacious, considering. I was tempted to scream down it to hear the echo and see how far it travelled. It wasn't worth the inevitable punishment, I just wanted to do something childlike; something to actually make me feel my age, for once. I shimmied further down the vent and started to hear voices. I edged closer to a small outlet that was, largely, for decorative purposes and too small for me to get out on the other side. I couldn't believe what I was hearing.

A rather assertive man was quizzing Father and he wasn't about to back down. The sounds were getting louder, as though they were walking and talking down the hallway.

"I'm sure you aren't used to these sorts of checks, however, let's call it procedure. A number of children are under your care and I'm here to check what's going on," the man said to Father.

"Absolutely. You'll find that they are all well cared for. Fed, watered, clothed, and most of all, loved." His final word hanging as though forced. I felt sick, knowing what I now knew about the cage.

"I won't beat around the bush; I know who you are, Mr Willoughby. I've heard the stories," the mysterious stranger retorted.

"Is that so? And what do you think? Do you think they are stories?" Father boasted.

"Irrespective of what they are, I'm not about to be intimidated by some lawless runt. In fact, I welcome it. I've been incredibly careful about my arrival here, multiple sources know where I am should something happen to me. I'm well connected too, Cyril. Do you mind me calling you that? I figure it's a mark of disrespect for the man that I'm calling out after all. I'll call you by your first name because from what the stories tell me, we are far from pleasantries.

Anything happens to me, and whatever you have going on will come down like a house of cards," the man gallantly spoke.

Father grunted and blasted some obscenities at the stranger. Mr Cyril Willoughby was his full name. I couldn't hear much more, as they were walking away and talking, and it was everything in me not to shout for help then and there. Something made me freeze, not knowing if it was another trick or game being played, something in me stopped the words coming out of my mouth. I felt trapped, scared, and almost afraid of redemption because I'd become a glutton for punishment.

I kicked and flailed in the tight space, angered with myself for my own inaction. It could have ended with one simple word: Help. I pressed on, as the only way was forward now. Perhaps Mallory's letter reached the right person after all? Someone was prepared to step up to the challenge of battling with Father. Someone was ready to play chess with the man and we were the pieces. A faint glimmer of hope, as I crammed myself further into the space of the ventilation shaft. Sadly, it was the one place I suddenly felt safe. The vent was mildly comforting as they were big enough for children, maybe not adults.

I came to the end of the vent, which brought me out into the reception area. At least it was an area I was familiar with, as we walked past it every time we were marched to the canteen area for breakfast, lunch, and dinner. Only this time, I was behind the counter. I didn't leave the vent. I

228

racked my brain, trying to think about what my next move was.

I felt as though I was left with an entirely blank canvas and holding the paintbrush. Empowered, motivated, and determined, I ventured out of the vent. I had to make it to the nurse's station, get word to Mallory that we were all okay. The only way I knew how to get there was through the vent and the maintenance room.

I made my way through the orphanage, creeping silently, avoiding any staff members in the process. It was fairly quiet, with few people wandering about. There were a few security guards, but no sign or sound of the mysterious stranger or Father. I opened the door to the maintenance cupboard, carefully leaving it unlocked. I scanned the room for any items of value, or use. I opened the locker I found the chocolate bar in, what felt like eons ago, and fortuitously stumbled across a fountain pen, and a zippo lighter. I placed them in the same pocket. Not really knowing what the zippo was, I figured I would take it, in an act of defiance. I took the same person's chocolate, why not their possessions to mess with them. I giggled a little, appreciating I was getting some element of childlike excitement out of the endeavour. I shimmied through the vent and eventually found my watch and Mallory's diary.

I opened the watch and admired my beautiful mother. I wondered what they would have thought, knowing that their son was living in a very real hell on earth. Looking at her smile reminded me of Alexia and that she said she loved me. I shed a tear in the vent, realising just how surreal the entire escapade was. I was sneaking around the orphanage, through the vent, afraid of who or what might find me and do to me if I was caught.

I was living by the edge of my seat, and strangely excited by it. Knowing I was contending with devils, beasts, and bastards. I was doing what I was doing for the right reasons. Motivated by justice, motivated by the good in the place. I was spurred on for my brothers and sisters, Mallory, the people who were all hurting and here by a sick twist of fate.

I opened Mallory's diary, and tore a page off. I wrote a small note to her:

Mallory, I don't know what to do. I'm trying to look after Robert and Alexia, but we are in a cage in the basement under the Chapel. Robert is really hurt. We need help. Please find us. I'll protect them until you get here. Sebastian.

Short and to the point. It was the best I could do. I left the vent to place the piece of paper on the gurney I slept on the night I escaped the dormitory. I thought about writing in the diary, but figured that if I did, then left it out, and the wrong person read it, that would only serve to put her in danger, or worse, result in the reader stumbling across the rest of the pages, or my watch.

I crept back through the shaft, evading staff along the way, retreating back to my cage to let my brother and sister know what was going on. I wasn't spotted or caught along the way, which was useful, but I had hoped I was. I had hoped the mysterious stranger would be the one to find me.

As my face emerged into the cage room, my sister squealed in excitement.

"Quiet, Alexia, you'll make him come back," Robert blasted.

She apologised, and I worked my way down from the vent, making sure to restore it to a visibly untampered state, moving the barrel to the other side of the room so as to make it obvious to the untrained eye there was nothing suspicious going on.

"I left Mallory a note to say where we are. Hopefully she'll get it in the morning."

"A note doesn't help us, brother," Robert stated, still wounded but running on adrenaline.

"It's the best I can do without putting us in danger. If they knew I was out of my cell, we'd be in bigger trouble, wouldn't we?"

My brother's silence felt like an agreement of sorts. I stuffed everything in the bag of sawdust: the rebar, the pen, and the lighter. I closed my cell door behind me. I had messed with the trolley enough to make it seem believable if I threw my shirt at it to pull food off it. Everything was set up perfectly for the next morning.

Despite the recent goings on, that evening was actually quite beautiful in its own way. Robert, despite being in pain, was in reasonable spirits. The rush of energy as we'd gotten away with a literal prison break was magical. We talked like children that night.

231

I broke the façade of happiness by asking Robert what happened to George. I knew it was tough for him to talk about it. He recounted every sad second of the story of George, a boy who had clearly been down here for a long time.

"He didn't look real. He was so thin I could see his bones. After that night, I punched our beloved father." His voice getting sarcastic. My sister and I listened intently, drawn in to the story.

"He dragged me down here by the hair, giving me the occasional punch. I fought back but not as well as I'd have hoped. He took me through to... THAT... room! I was dazed and couldn't really see what was going on. I must have passed out, as I woke up to the lights being on, blinding me. I remember trying to move, and being stuck to the bed, my arms and legs were strapped down. I begged him to let me go. The lights were turned up slightly which blinded me more, and I couldn't see who was there. We weren't alone; I could feel loads of eyes on me. Soon enough, sounds were happening in the background and they said this was a video that would make them quite a bit of money. Before long, George was brought in. He was made to sit on the bed with me and was laughed at. They joked about how they were surprised he was still alive. He looked weak, he looked dead. I only really recognised him because they said his name, and his eyes. I'll never forget his eyes. Then one of them told him to, touch me–"

Robert broke down in tears. He couldn't finish what he was trying to talk about, fighting sheer pain. I'd heard enough and felt a tremendous pang of guilt at asking. His sister tried to reach him through the bars to console him and when her fingers brushed against him, he recoiled in horror and shock. He kicked and flailed to the other side of the cell, clearly hurt by that night.

"After it was all over. We must have been there for hours. Loads of different people were gathered around, sitting in some chairs, watching. Father," Robert spat. "That bastard stopped 'the show' and told the men to dig deep if they wanted more. They opened their wallets, they wrote cheques, and promised to pay thousands more if 'the show' continued. I was in pain from the beating I had. They laughed as I screamed and asked for help. They told me to scream louder and threatened me if I didn't. I tried. I screamed until I lost my voice. What happened that night... I wouldn't wish it on any of you."

Tears streamed down his face and Alexia beckoned him to her, crying herself. I felt helpless and just watched the scene between biological brother and sister as she comforted him, stroking his head through the cell like my mother used to do to me.

I closed my eyes. I tried to picture my own mother comforting me. So desperate for that moment of bliss, I felt as though I transformed the dire circumstances around me and put myself in my old home. Brighter, happier, and devoid of pain. I could have sworn I felt my mother's hand against me in that moment, only broken by the sound of Robert talking again.

"We were brought back in here, me and George. He said he was sorry, then started to cry, saying he wanted to die. He said he had given up. So anyway, the next day, that bastard Gardener came down to empty the buckets, saying it was the best kind of compost, fresh and young. When he came back with them, he made George touch him, with his mouth. George bit down hard, making him scream. That's when it happened. He hit George so hard I heard a crunch. His body was so weak that one hard, desperate hit broke his skull. He took one of those bats on the shelf and hit him again and again..."

Robert was inconsolable by this point. The smell from the buckets, and the story was actually enough to make me vomit. I hadn't heard anything so terrifying before.

"He beat him so much I could see inside his head. I was made to clean it up. I was let out of my cell to mop up after him. He watched me scrub the floor, back and forth, blood and water meshed up. He laughed at me, Sebastian. He laughed and said that George would make an even better compost and the flowers would come in full bloom with him. I think he's buried in the garden."

I'd heard enough. I had to get us out. I wasn't about to stay put, not act and become the next child buried in the garden. I took the rebar from the bag of sawdust and left my cell. I took it and wedged it between the lock of Robert's cell and pulled and pulled. That's when I was interrupted. I heard the distant sound of Father's walking stick.

"Sebastian, hurry," Alexia exclaimed.

234

I hurried back to my cell, closed the doo..
rebar in the bag again. In record speed too, as
myself, the door swung open and Father's smug laugh ..
the room. The room was freezing but I shivered more at the
laughter from Father. I prayed Mallory would read my letter.
It was getting unbearable, to live on the edge waiting for an
untimely end.

"My, my, Sebastian. You really are a resourceful boy,
aren't you! I knew you were something special," Father
complimented, taking in the sight of our feast.

Knowing what he was, I didn't take too kindly to his
appreciation, but I figured I wouldn't taunt him any further.
He motioned to my brother and asked him if he had learnt
his lesson. Defeated and in pain, he agreed and apologised
to him, referring to him as Father. He was ushered away and
removed from his cell, much to our silent protesting. It
wasn't worth drawing any further attention to us.

We probably spent a few days down there without
Robert and I grew closer to Alexia. We survived on the
remaining food and water we'd looted from the trolley
Father had brought in. We learnt more about each other;
about our hopes and our dreams.

I was rather touched, because Alexia talked about
wanting to get out one day and have her own family. She
thought about having her own kids and making sure they
never went through the same pain we did. She even said she
would marry me because I wasn't her real brother. It made
me feel good to know I was wanted and cared for like she

cared for me. We were close before, but nothing like we were now.

In the darkest of places, we had found a ray of sunshine in our friendship. She was amazing. We hadn't really been able to speak so freely before; upstairs, you could get in trouble for talking too much. She was incredibly empathetic, and I found we had that in common. She said she felt it when Erin was beaten up, when anyone else was for that matter. I knew exactly what she meant. It was tough to find the words, but I knew.

We tried to figure out our next move, hoping the note I wrote to Mallory was found and something working in the background. We managed to build a story of hope in the dark. We made a pact that whatever happened, we would go on to live. That we would remember what we went through and live happily, and with pride, doing the right thing to make sure places like this would never stand a chance of running. She was the yin to my yang. Together, we were one.

Robert was brought back into the cell later that day, which almost shattered the dynamic of what I had going with Alexia, though I was glad to see he was okay. He'd alluded to being treated somewhat better, bandaged, and fed by Mallory. In my head, I knew it wasn't my place to say, but I felt it would make them feel a little better knowing the truth, so I pondered whether to share my knowledge that she was their mother.

We decided it was worth breaking the locks with the metal rebar, all climbing through the ventilation shaft and running out into the night. No one would think about chasing after three missing kids; what could they say? Three kids that are abused are missing? We planned to run away, get to the nearest police station and tell them everything, using our scars, bruises, and tales to bring the place down and save the other kids in the process.

There was a youthful innocence about wanting to do the right thing that made our plan seem flawless. We'd decided to wait until night fell before making a move. There was an excitement in the air, as tonight was the night it was all going to happen.

Something was different with Robert though. He critiqued our largely innocent ploy as pointless and that we'd end up like George. The light that was in the room started to flicker gently, as though the bulb was on the way out. Thankfully, I'd pilfered the lighter previously. We tried our best to judge when night had fallen, using our fatigue as a measure of sorts. Keeping each other awake by talking about what we would do when we were out. It helped get us through.

Eventually, the time came, and we were psyched. I used that as an opportunity to tell them about the first night I escaped the room and found out their true origins. It hit them hard. Robert's silence was deafening. Eventually broken with a simple question.

"She's known all along and let us rot here?" he asked.

I defended Mallory. I didn't pretend to understand why but told them she was in a difficult position. Alexia seemed happy at the revelation, compared to her brother.

I exited my cell equipped with the rebar and the lighter before managing to force my way into Alexia's cell. One down, one to go. The light in the room flickered some more and started to fade. Robert asked for the lighter and held it near his cell to illuminate the lock.

I pressed harder and harder, and nothing happened. I was struggling and didn't feel strong enough to win, but with my sister's encouragement and my desperate brother's plea for freedom. Sheer willpower gave me a final gust of strength and with a final push the lock released, breaking under the pressure. We were all free; our plan was finally in motion.

I knew where I was going so I led the way. I dragged the barrel over, to give us our stepping-stone. Removing the vent cover, I hoisted myself up, arming myself with the rebar in the event we stumbled across any trouble along the way. Robert helped Alexia up just after me and before long, like secret agents, we were all crawling through the vent space, waving goodbye to our cells and the horrible smell left behind from the buckets. It felt liberating.

In a moment of shock, I realised I was missing something; my father's watch. I refused to leave without it. It was the only link to my past, and I needed it. It had helped me through my time here.

I turned my back and whispered to them I had to go to the infirmary and get my watch. Robert protested that it was a stupid risk to take but Alexia, appreciating the sentimental value of it, discouraged his chastising.

I agreed to get the watch, come back and meet them in the main vent as it came out at the reception area. From there, we agreed to bolt out the front door. With some arm-twisting, we unanimously agreed to the plan.

I knew where I was going. I left the vent, leaving my brother and sister in it. As I pulled myself out, Alexia begged me to come back. I leaned down to see if she was okay. She kissed me innocently on the cheek and said she was proud of me and that whatever happened, she loved how brave I was.

I felt rejuvenated and alive. We were only kids but forced to grow up incredibly fast given our experiences and learnt to love and live with each other. Robert looked on, shaking his head in youthful protest at the show of affection.

I snuck through the hallway again; appreciating this would be the last time. As I crept forward and peeked around a corner, my heart jumped out of my skin and I froze. I was tapped on the shoulder and thankfully didn't scream, just exhaled in defeat. I couldn't alert anyone else to my presence in the event they found my brother and sister. I turned my head slowly, with the rebar in my other hand, ready to swing. I stopped myself at the realisation it was Robert.

"I'm coming to help you, it's the least I can do for you, little brother," he whispered.

Relief swept over me and my heart retreated into my chest. We inched through the halls together and I motioned to the maintenance cupboard. We crept in and as I crawled in to the vent to retrieve my prized possession, I couldn't sense my brother behind me at first. Eventually, he caught up to me and ushered me forward, telling me to hurry up. The most eerily sounding alarm started to ring.

That was it, we'd been caught. I panicked, thinking it was Alexia. Who raised the alarm? Father? Did he realise we were out of our cell.

"Keep going, don't stop," Robert pleaded.

I grabbed the watch and Mallory's diary and got ready to turn around.

"We can't go back, Sebastian. We've got to keep moving forward."

I froze in confusion and after being shouted at to hurry up, emerged into the infirmary. Robert followed closely behind, the alarm echoing through the halls and the orphanage. It felt as if the room was getting larger and expanding. The sound of the alarm was ringing so much in my ears I started to block it out. I panicked thinking about Alexia.

"Where is she?" I barked at Robert. He suggested she was safe in the other vent, waiting for us.

That's when he came clean and told me what he had done. Robert had started a fire in the maintenance room, using the various oils and flammable liquids to get it going; expressing that was why he took a while to catch up to me. He told me the entire place deserved to burn and the fire would light the sky enough to draw attention from the authorities.

I told him he was stupid and that wasn't the plan. Realising the only way was forward and the building was starting to come alive with screams, shouting, and panic, we pressed on. We had to get to Alexia and hope we could all get out together. I was furious with Robert. He put the plan at risk.

When I walked up to the door, the infirmary door was locked. We both started to panic realising we were trapped, as going back through the vent was suicide. Smoke started to follow through the vent, but I refused to give up.

All our fighting, all our planning and plotting was nearly for nothing. I started to bang on the door, furiously. The alarm was enough to drown out the banging. Robert watched from behind, with a blank face, appreciating his stupidity at this point. He pulled off his shirt and tried to cover the vent as best as he could. His bloodied bandages were visible. It was impressive that his youthful body could take such a battering and he could still stand next to me. He couldn't cover the entire vent, but he didn't stop trying.

We must have been in the room for a good ten minutes, trying to break our way out. It was terrifying. The entire time, I was thinking about my sister and how scared she must be. I banged harder on the door to the point my hand was throbbing in pain.

I grabbed Robert's shirt and pulling it away made a puff of smoke enter the room, causing me to cough. I wrapped it around my hand and picked up the metal again, striking the door some more. Eventually, it started to give way and one of the panels started to come off. We started kicking the panel, finally revealing an exit route. The glow of flames could be seen through the hole. I poked my head out trying to see what was going on, when the awful alarm, screams, and banging of footsteps from scurrying bodies started to take my focus. Robert collapsed, appreciating the magnitude of what he had done.

"The screams, Sebastian. It's my fault," he said with a remorseful tone. I grabbed his head by the chin, turned his head up to mine and told him that he would be damned if he didn't get up and help me find his sister, our sister. He nodded, and we forced our way out through the small hole in the panel of the door. It was a tighter squeeze than the vent, but we made it. I went first, and as I squeezed through, the watch fell from my pocket back into the infirmary. Robert turned, grabbed it and passed it to me, smiling in the process whilst saying he had his little brother's back.

Robert was a little bigger than me and struggled to get through the hole. I pulled at him and he screamed as his body was dragged through the wood. Eventually, he broke through the gap and we made our way down the hallway.

Staff members and children were being led out of the building, amidst screams. Selfish adults pushed by us to make it out, without little care or attention for who stood in their way. As we roamed the halls, we walked past one of the children from the dormitory, who had collapsed, possibly from smoke inhalation or from being trampled; it was difficult to tell. Their body was facing the wall, so I turned them around to see a familiar face: Erin.

I urged Robert to look for Alexia and that I would help Erin. I started to drag Erin, mustering all my might, starting to become overwhelmed by the heat of the fire. I was struggling to breathe, as flames were dancing around me. With my last ounce of strength, I pulled on Erin and everything went black.

I came to, being carried out by a man in yellow. I was fading in and out of consciousness, the ringing of the alarm occasionally breaking in and out of my auditory senses.

I snapped my eyes up to a handsome man who had given me his breathing apparatus, risking his own life to provide me air. He led me to the fire engine, shouting about where the ambulances were. My body weakly re-adjusted to what was going on, oxygen finally coursing through my body.

All I could hear were screams, echoing in the moonlight. Huge, orange flames filled the night sky as they raged uncontrollably; the blaze met the skyline without so much as making a disturbance to the vast cosmos. As peaceful as it met the night sky, it was causing anarchy on the ground.

I couldn't be heard because I could barely breathe myself, wheezing slightly. I looked down at my blackened hands, as a paramedic raised an oxygen mask to my face. I looked up and Alexia's small hands were hitting the glass of a window frantically at first but started to slow. I felt horrible, my sister was in mortal danger and I was doing nothing about it.

This snapshot in time would eventually become my mental genesis. That feeling of how it could have played out differently. What would have happened if I went upstairs? If I removed the flammables in the basement? Stopped the fire starting completely? This day was a living nightmare that would plague my mind and I'd re-live it constantly. I'd play it back like an old VHS where I would write a happier ending every time.

I jumped off the back of the fire engine and tried to run towards the building to help but only made it a few steps before collapsing again.

The kind soul that saved me grabbed me and told me to relax. I pointed at the window where Alexia was, and he gestured that I was a tough one. I'd battled the fire once before: I could do it again for her. Believe me, I tried but failed. My body had given up.

My arm dropped to my side, but my eyes remained fixated on the window. I felt as if Alexia looked right at me and our eyes met, despite the shroud of the smoke. I felt her love for me. I felt her fear. I felt the heat of the fires touching her soft skin, and sweet smile. Then the shroud took over and the window blew out with a crash of glass trickling like water to the ground below.

Servicemen shouted orders at one another, directing the flow of the hoses in a united front.

Like demons emerging from the fire, the last few bodies ejected themselves from the upper floors of the building. It was tough to watch them fall to the ground with an almighty thud. That also etched into my mind over the years. Dreams where I was falling constantly and couldn't wake up. Feelings of impending doom when I was having a panic attack, my heart sinking with butterflies in my stomach as I balanced in the flaming night sky, waiting to crash to the ground.

Whatever almighty being orchestrated this evening, at least I knew they had a sense of humour. I recognised Father screaming in pain as his tibia bone protruded through his trouser leg. What karmic justice. Father's walking stick lay next to him with the bone from his good leg pointing into the night sky. It must have been a bad landing, but he was breathing. The servicemen ignored his plight, focussing more on the children in need.

Through the smoke a serviceman carried out the lifeless body of a girl, arms and legs heavy, neck falling backwards; I looked on helplessly and watched it happen as if in slow motion. Everything went silent; I started to zone out and couldn't hear anything anymore. It was my beautiful sister. I promised to help her. I promised to save her, and I failed. That was one of the reasons I became a perfectionist and never stop in my pursuit of doing the right thing.

A nearby nurse's guttural scream filled the night, contending with the flames. It was Mallory. The shock of seeing her lifeless daughter obviously pushed her over the edge. The sound made me shudder. That same sound clearly hit someone else as a serviceman had pulled my brother Robert out. He looked on at his sister, lifeless, fully aware that he was the one responsible. He never uttered a word, never moved, his eyes wide open in defeat. His pain must have been unimaginable.

I closed my eyes and continued breathing deeply through the mask. I passed out.

Weeks passed, and as I was nursed back to health, I was visited in the hospital by the man that saved me. He visited every day, and his strength and bravery inspired me. I was proud to one day call him dad, the same man who would later stand next to me as I got married, Henry. The entire town, the world, was affected by what came out from Fort Rose.

My dad made a point of making sure I was never hurt again. He cared for me and his service made me decide to follow in the life of good. I was accepted into another family, as a brother, and a son.

I later found out that Mallory had Robert institutionalised, and then disappeared herself, with remnants of the staff at Fort Rose being held accountable for what they did to the children, except Cyril. Somehow, he got away, scot-free.

The pain from that part of my life subsided over time but left suitably deep scars. I dreamt of that night frequently, waking up screaming, waking up crying. I'd clutch my real father's watch and sleep holding it tight. I always asked myself whether I was responsible. The fire started because I went looking for the watch, whereas if I'd left it, we could have run into the night.

My new parents were incredibly patient, even managing to keep the other kids calm, who were afraid of me. They were afraid because I couldn't sleep without wetting the bed or screaming some nights. My whole family was patient with me, helping me, moulding me, and restoring my broken soul.

I grew up stronger than ever, with a passion for making sure that justice prevailed.

I grew up, swearing I would never let the damage of Fort Rose seep into my soul again.

Never would I allow myself to feel as helpless again.

Chapter Ten

The feeling going through me, the feeling of being lost took me back to that fateful night. My wife was in the arms of the devil and I was no closer to catching him. I felt like weeping, but it would do no good. I thought about the comfort of my biological mother's touch, caressing my head, as well as a tentative Mallory, tending my aches and pains.

Then I thought about the comfort my wife brought me and it brought me full circle. I thought back to the youthful innocence I had as a child, that was slowly, but surely, chipping away at me throughout my years; then I compared it to now.

Part of me wished I was a child again, as even though I lived amongst demons and predators, I never truly understood the gravity of the situation. I knew I was in danger, but how much danger, it was too great for my young mind to comprehend.

Now, I knew the ramifications of my failure to catch Arthur, the finite possibility of a future without my wife. My anxiety started to flare up, I felt dread. I ran every possible scenario through my head except the one that would actually make a difference, the positive outcome.

I felt a creeping loneliness washing over me. Michael wasn't anywhere to be seen despite his offer of support; perhaps he was scared off by Arthur's latest move. I didn't hold it against him. Like my younger self, I was shouldering the burden of the situation upon my own shoulders, though the sheer weight was dragging me down. Like Atlas holding the world, I felt powerless.

Wait.

Atlas? The titan that was condemned to hold us to the celestial heavens, often pictured as holding the world. A penny in my darkened thoughts dropped. I thought about Atlas. I thought about the clues and the riddles and enshrouded in solitude, felt a spark of hope. Re-energised with my mind giving me a clue. I had to find what everything meant. From the lucid dream, to the riddles and clues, it all had to tie together into a nicely wrapped package. One that could blow up in my face.

I lifted my head up from my dining table and took in the view of my work. It felt quite pointless. Days, weeks, maybe even months of time poured into finding Arthur Henderson, and I was always behind the curve, never ahead of it, and now my wife was in danger. I had enjoyed my job, up until now, protecting those that deserved it.

It took a long time for the scars of my childhood to heal, though in the space of about thirty-six hours, Arthur stuck a knife in them and made my mind enter that terrible place again. I wished Henry were still with me, I could use his support right about now, or even his wife Isabella. Both were no longer with this world, but two shining stars that burned brighter than one hundred suns.

Those people were living, breathing angels, I'm certain of it. I remembered how proud they were of me as I graduated from the Police Academy and when I got my first detective's badge, Henry and I celebrated with one too many drinks, much to Isabella's distaste. Despite everything, she still thought that one night was enough to be a bad influence on me.

I remember how strong my dad was when he sat through my therapy when I was younger. When I talked about what I witnessed when I was in the cage, and escaped, he himself lost control and shouted at my therapist, 'How could bloody animals like this walk the earth.' That made my mum cry, but they both stood by me, helping me come to terms with what I suffered, what I survived.

I felt mildly empowered, mildly stronger just thinking about them. The very thought of my foster parents and the penny dropping about the clues seemed to remove the cloud of anxiety raining over me. That spark of hope rejuvenated in me.

Minutes later, the phone rang. My heart started racing, thumping through my chest as I read that the caller was Arianna.

I answered without saying a word.

"Now, detective, that was very rude. Most people greet their caller, especially if it is their beloved," Arthur taunted down the line.

Assuming the worst, I thought I heard the muffling of my desperate wife down the phone.

"I told you, if you hurt her…"

"Detective, this is no call for empty threats. I was interrupted on my last call. In fact, I called to say how much I

250

admire your wife. How very brave. The bitch actually broke my nose with a head butt."

My heart stopped as he laughed at it, and very suddenly, as much as I was proud of her and wanted to laugh in his face, I chose not to follow suit. As much as I was proud of my gorgeous woman breaking one of his bones, I didn't want to laugh with the prick that had her. I'd wait and laugh as I broke the rest of them.

The most profane of words fought to exit my mouth but subconsciously, I suppressed them so as to not aggravate him. Strange really, being so subdued and restricted with everything. As much as I wanted to scream, curse, and threaten him, I couldn't get a single word out. So much so that Arthur must have expected my retort instead of silence.

"Are you still there, Sebastian?"

I grunted in response. I couldn't tell if this was him trying to assert his power over me. Was this Arthur trying to get one over me, to frighten me into submission? It seemed to annoy him not responding, so I felt as though I'd keep my vow of silence. The ground was beginning to crack beneath my feet, ready to swallow me whole as I made the conscious decision to stay silent and taunt him back.

"I have to admire her. I truly do. I'd tell you the full story about how it happened, but I feel pressed for time, you know, in the event you are tracing this call. Instead, I'll give you the short version. I set up a video camera and was ready to have my way with her when she cried. You see detective, I had her tied down, spread-eagled across the bed, barely able to move. She was a little bruised around the ankles because she'd been fighting so hard to escape." The bastard laughed at his final comment.

Fuck you. I responded in my head, instead of through my mouth, still choosing to keep my vow of silence. I clutched the phone, desperate to hear her. Desperate to know she was okay.

"Fucking answer, Sebastian," Arthur spat, clearly annoyed I wasn't giving in to his power trip. He began to lose control of his own emotions and I laughed down the phone at him. I was laughing maniacally to let him know I wouldn't be intimidated.

In his final ploy to get one over me, he spoke. "She gave me that same fire when I started to undress. I wanted what you had. I was going to rape your pretty flower and make her my own. I was going to fuck her brains out until she begged me to continue. That fine specimen was mine to taint."

I finally chose to speak, deciding to fuck with his head at the same time.

"Then, she cracked you on the nose and made you bleed. Poor, little Arthur. You are so fucking soft that a woman tied up managed to get one over you," I continued with a laugh.

"Laugh now whilst you can, detective fucking clown. You won't be soon," Arthur responded, clearly angry with the way the conversation went.

The call was cut abruptly, seemingly out of anger and then mine buzzed. A picture message of her spread out on the bed was eerily reminiscent of old memories of the basement near the cage that I felt sick thinking about it. However, I felt mildly okay given she wasn't harmed and hadn't been defiled. *Stay strong, Arianna.*

Refocussed with thoughts of her being okay, the memories of my foster parents, and the penny dropping about Atlas, I was ready to tackle some of the riddles to find the hidden message.

I knew Arthur would regret leaving me hints soon enough, because I was on his tail. He'd be the one begging me not to hurt him by the time I caught up to him.

Formed in an instant, lasting a lifetime; I draw you back to where it began.

A bare-faced lie; he carried something new, weightless unlike the guilt of the past.

Deities Apollo and Artemis protect us, he defiles us.

Chronos mistaken affiliation, despite devouring his own, puts reflection on who the victim may be.

I read it, then read it again and again. I wasn't seeing the answer, so I dusted off an old book I had on mythology. I scrambled through the pages to find excerpts on the named Gods. Apollo, Artemis, and Chronos. I knew Chronos was the God of time, but what was being alluded to, I didn't know.

I flicked through the pages and highlighted anything remotely related to Apollo and started to read, focussing my efforts in what the solution could be. I read through the

Apollo sections for hours, trying to make something fit. That's when I began to write everything down.

Apollo – Olympian Deity, Greek.

God of music, prophecy, truth, healing, medicine sun, light, poetry, archery, and plague?

Complexities, contradictory. Healing and plague?

Son of Zeus and Leto, sister Artemis.

Viewed as the most handsome God.

Archery – target, 'X' marks the spot?

God of foreigners, hosts dominion over colonists.

Protector of fugitives, refugees, and young boys, nurture to adulthood.

Giver and interpreter of law.

Patron of herdsmen and cattle, flocks and fertility.

Wards off evil, averter of plague, but giver of it?

I was trying to understand why Arthur would refer to Greek Gods but continued the task and moved on to the next God in the riddle.

Artemis – Olympian deity, Greek.

God of wilderness, hunting, wild animals, the moon, and fertility.

Helper of midwives, and Goddess of birth.

Daughter of Zeus and Leto, twin to Artemis.

Patron and protector of young girls, able to inflict disease upon women, and relieve.

Contradictory again, healing and plague?

Gods of healing, and plague? Could it be a suggestion he has the power to take and prevent himself inflicting harm? The complexities and contradictory natures of the Gods. Was there something in it I wasn't seeing? Of course! The second crime scene in the hotel, with the lamb head. Was that linked?

I thought about every possible Greek monster. The chimera, was that it? Flicking through, it wasn't. Damn it! I wasn't thinking clearly enough, it wasn't fitting. Knowing the stakes, I was getting impatient and frustrated. Terrified the phone might ring again and it could be him with another taunt, or perhaps I had angered him enough to do something stupid. Fuck!

Stop Sebastian. Think. The riddle. Stay on course. I had to breathe, I had to take it slow. What am I being told? Artemis and Apollo protected us. Who is us? Protectors of boys and girls, men and women. The riddle read they protect us, but 'he defiles us.'

I thought about it in terms of the riddle, and the theme of mythology. Someone powerful enough to overthrow the Gods? It could only realistically be Zeus. Of course, Arthur feels as though he has power and dominion over boys and girls, referencing little Sebastian and his mother at his first heinous murder. So, Arthur views himself as the God with power over the protectors?

I struggled to find what the sudden fascination with Greek mythology was. Arthur was specific in his previous crime with Jessica, where he viewed himself as the devil, capable of snuffing out his own son. Was he the proverbial Hades, not Zeus? I felt like I only had one part of the riddle and not enough for a eureka moment, so pressed on and continued with the task at hand.

Chronos – God of time.

Three-headed serpent: a man's head, bull's head, and a lion's head.

Daughter Ananke, Goddess of inevitability.

Revolves around primordial world 'egg,' split with daughter to form planet Earth.

Gave birth to Chaos.

Often infuriated and not to be mistaken with Titan Cronus.

That's the mistaken affliction? I flicked some more pages and dug up what I could on the Titans, specifically Cronus.

Cronus – Titan, leader of the first generation of Titans.

Youngest son of Uranus and Gaea.

Ruler of all Gods and men for a brief period.

Rebelled against his father, grew tyrannical.

Imprisoned the cyclops and hecatoncheires.

Viewed as Father and Lord of Time.

Swallowed and ate all of his children except one,
Zeus.

That had to be it, it seemed to fit the riddle. Artemis and Apollo, despite later being offspring of Cronus' surviving son Zeus. He was the almighty that gave birth to the almighty Zeus. That felt more like Arthur. Devourer, destroyer of families. It seemed to fit. The excitement of finally starting to break through and get to the hidden messages within.

That was just two lines of the riddle though, and oddly, working backwards – I seemed to be making more headway with the final two lines. I mulled over the others.

Formed in an instant, lasting a lifetime; I draw
you back to where it began.

A bare-faced lie; he carried something new,
weightless unlike the guilt of the past.

Formed in an instant, lasting a lifetime, I draw you back to where it began. I read that over and over, trying to break it. Formed in an instant, lasting a lifetime. A thought? A memory? Drawing me back to where it began. The night he killed Sebastian? That's when I started my hunt for him, to hunt, like Artemis? It all seemed to connect.

A bare-faced lie, he carried something new, weightless unlike the guilt of the past. That's where I hit the proverbial brick wall. No matter how much I pondered that line, I couldn't make anything fit. He wanted to draw me back to where it began, so I was going to the Jessica and Sebastian McColm residence. Nothing seemed immediately visible in the photos of the crime scene.

257

The phone rang, breaking my concentration. I couldn't bring myself to look at it. The ringing continued. My entire soul crashed, thinking I may have spurred Arthur into doing something stupid to my wife. I looked over and it was Michael. I let it ring off. I'm sure he meant well but I didn't feel like talking to anyone. If Michael did back off to protect himself and his family, which was just sheer conjecture on my part, I was doing him a favour not hindering him with the news about Arianna.

I ran out the door and something inside me decided not to lock the door, ever hopeful that Arthur would be stupid enough to come to me. If I left it unlocked, it gave me an excuse to be more cautious going back into my house as well. I shrugged it off as borderline insanity, perhaps borderline ingenuity.

I had other places to be, namely – going back to the beginning to try and find some clues. It was a fairly uneventful drive, as I could only focus on the clues I had been left up to that point.

"A bare-faced lie, carrying something new, weightless," I said out loud. The final part of that riddle was spinning around my head. Weightless. Knowledge? Power? Desire? Emotion?

There were so many options that it distracted me enough until I got to the McColm residence. I parked at the side of the road and stared at the door. It was still covered with 'do not cross' tape and the front garden had become mildly uncontrollable, seemingly only tended briefly by neighbours when it started to intrude on their side of the adjoining gardens.

I exited my car. Walking up the pathway to the door was disturbing. I didn't know if I could expect to find anything, if at all. Maybe I was miles off and searching in the wrong area. If so, all I was going to do was to re-open old wounds. The feel of that room when I walked in to it still stuck with me; and very few situations in my time did, most of which stemmed back to Fort Rose.

My mind teased me by flashing back to the night I walked up here after getting the call. Mental images of the blue lights flashing against the walls, the sounds of colleagues in despair; crying and cursing the bastard that inflicted the torment he did on that poor child.

I knew devils existed from my childhood and Arthur was the first one I had encountered in decades. My hand reached out to the door, and almost as if I was living that moment in the past, I broke through the tape as if it wasn't there. The sound of people still ringing in my ears got louder, notably, one of the paramedics tasked with taking little Sebastian's body away. I remembered how loudly she was crying, having caught a glimpse of the scene, decorated with tags and numbers, bloodied and brutal. She took one look and couldn't even face zipping up the body bag, leaving it to her hardened colleague. I watched it all from the hallway after assessing the original scene.

It came flooding back. Knowing the clue was leading me back to here, if I was right, was harrowing. I didn't know what else I could possibly find. We went over the place with

259

a fine-toothed comb and came out pretty empty handed. Guided by disgust for the man that had inflicted the pain and committed the murder was all any of us came away with.

I felt sick thinking back to that night and how I almost admired the evil nature of the man I chased. The excitement of always being up close to evil was like an aphrodisiac to me, albeit, without the sexual implications. My heart raced in a different way, reminiscent of meandering through the Fort Rose basement looking for the metal rebar. It truly was the excitement of dancing with devils that got my heart racing.

This time was different. This time, it had become personal. I'd matured and grown from my experiences and all of a sudden, the person I cared most for in the world was in danger. My mind flashed back to that room one final time as I looked around and then I snapped back to reality, realising just how vacant and empty the place was.

Some items were still left in position. Some sad fanatics for Arthur had followed the news and broken in and tagged the walls with gang signs, leaving some of the personal belongings in upheaval. Smashed photo frames, upturned bookcases, general dirt, and mess had left the house in a state of disrepair. My heart truly sank for Jessica, as she'd clearly opted to wash her hands of any of her old belongings, perhaps not wanting any reminder of what happened to her son.

I wished I could have said I understood what she was going through, but alas, I'd be doing them both a disservice if I put any such words to the gesture.

As if the place was cursed, the rest of the house had strangely been left untouched, other than the tags in the room where it happened. The riddle ran through my head: *go back where it began*. What was it trying to tell me? Why was he trying to tell me this? Was it a clue to his whereabouts, or a clue as to the motive? Perhaps understanding the riddle fully, I could harbour a guess as to his next step.

A lone wolf doesn't just stop hunting for its own perseverance, it does it to survive; and something in him needed to inflict pain and torment. I truly felt as though I was humanity's last hope at stopping him. Armed with a personal vendetta, it was clear the chase was entering darker territories, and I would have to make a decision as to what my moral code was when I faced him. Right now, I wasn't going to battle with my own internal thoughts, as I would have only stagnated and stopped myself from pressing forward and finding the solution.

I started to observe the untouched parts of the house. I couldn't understand why no one who had the gall to break in and set up a graffiti epitaph to Arthur would decide it suddenly wasn't okay to see the rest of the house. Valuables still lay out in Jessica's bedroom, gathering dust as though they had been lost to time. Photo frames sat with a thick layer of it, almost blocking the sun and the smiles of the happy mother and son.

It depressed me looking at it as I was in the position where I would have killed to be with my wife, and to start a family. I had always dreamt of starting a family, but the job got in the way, and despite numerous attempts to try for one, it fell flat.

If I could rewind the clock and control time, I would change a lot of things. Perhaps I would change the day I decided to take on the Henderson case, and let this fate befall someone else. Perhaps I would have stayed in Fort Rose and tried to save my brothers and sisters. Perhaps I would have found the lighter to stop the fire being lit. Perhaps I would have stopped my parents leaving that day, feigning an illness. My life could have taken a multitude of different paths, yet I was on this one, committed.

I searched that house high and low, scanning for clues, scanning for a hint or suggestion as to where the riddle was taking me, and found nothing.

I moved on to the next crime scene, the hotel where I found Jane Doe; the woman who had not been identified. What a tremendous waste of time that was. The room had been deep cleaned and bleached beyond any possible forensic capturing. The proprietor of the establishment, extremely embarrassed by the happenings in that room had obviously gone to tremendous lengths to hide what happened there, so I ceased my search upon entering the room, accepting it was pointless.

My phone buzzed, there was a voicemail. Then it buzzed again. Then it buzzed again. Michael was sending me texts now. I read them, and they urged me to phone him. As I was reading, another one came through: *I know what you are doing, if you trust me, you've got to make yourself scarce. You've got to hide. Meet me behind the bar in twenty minutes.*

I hopped in the car, then drove down to the bar, as it wasn't too far away, perhaps fifteen minutes. My mind was reeling at the fact I had finally made some headway with the riddle but hadn't quite managed to figure out the last few parts, something wasn't fitting. I hadn't really had much opportunity to think about it given the phone call I had received moments after opening the bus locker, the moment I found out about Arianna being taken.

I mentally distracted myself by turning on the radio, banging a drumbeat on the steering wheel to the inane tune. My drumming did get quite aggressive so for the good of my steering wheel, it was lucky the journey was fairly brief. The battered wheel turned up behind the bar, through a tight alleyway that led to a car park for about seven vehicles. My car barely fit, though I recall the lawman in me did appreciate it because if anyone ever got too drunk and attempted to drive home, Kirsty would get out from behind the bar, push a large dumpster in the way and nothing could get in or out without doing a silly amount of damage to the body of their car.

Michael found that out the hard way once and explained it away with a weak story of chasing a fugitive, to our own laughter across the office, the bar, and anyone I dared tell the story to, to his unwelcomed shame.

Kirsty was petite, gorgeous, and ultimately wicked when it came to making sure her patrons didn't do anything that might jeopardise future customers or driving licences and I appreciated her for it.

In another life, we might have been married and I could have been trying to save her instead. However, immediately after the thought crossed my mind, I chastised myself for wishing Kirsty was trading places with Arianna, under the guise of, 'I could have married her.'

It was quite pathetic and evident that I was trying to brush aside any sense of urgency with the situation in case I failed; emotionally detaching from the responsibility that was in my lap. Truth be told, I probably would be going crazy if Arthur took Kirsty instead, as I had grown fond of her. If I had any sense of duty and goodwill, I'd do the same for anyone I knew, liked, and respected. Perhaps even those I didn't, because I felt as though I was a good person, with a moral compass. It was just cracked slightly right now, as conflict battled with the proverbial angel and devil on my shoulders.

Speaking of the devil, as my mind wandered, that's when she emerged from the back door of the bar, with a case full of empty glass bottles. She threw them in the dumpster, spun around in a graceful pirouette, then waved as she embarrassingly noticed my car mid-spin. She probably thought no one was watching, so she waved with a beetroot red face and retreated back in to the bar.

I sat in the car and waited. I deliberated going in and telling Kirsty what was going on but feared coming back out in a state fit enough to do anything about what actually mattered. It was a sad state of affairs but after Arianna left, I did have my own demons. I often tried to drown the sorrows with alcohol, which only made me feel worse in the long run, so the angel won with that conflict; the bar idea left my mind. I waited patiently for Michael, even going so far as to answer his next call in which he promised me he would be five minutes.

There was little that occupied my mind in that time. Thoughts of being in a happier place, from my parents, my engagement, the wedding and every single second I spent with that amazing woman. Why I pissed it away, I don't know. I'd become so hell bent on capturing the most sinister evil I had encountered since Cyril in Fort Rose.

My mind fleeted to being a child again, with strength, bravery, and utter vulnerability. There was a lot to be compared to, minus the age gap of course. I was interrupted by Michael, who sped through the alleyway, even scratching the side of his car again, to my slight amusement.

He was in a fierce hurry and I couldn't wait to understand why. Had he found Arthur? Did he have a lead? Jumping out of our respective cars with symmetrical grace, mirroring one another perfectly, closing the doors at the same time. We couldn't have timed it better in fact.

"You've got to lay low. You've got to find this guy without the department," he blurted out.

"What do you mean?" I quizzed, not intending to involve them anyway given the close ties I had, and the fear of being benched from the main event.

"A package was delivered to the Chief. It had a message in there, for you. Signed by Henderson."

"What? What did it say?"

"It said that your wife would be the next person delivered in the package. As a precaution, the Chief wants you under watch. Protective detail, and... how do I say this. He said he wants to rule out any possible chance you are a suspect–"

"That's fucking ridiculous, Michael, and you know it," I declared, aghast at the implication, even if it was protocol.

"I know, but you know these things. It's nearly always the spouse. Precautionary move by the Chief. Not to mention, he wants to make sure you are kept an eye on because you can't work this if your wife is in danger. Your wife as a possible victim. You are too close to it now. The Chief won't want Henderson to walk on technicality bullshit. The fact he only got jailed for rape was a joke in itself. Anyway, I got word from some of the guys that owed me one, that's when I called you. As far as I know, they'll already be at your house."

I started to laugh, considering the ridiculousness of the situation. Everything had begun to spiral.

"What?" Michael asked.

"I know it's not me, Michael, but how is it going to look? The previous crime scenes practically spread-eagled across my entire dining room wall. Latest theories, thoughts about elements that weren't even at the crime scenes. You know the Xavier Hardiman case? I may have pocketed the key card to a bus locker to search the thing instead of logging it as evidence, to get a warrant. So, I've acted outside the normal parameters of justice, to get a head start. That's why I'm laughing. I even left the door unlocked for the guys to waltz in to the damn place."

Michael questioned why I would leave the door unlocked and my reasoning wasn't acknowledged, laughed at, or even inspired. Simply heard.

"There's something else you should know, Sebastian. The package the Chief received? It didn't just contain a letter and a threat, it's pretty damn serious."

My heart sank; I panicked and demanded an immediate response to what was in that package.

His answer to that question made my world fall apart. Any reservations I had about arresting Arthur and making him come quietly were about as far gone as they possibly could have been. I was furious, I was beyond despair, I was inconsolable to the point that my shouting alerted half of the bar and I was the Shakespearean tragedy performing in the seedy car park. My screams were similar to that of a banshee, alerting anyone nearby, crippling the eardrums of those that could stand to listen.

I'd never lost myself emotionally like this before. Michael consoled me and he hugged me so tight that I started to push him away, my fist crashing on his chest in a weak, desperate plea. The only question I could ask was why?

Rage fuelling my every action, I took the keys to Michael's car, appreciating if I was to be under watch, a classic car would be immediately found on an APB. He didn't even try to stop me, no one did. Kirsty looked on, almost traumatised by what she had witnessed and heard. It looked as though she wanted to console me but stared in sheer disbelief, powerless.

The sun started to fall, and night was soon upon us. My favourite time of the day, because that's where I was more likely to find the kind of beast I was hunting.

My mission was simple, it was time to get to the next crime scene. I put my foot down and sped to the Xavier Hardiman crime scene, desperate for an answer, desperate to understand why these stupid fucking games were being played.

I couldn't think clearly, wrought with sorrow and anger; an epic mixture of every sinful and despairing emotion in the book. With bleary eyes, unable to see the road clearly through rage, I drove. Every fibre of my body was on fire; every fibre of my being was crashing. I felt anxiety sweeping over me, realising I was failing in my mission, realising I failed to protect and serve those unable to do so themselves. I cursed Arthur Henderson. Michael tried to call me, and I purposely let it ring out.

Despite being a reasonably recent crime scene, only tape blocked the way to some answers. I rarely took my service weapon, but luckily, I was in Michael's car. I grabbed it, unsure as to what I could expect as I entered the house. With one swift kick, fuelled solely by adrenaline and anger, the door flew open and I ripped the tape away as I walked through it.

I headed to the study, in the distance, I could see that the case holding *The Gutenberg Bible* had been smashed and the book taken. Arthur, or perhaps an attending officer, had obviously returned and decided to pillage the priceless treasure.

Flashes to that crime scene flickered in my head, being immediately broken by another phone call. Not now Michael, then as I snapped into detective mode, I realised I had to get rid of it.

If the Chief wanted to side track me that much, I wouldn't be surprised if he'd run a trace. I wasn't in the mood for fucking talking, so just as I ran the scenario through my head, ready to eject the phone across the marble hallway of Mr. Hardiman's home, by sheer good fortune, I noticed Arianna's face appear as the caller.

"You've got a fucking cheek calling me, you sick cu–" I cursed at Arthur in the most profane way.

"Oh, but, Sebastian. I had to let you know I was serious," he sneered back at me, having the audacity to laugh at me.

"She had better be okay, because I'm coming for you. I'm following the little trail you've left me. I'll figure it out, then I'm going to kill you. You don't deserve to breathe, Arthur.

You're sick. You're fucking sick!" I screamed, the echoes filling the marble hallway

"She's still breathing, just. I have to say, I am so impressed. I said I would kill you, and in a way, I did," Arthur taunted, twisting the knife he stuck in to my gut, and hers.

Time stopped as he spoke. Arianna was pregnant. The package he delivered to the Chief was the foetus of our unborn child he had gutted out of my wife. I felt sick even talking to him, knowing what Arianna had gone through; that the past had repeated itself and he made another mother witness the un-birth of their child.

That bastard had them both and I didn't even know. That must have been what she needed to talk to me about. I would have given up everything if she'd told me. I'd have quit this God forsaken job and moved on to be with them. I'd have been a great father. I would have made sure that our beautiful baby never had to experience what I went through as a child. I'd be their saviour, their protector. Only, I wasn't.

In full contradictory fashion, I started to punch the wall realising that everything I wanted to be was on the opposite side of the gorge I was proverbially standing over.

My baby hadn't even breathed life and he took it from me. He had killed me, part of me. Part of Arianna. Regret washed over me for even taunting him earlier, trying to walk away the more powerful one. I understood now that he was, he had won. I was broken.

"I'll admit, I was moved by her pleas that when I went to defile her, I didn't," Arthur said calmly.

"Where the fuck is she, you fucking animal. You said she was alive, just. Please. You win, just tell me where she is. Please just let me save her," I begged on deaf ears.

"You really pissed me off, Sebastian. Your relentless turning of stones just to find me. You prodded the bear and I wasn't happy. I'll admit–"

"I'll fucking kill you, Arthur. I don't care anymore. You are mine," I bellowed.

"You'll never find me. Which is why, I figured I would give you this final farewell. It was fun, watching you from afar. I was always watching you as you turned over those stones, even leading you down some garden paths, so to speak."

I contested whether to try and talk him down, go into police mode, keep him on the line to prolong the situation, or whether to listen, and then find him. Panic overtook reasonable judgement.

"I wanted to kill you. I succeeded," Arthur protested proudly.

"Do you believe in karma, Arthur?" I spat back.

"By killing your unborn child, I've killed you."

"You motherfucker."

I started to swear down the phone. I was incensed with anger and sorrow that I couldn't take it anymore. The cracks at my feet opened up and I felt myself being swallowed by the abyss. My life couldn't mean so little any more. I punched the wall in front of me more times than I cared to count, I led myself into Xavier Hardiman's study and defiled the place of his death. I started to throw books across the room, pushing over various stands in anger.

I could still hear Arthur's voice down the other end of the phone and his final words stuck with me before I snapped the phone and ejected it across the room.

"You are going to die a slow, painful death without them. Just listen," he said sadistically.

"I... love... you... Sebastian," Arianna said softly, exhaling densely towards the end.

"Arianna! I love you, too. I'll find you. I'm coming," I cried out desperately.

"It's already too late. The same knife that cut out your child. The same knife that killed your unborn daughter has just plunged into her heart," he said as I fell to the floor powerless. "Maybe I'll succeed in the end because when you realise that you'll never find me, or your wife for that matter, you'll realise the only way to end the torment is to put a bullet in your own skull. I'll have killed you once, twice, perhaps three times over. Have a nice life, detective."

His final monologue would be his last taunt. His last song and his last fucking dance. I tried to call back and it went straight to voicemail; it was over. I battled with the thoughts of injustice in my head and the scales were tipping far to the wrong side, the side I'd only ever considered exploring once, as a child, holding the screwdriver atop the Gardener's neck as he slept.

I chose to walk away that day, realising I didn't have it in me. Now, though, maybe I did? Arthur-fucking-Henderson brought out the worst in me. Something in me knew I would catch him. Something in me knew I would have the pleasure of snuffing out his pathetic little life.

I screamed uncontrollably for a while, not truly knowing how long I had. I trashed Mr Hardiman's library, screaming until my voice couldn't sound off any longer. I cried for my wife, realising I would never see her smile, never look into her beautiful eyes, or make love to her like I did just a day before.

How fleeting life is. How wasteful it is, knowing that creeps like Arthur can walk the earth without being struck by lightning from an angered God.

I felt as though I was truly alone. I was at rock bottom with no companions, no Gods, nothing.

My only motivation now was to find the prick that took everything from me and take everything from him as well. As I trashed the library some more, I stumbled across a hidden secret. A switch in the wall, stuffed behind the books I had thrown across the room in my rage.

Stunned at the chance encounter, I pressed it to hear an almighty click that killed the newly-achieved silence. A small doorway opened. Of course, someone as rich as Xavier Hardiman would have a secret room.

The door led to a small opening, so small it was how the room could remain concealed when considering the layout of the property. A switch sat on the wall as I stepped into the secret alcove, and I flicked it. It lit up a very steep staircase that traversed into a deep basement. There was nothing to suggest this property even had a basement, no other entry points around the property, no windows, just the artificial light.

Led only by confusion, I worked my way down the steps. The room had many trinkets, and collectibles Mr Hardiman had elected to collect and stash in secret. A mannequin faced the wall looking away, towards a small bookcase of old Betamax tapes, journals, trophies, and trinkets.

I stepped closer to the mannequin, taking in the sights of the hidden secret we all walked over when we assessed the crime scene. We had no reason to observe any deeper than we did. We wouldn't have thought to remove the books and journals to reveal secret access points.

I felt as though I was living in a fantasy, as secret rooms always felt quite far-fetched until I thought about the cage in Fort Rose. I turned the mannequin, and everything suddenly made sense. The answer to the riddle came to me in an instant.

Formed in an instant, lasting a lifetime; I draw you back to where it began.

A bare-faced lie; he carried something new, weightless unlike the guilt of the past.

Deities Apollo and Artemis protect us, he defiles us.

Chronos mistaken affiliation, despite devouring his own, puts reflection on who the victim may be.

Formed in an instant, lasting a lifetime, a memory. A bare-faced lie, he carried something new. He did, he carried a new name. Deities Artemis and Apollo protect us, they protected boys and girls. The Chronos myth, he ate his children. His mistaken affiliation, 'Cronos;' the Titan Father Time. The deities did protect us whilst he defiled us.

Xavier Hardiman's missing face had been found. It sat on the mannequin in front of me and it was an aged Father Time. Father, Cyril, my past coming back to haunt me in the most twisted way.

X did mark the spot; it marked the spot of my past.

The flowers from the crime scenes, they immediately made me think of flowers from the Gardener's garden in Fort Rose, a link I'd have never made if not for the haunting view in front of me.

Not to mention the links wouldn't ever reveal as that part of my life was over, closed behind a door I had mentally bolted shut. I didn't see it because I refused to accept that it was even a possibility.

Everything started crashing down on me and my throat started to close, I entered a full-blown panic attack. Air struggled to enter my lungs, I clutched my throat, undoing the top buttons on my shirt to try and trick my mind into thinking that I wasn't choking, wasn't being strangled. I reached out to the nearby trinkets, trying to grab anything to help me find my feet, then I noticed it: the old walking stick. The thudding against hard floors started to play in my head and I lost consciousness.

I awoke, unsure how much time had passed. No vivid dreams, nothing. As I came to slowly, I didn't even move from the floor, just looking up to the ceiling, trying to take it all in. It was impossible.

Everything that brought me to this moment was like a giant sick game being played and I was the pawn. I was truly a man who had lost everything. My wife, my unborn child I found out about in the most harrowing way possible. I had no biological family to speak of, my foster parents had left this world. I had two friends: Michael, and Kirsty.

I was a broken man, not even afraid to admit I couldn't even weep in that basement, conflicted and torn between helplessness and whether there was even a point in pushing on.

I had Michael's service weapon, I placed the end of the gun in my mouth and as I went to pull the trigger, felt my entire harrowing life flash before my very eyes. I pressed the trigger and it clicked. Nothing. In a twist of fate, the gun didn't fire. I removed the barrel from my mouth and sat up slightly to inspect the gun. It made no sense whatsoever; as the clip wasn't empty.

Michael was a stickler for keeping his gun immaculate, so a jam or misfire from an unmaintained weapon wasn't the case. Suddenly, a bang went off. A hang-fire shot out of the barrel and through the mannequin's head, creating a satisfying hole through Father's head. Something I had always secretly dreamt of.

I could have attributed the hang-fire, an extremely rare occurrence with any weapon to whatever God, or Gods I cursed as not being out there if people like Arthur could walk the street. Something clearly shone on me that moment, and whether budget cuts within the department caused us to get in bad ammo, whether the incessant rain we'd had for weeks had caused the rounds to go wet, I couldn't tell and frankly couldn't care.

Looking at the hole in Father's head, aka the missing face of 'Xavier Hardiman' attached to a mannequin; the stroke of good fortune amidst the recent heartache was enough to rejuvenate me. Despite hitting rock bottom, I failed in my attempt to kill myself.

I had failed to let Arthur win outright.

I stood up, kicked the mannequin over, spat at the ground and left the basement, deciding I still had something to live for: justice, revenge, vengeance, time would tell.

I was going to the ruins of Fort Rose. I was going back to the beginning. I was going to find answers.

Chapter Eleven

Images of flames were still scorched in my mind. Through the eyes of a child, I witnessed people I cared about, burn. I was surrounded by pain growing up but witnessing death in such magnificent balls of flame was a lot for my young mind to take, mentally draining and defeating me.

I truly believe that a small part of me died that night, irrespective of the beatings, the loneliness, and the sadness I had gone through. I hadn't had an opportunity to process death properly as I hopped between Miss Battersby's house, Madam's cupboard, and finally Fort Rose.

The flames purified any other pain, allowing me a chance to soak in death. That night, I mourned the loss of brothers and sisters, as well as previous losses inclusive of my parents and even myself.

My life was truly owed to my foster parents, Henry and Isabella. I was quite ashamed having reached the point where I pulled the trigger of a live weapon whilst the barrel was in my mouth. That said, there was something freeing about failing to kill oneself despite an actual well-aimed attempt.

Fate intervened and invincibility was quite a trait. My anxieties seemed to stop; the depressive thoughts stopped. I failed to kill myself in that basement, but I killed my demons. I felt new and alive. Had that round of ammunition been fine, had the hang-fire not occurred, I wouldn't be driving to the scene of my childhood; the scene of the flames. The heat, the burning imagery of the flames were quelled with my rejuvenated freedom.

It didn't wash away the loss of my wife and unborn child, but it made me feel free to act upon the actions of Arthur Henderson. I was ready for what I was going to face. I knew that I could face him without another panic attack, without helplessness intervening. Like a phoenix rising from ashes, a new man, I felt like I was about to start a new chapter. Without delaying the inevitable, I just had to finish the last chapter, absolutely and without remorse, whatever my decision. Arrest or kill.

My phone rang again, and I answered. It was Michael. He told me that a tip off had taken the Chief and him to an abandoned warehouse. That it was Arianna. I knew her fate but didn't share. The only thing I did know was that Arthur wasn't there. I ended the call without exchanging much in the way of words. Michael tried to ring back, so I threw the phone out of the car as I made my way to the orphanage, free from shackles, smirking in anticipation. If Arthur wasn't at that warehouse where my wife's body was, I had a reason to believe where he would be.

I parked the car about a mile down the road from the orphanage. It was practically a huge ruin now, untouched. It had never been bought, renovated, or seemingly touched since the fire. I had never thought to return, appreciating the ties it held to my mental state. The ties back to my childhood.

My foster father, Henry, was dead against the idea when it was suggested in therapy, insisting there was another way to help me. He spoke with such passion and regard for my well-being, I remember it was the moment I truly respected and loved him. I finally felt safe.

With the pistol in my hand, I crept up to the building. It was still as ghastly as memory served. The hallways were empty, dusty, and desolate. I crept through the halls, silently clearing the rooms with the pistol in front. Some rooms were impossible to see all the way through, though I was confident they were clear. One particular area sparked memories, as I realised I was going to the old dormitory we stayed in.

The thick frame for the double doors stood intact, with one of the old doors charred and barely hanging from the dingy hinges, and the other having burned and crumbled to dust. I pointed the pistol in, looking around. The old blackboard eerily gleaming from the corner, lit up by moonlight, the furthest part of the dormitory largely untouched by flame. Nothing had changed from what I could remember.

My older self wished I were breaking in to the room a few decades earlier, to save my brothers and sisters, united in tragedy.

A sound in the distance rattled me, though a large cat-like rat was the sole perpetrator of the disturbance, it was left undisturbed, just in case there was something, or someone here. I worked my way around the hallway, clearing the way forward, being sure not to make a noise.

That's when the hall branched out to the old pathway to the garden. I fondly recalled Mallory treating me and tending to my twisted ankle the very moment I was lifted up and threatened by Jack, the Gardener.

A light could be seen from the old cabin in the garden. For all that was scorched in the orphanage, the cabin outside in the garden was largely untouched by flame, just old and tattered. In the distance down the garden was the remains of the old garden, still showing a cross, made from wood, in the soil. I thought back to George; the boy I fleetingly witnessed disappear on my first night, was buried there. The Gardener's threat about him being good for the soil.

Every stained, harrowed memory flooded back to me from my time there, but it didn't slow me or strangle me, it fuelled me. The lights from the cabin were dim, some of which flickered through older cracks in the wood. It was elevated somewhat, a detail I hadn't recalled from childhood, in an Aspen cabin design. As I crept closer trying to mentally imagine whether this was the correct building or not, my thoughts were interrupted with some whistling.

My heart started thumping with excitement, feeling that I was close. Using the faint whistles as a bold theme-tune of encouragement, I realised I was a step ahead now. My prey was unaware of my arrival. My target had no idea I was nearby. I tried to peek through one of the cracks where light was escaping but it was far too small to see anything, other than some shadows dancing.

The whistling got louder as I worked my way around the edge of the cabin. Climbing up ever so slightly from my kneeling position, I tried to peer in one of the windows and based on the height, struggled to see in.

All I could see was the shadow reflecting from the lanterns or candles that were illuminating the property. It had to be him, though his face was obscured, I couldn't see. The window was firmly closed and too high anyway, so wasn't a suitable point of entry.

There was no way to get under the property that was immediately visible so I couldn't break the wood and try to find a trap door, as that would alert whoever was inside. I had to climb the porch and head to the door. Now or never. Kick down the door, start firing and ask questions later.

I stood at the bottom of the stairs, mentally counted like I always did as a child. *One, two, three*. Then crept up. A slight creak on the first step halted my progress. I waited a few seconds, keeping a close eye on the windows for movement. Nothing happened, so I continued, the slight creaking averting my eyes to the windows again. That's when I realised, I was no longer a step ahead. As I motioned past the final step on the porch, I fell into a different trap. I tripped a wire, that rung a small bell. The occupant was clearly paranoid to the last moment.

"I've been expecting you," the voice said. "Come in and talk."

I burst through the door, pointing the gun firmly in front of me. I looked forward, clear. I looked right, clear. As the gun turned to the left, from behind the door, my arm was stopped, and I was disarmed by a familiar face.

The face looked back at me and would have seen nothing short of utter confusion.

"Hi, Seb," the voice spoke, rendering me speechless. "You got my message then?"

He waited for me to respond and I simply couldn't. He was stocky, bald, and I recognised him. This wasn't the person I was expecting.

"I half expected to hear your car coming up, in its old-fashioned glory, but then again... you always were a sly one," he said.

"Wha...?" I forced out, unable to finish the word. I didn't feel in danger, so started to relax.

"The messages I left you obviously brought you here." The man laughed and turned his back to me, heading towards a small table with seats either side. As his back was turned, I noticed the birthmark on the back of his head again.

"You. You fixed my car that day. I bought you a drink in the bar. Al, right?" I said.

"Alex, yeah. You've got it," he said. "I'm so happy you got my messages. You always liked secret messages and codes, didn't you?" Al said.

"I don't understand, I was expecting to find someone else here, Al. What are you doing here? This doesn't make sense," I responded, incredibly confused.

There was no Alex in Fort Rose that I remembered. He sat at the table and I stood at the doorway, the gun at my feet having been disarmed from the surprise attack. He motioned for me to sit down, and then noticed me assessing the room, the chairs at the table, and caught me looking at the gun.

"You don't need to do that, I'd rather you didn't force me to have to defend myself," he said calmly, though I didn't feel threatened.

"I don't understand. You shouldn't be here. Arthur should. Arthur Henderson led me here," I exasperatedly retorted.

"No, little brother," the man said, and that was it. I knew who this was. Only one person ever referred to me as little brother. Robert. *This was Robert?* How?

"Robert?" I quizzed.

He exhaled, incredibly relieved at the fact I knew. The fact I guessed who he was. I had never seen a birthmark on Robert, ever. Then again, he was bald now. There was no reason to ever assume it was him, or to expect him to be anything other than 'Al the mechanic,' who kindly fixed my car.

"I've waited for this day for a long time, little brother. I've missed you. I don't know if we should, you know, hug it out or something?" he suggested with a laugh, but it fell on deaf ears.

I was still too confused. I sat down at the table, pondering everything. I was so blinded by desire to find

284

Arthur, that everything I pieced together, I tried to make it fit. I forced every crime scene to be Arthur Henderson because of the twisted God-like symbolism left behind.

"You probably have a million questions, and I have a million answers. You look very confused, little brother, so I'm just going to talk. You can interrupt me at any time, and I'll answer, okay?" Robert stated, as if he were still the dutiful older brother. I could only nod my head in agreement.

He started to talk, and I barely listened, confused as to how this moment even came to be. It wasn't at all what I expected. I tried to run every scenario through my head. Arthur had only killed Sebastian McColm? As the other crime scenes were decorated with hints and clues. Jane Doe didn't make sense though, as that branded the individual a liar? My mind was ready to blow. I started to tune into Robert.

"As much as it pains me to say, I was responsible for a lot of hurt. I started that fire that night. I seized an opportunity to tear the place down. I know our plan was to run off into the night, you, my sister, and me. Something in that cage made me change. The things they inflicted on me, Sebastian, were cruel. They shouldn't have happened to anyone. I took a lot of it over the years, to protect my sister and I ultimately caused her death. It hurt. When I watched them pull her body out of the fire that night, it broke me. I didn't speak for years; I was put in an institution. I was cared for better than anyone ever cared for me in this dump."

I still couldn't believe it was him. My hardened stance softened with the knowledge that this was my big brother. I mentally and physically struggled to cope with the fact he was here. It didn't make sense, and reflecting on everything in that moment, I struggled to accept that he had evolved into a ruthless killer.

"I don't understand why you are here though. Why did you do all this to meet me? You could have knocked on my door?" I asked.

"I couldn't. I was afraid. I was ashamed. You were the only person I really cared for after that night and I honestly didn't know how to face you. I didn't know how you'd react if you knew it was me. That's why I left the messages. I figured if you followed the clues, played some games like old times, you'd have followed them to me," Robert said, almost proud he had delivered death.

"You killed people, Robert, just to say hello to me? I'm…" I had to think carefully about my next words given I had come here with an intent to kill Arthur. "I'm a detective, an upholder of the law."

"I killed Father for you. For us. The bastard that took us in and hurt us. You should be thanking me." His voice raised as he stood up and looked down on me. Realising his action, he sat back down and calmed himself.

"What about the other body, who was that?" I asked.

"You mean the bitch that had every opportunity to save us. The bitch that put me in a mental home instead of protecting me? My darling mother, of course." He spat physically as he thought about her.

It broke me to know that all this time, Jane Doe was Mallory. The amazing woman that acted like a shining star in my time at Fort Rose. I'd read her thoughts, her mind, her diary. She was as much a prisoner in that place as we were.

"You don't understand, Robert. Father–"

"Don't fucking call him that," he blurted out loudly.

"Cyril, Xavier Hardiman, whatever his real or fake name... imprisoned your mother too."

I told Robert about the time I escaped the bedroom to look for him. I worked my way in to the ventilation shaft to see my real father's watch, and I read his mother's diary. He seemed mildly guilty at the revelation his mother tried to save herself, tried to save her children, and ultimately, had made attempts to try and save us. All facts he genuinely didn't know, had chosen to ignore, or just didn't care about.

My heart sank for Mallory. I'd never so much as taken the time to think about finding her, though I would have liked to. I talked to Robert about attending therapy growing up, and I had blocked a lot of what happened in our childhood out of my mind. I told him about the occasional dreams I had where snippets of that night would come back to me, though I struggled to piece them together. We acted like brothers for that short time.

He told me he barely spoke a word for almost twenty-seven years, that he re-lived the moment Alexia was dragged out of the flames in his own dreams as a constant reminder of his guilt.

"I thought I killed you that night. It wasn't until I was in the institution's break area that the TV was on, and you were on the news. Your name struck with me immediately. Your face, your eyes. That's when I knew I would work at getting out of that place. I spent over a decade proving I was sane just to get out. You were my prize. That is why I was so afraid to talk to you," Robert admitted, proudly, yet sorrowfully.

"But why go to the lengths of killing Mallory and Cyril to get my attention? It doesn't make sense."

"I'll admit, there was an element of personal vendetta in there. I was angry with my mother as I was certain she abandoned us, left us in this dump I've miraculously found myself back at. I was furious. If she cared, she'd have taken me in, regardless of my mental state. Fucking Cyril on the other hand. That was admittedly, for the sheer enjoyment. He inflicted so much hurt on us all over the years. The beating he gave Erin, if you remember."

I nodded, appreciating exactly what he was referring to.

"That was nothing compared to what they had done to me. I was beaten, I was cut, bruised, raped, filmed, paraded naked; all for a quick buck, and some twisted sexual gratification for faceless strangers and willing bastards I barely knew. I vowed to get them all. I vowed to snuff out every last one of them. It took me years to find some of them. That bastard Gardener, he was all cooped up in a

288

home. I got some fake ID; let on I was a nephew of his and checked him out under the guise I was going to care for him or send him to a better hospital. I brought him back here and kept him in that fucking cage downstairs. Can you believe it? It's still fucking here! Anyway, he didn't remember much but he did give me a few names. Shame really. Alzheimer's was a gift for that bastard. I wanted him to know why I was doing what I was doing. He cried when I dug up George's body and he realised for a split second who I was. I killed him and buried him in his own fucking garden."

I struggled to listen because part of me understood, hell, even appreciated and accepted what he had done, but the small, dim light of law enforcement still burned in me.

"How many people have you killed, Robert?" I asked calmly.

"Forty-two, if you don't count the people in that fire."

What surprised me more was how effortlessly that number rolled off his tongue. He'd not only kept count, but said it so passionately, so chillingly calm. I asked about the victims, I asked about the reasons, and why they all made sense. They were people involved in the making of the orphanage, and the underlying paedophile ring that sat atop it, practically funding the entire operation.

The bed in the basement was not just a symbol of the entrapment in our lives, of children and teenagers being stripped of their innocence and identity, but it was allegedly a trophy amongst the paedophile community. Betamax videos, images, and underground literature all fed sick fantasies of many people bound for hell.

Worryingly, some of Robert's victims were powerful people as well. Retired police chiefs, retired politicians, even high-ranking military men; his victims even included throes of women who had acted as halfway houses to Fort Rose, inclusive of people like Madame. The ring was very sophisticated, which made sense as to how it could go on so long, how people who Mallory alluded to in her diary would suddenly go missing, and how people could barely make a dent in their investigation into Cyril.

Ultimately what took Robert so long to find Cyril following his name change, was unravelling the web of deceit and lies. He was even quite bitter about how some of the people had died peacefully from old age, feeling as though he was the one who was almost guided to reap their souls. Robert truly felt as though his epiphany, once he realised that I was alive, was to avenge everyone that'd had a hand in hurting me. Not him, not his other brothers or sisters, me.

I was almost honoured that I meant so much to him and he felt the need to do it, though, as swift as the hammer of justice was; some of these people would have evaded it if he hadn't acted. Knowing I was once a child from here, that running into the night probably wouldn't have solved anything, I actually had to agree that the fire, as destructive and devastating as it was, was probably the only way to expose what lay underneath.

"Robert, as difficult as it may be to hear this... I not only forgive you for starting that fire. Something in me thinks, given everything that went on, it was the only way. You probably saved more people than you harmed." I couldn't believe the words that fell out of my mouth, but I meant them.

"You have no idea how much that helps me," Robert said.

We spoke a little longer, I asked why he referred to himself as Al, and of course, it was a means to honour his sister Alexia. I told him that he effectively acted like the black ops of law enforcement, dealing with the people and finding them, through measures I couldn't follow through the correct channels. We had taken different paths in life. He'd just walked down the road I could have if I had stuck that screwdriver in the Gardener.

We were completely different yet riddled with comparisons and likenesses. I sat across a small table with a serial killer, my non-biological brother, hardened and shaped by similar harrowing experiences as a child; everything about the encounter felt like the most natural thing in the world.

"There's something you should know, Seb. I am sorry for something else. I wasn't quick enough."

"What do you mean, Robert?"

"I watched you from afar for a long time. A very long time, trying to pluck up the courage to just say hello, to rekindle what we shared in this place," he shared passionately.

"But what are you sorry for?"

"As I watched you from afar, I noticed someone else was too. The man you spoke of earlier, Arthur Henderson."

The reality of why I was here suddenly crashed down on me. I'd been so side-lined with this unexpected and unequivocally awkward, taboo sit down. My eyes widened, as I realised this was my last clue. My last lead to finding Arthur. I held my head in my hands as it collapsed under the weight of disappointment.

"Little brother, as I watched, I learnt his patterns. I wanted to understand who he was and why he had an interest in you. I'm sorry because I couldn't stop what he has done. I couldn't stop it and I am truly, deeply sorry," Robert said, clearly distraught.

Though, I couldn't understand why and how he knew.

"Over the past few weeks, I've seen you chasing him and enjoyed watching you. Seeing you work fascinated me. You always were a smart one. My, messes, shall we say, did send you off in the wrong direction, and I always intended to share with you what I knew and how to find him once we had this discussion. Once you got my messages."

"You knew where he was, and just sat on it? Where, Robert? Where?" My voice raising, realising all hope was not lost.

"I'll tell you. Just let me explain. I was too busy piecing together my planned reunion here, that after killing Cyril, I took my eyes off him for a moment. I appreciated you had a happy reunion with your wife, and I'd have loved to have met her."

I was starting to get impatient. The thought of letting my beautiful wife meet a serial killer, who I happened to grow up with, was completely out of the question but I daren't say anything as he was sitting on critical information. The key to my hunt. Key to my vengeance. Key to my promise to Jessica McColm.

"I followed you to that bus station when you got my clue. I hadn't noticed or realised he had taken her at that point. My worry was that you figured out my message straight away, that's why you were screaming. I thought you knew who was sending the messages and you didn't want to see me. Do you remember that kid you beat the shit out of? I paid him to peek through your window. I didn't expect you to chase him down the street." Robert laughed. "Then again, I didn't know what you were going through. I went into your house that night and looked at your dining room setup, I looked at everything you'd pieced together and realised you still hadn't figured it out. That's why I couldn't understand your pain. I only knew pain like that when I looked into the fire that night."

He could see me getting impatient.

"I'm nearly there. I promise. Anyway, I kept following you, I watched you go to the crime scenes. I could feel you getting closer and yet, I still didn't understand your pain. You hadn't revealed. Before you went to Cyril, sorry Mr Hardiman's house," he said sarcastically. "You detoured to

293

the bar. I'd drunk there a few times, no one thought to suspect me so when you started screaming at your friend, that's when it clicked. You raced off, I raced in a different direction, sensing it was the man Arthur, who had been watching you."

Robert hadn't shown much emotion at all through the night until now.

"I was too late. By the time I got there, he was taunting you down the phone and had already stuck the knife in your wife. I snuck up behind him and as he ended the call to you, I hit him over the head with a brick. You tried calling back and I couldn't answer as I was doing my best to keep her alive. I guess I did meet her, but not properly. She was beautiful, like my sister was. But... I failed you, Sebastian, again. I'm sorry I couldn't save her."

My heart ached at the thought that my wife died without me there, but a ghost from my past had tried to save her, tried to make her live just moments longer, and it was eerily comforting. I punched the table, angry at the thought she was no longer here. Angry that if we hadn't been playing this stupid cat and mouse game with clues and riddles, I'd have been able to save her.

We could have united our intelligence and got to the bastard. I made a point of letting my brother know how disappointed I was that he was too much of a coward to approach me sooner, that those games resulted in her death, and he certainly felt it as he tried to grab my hand and console me.

I ripped my hand away from him, suddenly aware of one key fact: Arthur still lived.

"Where is that motherfucker?" I asked through gritted teeth, fuelled with rage once again.

"I've got him downstairs. For you. He's in the cage."

Robert barely had a chance to finish that sentence and I was already rushing out of the cabin towards the main orphanage building. I bolted through the hallways, being beckoned by my big brother to slow down. Vague memories guided my path through the building, through rubble and dust until I noticed a familiar plaque above an ornate door.

Time and consequence had made the plaque blackened and illegible, but this was the one. I burst into the chapel room, Robert following closely behind and made my way down the stairs into the basement after ripping up newer pieces of wood, clearly untouched by the flames of old.

As much as my redemption following my suicide attempt seemed to kill off any feelings of anxiety, knowing the ultimate decision could shape my life lay before me, I started to slow, sensing a panic attack. Robert was seconds behind me, but I carried on through the old basement, recalling my path as a child, bursting through the old, hidden door to the cage area.

There he was, right in front of me, Arthur Henderson. He was bound, unable to move.

"So, the beast is alive. The bear I prodded is in a trap. You son of a bitch. *Have a nice life, Detective?*" I spat at him, infuriated by his final words.

Arthur still had the audacity to laugh at me, despite his current predicament. He laughed at me, psychopathically communicating without so much as a shred of remorse. Whilst my big brother was a killer, he seemed to at least feel something. He was guided by the shadowed hand of justice; he was doing the good the law couldn't. Here I was, infuriatingly defending a serial killer given the fact that bastard was still laughing at me.

I opened the cage and kicked him across his face, causing him to recoil back in pain, yet he still laughed.

"You." I kicked him in the face. He still laughed.

"Took." Another swift kick. He still laughed.

"Everything." I spun him round, mounted him, and punched him hard through his laughter.

"From." Arthur's laugh started to weaken.

"Me." Another swift punch to his eye, causing it to bleed silenced him.

"I–" Arthur started to speak weakly.

"What?" I spat, venomously.

"I... fucking... love... that... I... did..." Then he spat blood at me.

The bastard had the cheek to still taunt me. I head-butted him and knocked him out in the process.

"Ease up, little brother," Robert said.

"Ease up? Ease the fuck up? He robbed my life, he killed me wife. He killed my unborn daughter."

I started to lose it, overcome by emotion. Robert pulled me away from him and hugged me.

Through my sheer despair I welcomed it. My life had gone from bad to worse in a matter of days. I cursed my job, my life, and everything I had done since Arthur took the life of that little boy. Spurred by my desire to right that wrong, I chased someone who had a bite worse than his bark and he robbed me of my own chance of a family.

Robert pulled me away from his chest and looked me directly in the eye. I felt like I was a little boy again; the way he looked me in the eye and spoke to me like he did in the past.

"Let's get out of this room. There are too many bad memories. You grab his legs," Robert instructed.

I blindly followed his instruction. We dragged Arthur out of the cage. This was wrong. Completely and utterly wrong. I had crossed the line and knew what I was going to do. I'd made my decision. Robert dropped Arthur's head and it hit the stone floor with some impact. The good in me even stopped to hope he was okay; that was too good an end for him, too swift an end.

Robert caught me off guard as I kept a hold of Arthur's legs, and he knocked me back, forcing me into the cage, locking it as quickly as it took for me to react and jump up.

"Let me do this for you. I couldn't save your wife or daughter. Let me save you."

His words fell on my ears like a sweet symphony. I knew he would do it as well and save me the arduous mental strain of walking the road of becoming a killer. As much as I felt like one by proxy, and as much as I wanted Arthur dead... from behind the same cell doors where I learnt and ingrained good and evil in my mind, I couldn't allow it to happen. The statue in the police station entered my mind and the words of justice and equality plastered on it.

"Robert, no! Let me out. Let me take him in. Let me arrest him," I pleaded.

I wasn't heard, rather, I was ignored. Robert knew what I wanted deep down and he intended to deliver, whilst giving me some element of plausible deniability. I kicked at the door of the cage, but the lock was too strong. I tried again but admittedly didn't kick too hard, battling the injustice and conflict in my own mind in the process.

There was little to no point, Robert had taken the decision out of my hands, almost accepting an element of responsibility for the death of my wife and child, he wasn't prepared to do nothing. He had it in him, the power to give life, and snatch it away were in his skill set. He'd moulded them from the day he set that fire.

Realising my fate in the cage, I actually felt the early onset of an anxiety attack. I cursed myself for being so weak as I passed out.

I'd obviously been out for quite some time, and I finally awoke to the distant sounds of my colleagues. I was eventually helped out of the cage, freed by a lawman in an ironic state of affairs; the very wish I had hoped for as a child.

I couldn't understand how they'd come to find me, and to view me as a bystander, a victim in this whole thing. Michael followed closely behind, stating the next room was where the body was.

The entire episode from Fort Rose, being led by servicemen felt strangely familiar and another suitable end to the entire debacle of that building.

I was led to the station to be debriefed by the Chief himself. He gave me some lecture for running off into the night and going rogue as he put it, citing that a suspension would be more than justified. He asked me how I found Arthur, and I told him a half-truth of sorts, giving him the whole story of 'forgetting' to log the bus key card as evidence and instead following up on the clue. I gave a weak explanation of the riddle and deities being why I was led to Fort Rose as the only nearby orphanage, though closed down. I didn't allude to knowing, or even acknowledging its existence.

The Chief quizzed me on whether I found anyone else, whether I knew of anyone else being in the building. I flatly denied it. He showed me a video that went viral, posted as a live stream online.

A masked individual, obviously Robert to me, announced that the man chained to the bed had something he wanted to say. Then Arthur miraculously apologised for what he had done. He confessed his crimes, with the addition of some new ones, inclusive of what the police accepted as Jane Doe and Xavier Hardiman. Following his obviously forced but verbally stated, 'heartfelt apology,' Robert shot Arthur in the head, killing him instantly. It was mildly satisfying to watch.

At which point, Robert turned to the camera and said a few words:

> *My name is not important but know that I was lucky enough to escape this man. He had me locked in a cage just down the hall behind the camera and I came back here to seek retribution. To my surprise, he also has a police officer in there, where I was also once held captive. My understanding, following our discussion is that he baited and led the officer to this building following a brutal escapade where he killed both his wife and unborn child as you just heard him confess to. I shall reveal my location to the local police department in a call separate to this video. The key to your colleague's cell is on the table next to this beast. To the police officer in the cell, if you ever watch this, I hope you can find peace knowing what this man has done to you. Be at peace, brother. To the police officers who will have a duty to find me, do not. You won't succeed.*

Robert made a point of clumsily revealing his birth mark on the back of his head, keeping his face hidden before turning off the video. I felt like laughing. I felt like crying. Although incredibly polished and suspect, it was evident I was not the one to pull the trigger on Arthur.

I was quizzed for days, weeks even, keeping true to my version of events and ultimately given the all clear by the end of the proceedings. Michael always sensed there was something I was hiding, as he only knew me to be hunting Arthur alone. The plausible deniability Robert gave me was exactly what I needed to keep the truth buried.

Everything from who started the fire, the child abuse ring, to the identity of the newly-dubbed 'Masked Murderer,' yet another truth was destined to remain buried under the ashes of Fort Rose.

Epilogue

I took a few weeks off to recover after the proceedings, using the time to question what I really wanted in life. The hardest part of those few weeks was burying my wife and burying our unborn child. I carried the tiny coffin of my daughter alone, surrounded by colleagues and friends who helped carry Arianna, including her sister. It felt like another, proverbial, bullet had been dodged with all the recent accounts.

I took most of the time recollecting the case, packing down the operations room I set up in my dining room, and mainly looking in the mirror, reflecting upon myself. There hadn't been so much as an anxiety attack since being locked back in that cage. Perhaps the poignant saving from law enforcement colleagues had helped to seal the memory. Close the chapter finally, I'd hoped.

I went back to work not long after the funeral, to the surprise of my colleagues. Walking through that hallway, with the statue and the echoing footsteps wasn't quite the same feeling as previously. I took the lift, and instead went to see the Chief. He welcomed me back with open arms, then assigned me the task of finding 'the masked murderer,' citing me as the most equipped person to do so as I had a knack for figuring out the impossible.

I shouldn't have let him speak first, because the reflecting had made me reach the consensus I had reached the end of my time in law enforcement. I was heading up to his office to resign. Few protests to try and change my mind did fly across the desk, but we both knew, what I'd gone through for the job just wasn't worth it anymore. I resigned effective immediately.

The Chief was firm in his assessment that if I ever changed my mind, he would welcome me back gladly. Michael was fortunate enough to benefit from my resignation, as he was given the open detective slot, following passing the exam. Proud would be an understatement; he'd worked incredibly hard to prove himself and not be the typical ex-jarhead. This line of work kept him focussed and he even went so far as to start a scheme for ex-military and ex-servicemen that wanted to start fresh, like myself.

It started as a charity that I initially helped him set up, sorting out work locally, nationally, and internationally; security work, private detective work, ultimately anything that could help utilise the skills of the people we worked with. Those without combat experience were supported in other lines of work as well, inclusive of engineering and craftsmanship.

It has been about a year since the events from that final night when I lost my wife and child. I woke up to Colin Hargreaves on the radio again today, much to my amusement. Next to me, Kirsty slept softly, groaning about the irritable man, hence my pleasure for our shared annoyance of the man.

We didn't act too fast following my wife's death, I mourned for about six months, some of which was spent in that bar, asking for advice and support in where I should go.

The idea for the charity scheme for ex-serviceman was actually an idea that blossomed across the bar.

I had a chance to learn a few other skills as well. To Kirsty's amusement, I helped pour pints rather than sink them some nights just to keep the cash coming in, and I obviously got a lot closer to her, which allowed our friendship to blossom into something more.

She truly was a rock for me when I felt as though I had no one on any particular level. Talking in that bar until the wee hours when all the patrons had left; about my past, the case, my experiences, actually gave birth to a brand-new idea, probably the best idea that came from my time there.

Using the skills from some of the men and women from the charity scheme we set up, Kirsty and I found a large building that used to be a small hotel in the city and started our own orphanage: *Meadowbrook Homes.*

Our mission was simple, given what I'd experienced in the past, we would make a strong point of caring for the children, protecting them, and ultimately ensuring they went to well vetted homes that would continue that trend when would-be parents wanted to start families.

Various skills from the ex-military and servicemen and women allowed us to dig deep, almost as deep as Robert did when he found the perpetrators from the Fort Rose ring, ensuring that anyone not suitable to house any of the children were reported swiftly.

It was a highly rewarding experience setting it up and still is to this day. I go to work, still in my old Chevrolet, happy with what I have in life and fully intend to move in to the property and live there permanently once my house sale completes.

I didn't want to rush moving out, until I knew I had mentally closed the doors from the harrowing nights of the past when I lost Arianna. To put it in perspective, I still looked out the window every morning to see if Robert was watching from afar. If he was, I never noticed but that paranoia wasn't really what I wanted to bring into Meadowbrook.

My birthday at Meadowbrook was special. Kirsty and the kids we'd already taken in made it a truly memorable and joyful experience. Our receptionist was none other than Jessica McColm, whom had bought into our mission and used the place as a stepping-stone to try and get over the death of her son. She was the first person I went to see after I was cleared of any wrongdoing with Arthur.

I never told her the full truth, but we were bound by pain inflicted by Arthur that she knew. That unspoken acknowledgement I would avenge her son seemed to bind us to a mental understanding. I felt her approval as much as anything I'd ever felt before; she hugged me incredibly tight that night. It was nice to see the goodwill in Meadowbrook bring out her smile. I was beginning to see flickers of the woman that she was before her own trauma.

Only one thing that darkened the day was a birthday card I received in a golden envelope. It was addressed to the home, directly to me, and had been dropped off by hand, to Jessica. She had no idea that the man responsible for ending her son's killer was inches away from her when she did. I did battle with the fact he was out there.

My emotions the night we rekindled our lost connection clouded my judgement, irrespective of the ties and sins that bound us. I was tempted to encourage some of the private detectives at my disposal to try and bring him in but feared the repercussions of whether I sent people out to find him. Not only because the truth of that night in the basement could come out, but it ran the risk of putting the children in this home at risk.

His birthday well wishes within the golden envelope were heartfelt, and I brushed them off by simply hiding the card in my desk.

Happy Birthday Sebastian. It was good to see you, and for what it is worth, I am sorry. Forgive my inability to save your beloved. Forgive my actions that night of the fire. Be well, Little Brother.

P.S. I've sent a donation to your site. I took The Gutenberg Bible from 'Father' and sold it privately. Use your share of the money to do good. I'll be using my share to finish what I started.

An anonymous donation would be great for us, despite the fact it was blood money tainted with the whiff of Cyril. Perhaps it could be the only redeeming factor of his wastefully evil life; a gift from the grave.

I was angry with Robert for putting me into the position where I would accept the money, begrudgingly. The fact he called me 'little brother,' and tried to act as though we were all young kids, happy in our own company again was quite frustrating. The fact he set foot in this building, a building full of hope, dreams, and goodwill, vexed me even more. More so than the fact he was obviously still watching from afar. I knew, that one day, I could very well close the chapter of Fort Rose once and for all by bringing Robert in.

I'd danced with devils for most of my life, even coming close to losing myself in the process. He was a devil arguably worse than Arthur given the body count he'd alleged to accumulate. Driven by a false sense of righteousness taking out the scum of the earth that had evaded justice was mildly pleasing, but still not right.

If anything was to ever draw me back to that night and that tainted basement, it would be to turn in another monster to the scales of justice. Only this one was one that I knew quite well. Perhaps I'd speak with Kirsty first.

Either way, see you soon. Big Brother.

Acknowledgements

I want to thank my partner Katharine, who just let me get on with this without interruption when I was in the creative zone. More than that, you are my rock and were integral to me staying sane in the months leading up to this story. I've never met anyone quite like you, or someone that just 'gets' me. You are the best thing that ever happened to me and the words alone don't even do the statement justice. We can talk about everything and anything, as best friends and soul mates. Words just cannot describe how I feel or can ever thank you enough for what you do for me. In truth, I've never felt like I belonged until the day you said 'yes' at the top of the London Eye and I inadvertently joined your family. Hopefully immortalising this brief acknowledgement in text is enough to suggest how grand a gesture this is.

I want to thank one of my best friends, Kayleigh Ford – she says she is my 'bestie' and it's a sad reminder of how few true friends I have when she gets a mention... Joking aside though, you're incredible, you and your little family. You were the person who kept me laughing and joking when I was going through my antisocial slump of 2018 and dropped off the map. You were too loud and always found a way to break the silence, which wasn't a bad thing. I shall refrain from reiterating the kind of things you sent me in the event you eventually grow up and learn the art of embarrassment. Is that enough for 'ee'? Additionally, a thank you for allowing me to probe and question your anxieties as they are ultimately what helped build up my main character, amongst my own personal thoughts.

Ryan Webster, the brother. Don't really need to say much as we just get it and we always have. We are eerily similar in many respects, but you'll always be known as the one that took and ruined my trousers that fateful night. Bollocks if you believe they were yours. I said that I would stand by that until the grave, and you did too, so our equal stubbornness is to be commended. Just know, now the words are immortalised into eternity — and the discussion will forever continue beyond the grave. Keep being you: simple, effective, and never beating around the bush. Casing point, "That's your gran 'deid,' what are you going to do, eh?"

Other family members — too many to mention.

Richard Williams, Iain Murray, Dean Purves, Haydn Meredith — all reprobates and the harsh truth of my 'patter being shite as I wasn't around enough,' was enough to instigate changes in work/life balance. Just know that if it happens again and I drop off the map, it's because I've come to learn that your patter is as equally shite and it won't be work related. It's why we are all friends. We all seem to work for each other and help one another in our own way. Friends like you are my real family I guess.

Stephen Logan, Gavin & Jo Burton, Craig McMichael, Elaine Brachtvogel, Brad Symcox, Antoni Saunders, Laura Casey, other admins/mods — and the people in the Touchdown House group that kept things ticking over as I wasn't around, but still checked in with me. This story actually started growing arms and legs around the time of our last sesh, at the SB party when I was in the hotel feeling worse for wear (self-inflicted).

I want to thank the 'F-n A-Team' of Kerry Worgan, Joe Griffiths, and Lou Barnett. You were all amongst a group of people who kept me sane in the workplace during the 'washing machine,' long working days in 2018. Kerry, you specifically encouraged me to share the first few chapters of this story with you when I was just playing with the idea of doing it. Your love of the character and the story are probably what made me stay true to the project and ultimately whip through it in such a short space of time.

Robert T C Rooney, an old friend with similar creative outlets. You once put me in the acknowledgements of your book. It's only fair, right mate?

And anyone else that ultimately had a hand in reading early drafts or helped me to create this in whatever capacity.

About the Author

This is Scott Webster's first venture into writing a novel. He does have other comedy writing experiences under his belt: a play with a friend, a few concepts for a TV series, small stage shows, and some radio sketches, but this is the first serious piece.

He looked into the proverbial mirror and realised he wasn't being disciplined, or versatile as a 'self-proclaimed' writer. He has a terrible knack for being easily distracted and not completing creative projects, so he told himself he was going to write a novel.

The beginning and end, cover to cover is the perfect beginning and the perfect end. Additionally, he considered it a bucket list item: something more lasting and immortalising than something one would do for fun, like the comedic outlets.

Scott mapped out the story into chapters and bullet points, then sat down on February 2, 2019, and began writing. He would tick off the bullet points as he went along, one chapter at a time. He finished the first draft on March 23, 2019, in a hotel room in India, incredibly ill.

This project, out of anything creative he has ever produced, is definitely the one he is most proud of. He set out with two targets in mind: to write a novel and to ensure, at least, one person enjoyed it.

The fact you are reading this means he succeeded in one of those objectives. Enjoy, and help him achieve the second.

Printed in Great Britain
by Amazon